THE SILVER ORCHESTRA

THE SILVER ORCHESTRA

A NOVEL

Amin Bardjeste

authorHOUSE®

AuthorHouse™
1663 Liberty Drive
Bloomington, IN 47403
www.authorhouse.com
Phone: 1-800-839-8640

Published by AuthorHouse   02/09/2012

ISBN: 978-1-4685-5294-2 (sc)
ISBN: 978-1-4685-5293-5 (e)

Library of Congress Control Number: 2012902686

PROLOGUE

A cold breeze, rising off the Saone River, was blowing through the picturesque streets of Lyon, where the French city was hosting the G8 summit. The world's superpowers were gathered to decide upon their response to the bio attacks which had taken hundreds of innocent lives. On the table was the plot of the operation to strike at the secret city built by the descendants of the Nazis as their renewed empire, to rule over the world.

All routine flights to Saint-Exupery International Airport were canceled. The security level in and around the airport and all over the city was high. Every street was guarded by police cars and a large number of the intelligence forces of all eight countries. Diplomatic planes landed one after another at the airport. People were gathered on the sidewalks, holding banners above their heads; the most conspicuous of these read: *NO MORE WAR.*

The President of France was present at the airport to greet his guests. And, finally, the leaders of the eight countries were transported to the banks of the Saone.

About four hundred kilometers away from the location of the summit, in the underground level of the secret garden of the secret city, the five founders of the corporation were talking in their conference room.

The controversial and secret compound of *Der Kristall Hochburg* was not recognized on any map. No satellite could spot it and no government had been officially aware of its existence until that day.

'Professor, tell us about Project Beethoven,' said the chief of the secret meeting.

'It has come to the best condition we could possibly imagine,' said the professor. 'Everything has gone well; far beyond our wildest dreams. Plus, the Forum is ready, too.'

'Then I guess this is the time. We need to bring him in. The genius of the past will give us a huge amount of credit for the future. What is his state of health?'

'Perfect.' The professor grinned. 'He has got what we want: talent and ambition.'

CHAPTER 1

Dear Grandpa,

I can hardly say how much I miss you and the village. Everything is fine here in Rome. I am taking my last exam tomorrow, which I am not nervous about at all. I guess you know why! I have passed all the music theory courses and now it comes to my favorite test. My professor has asked me to perform a solo in front of the Dean. This is the moment I have been waiting for. If he likes my performance, the university will grant me all the costs of publishing my first solo album.

When it comes to composing, the turmoil of city life doesn't agree with me. I will have to spend the summer in Oria and complete my album there, where one can breathe the air and be among beauty. This album will be my graduation project, entitled Music in Curing Cancer. *I will be there with you in a couple of weeks, when I have sorted out things here.*

I can't wait to see the villagers. They always cheer me up with their kind smiles and their jokes, and recently with the puzzles they keep sending me. Here is one of them:

'Snowfall, Solo, the Sailor. The birds are coming!'
K H

    I'm sure my brilliant grandpa knows the answer. It was written in crimson ink on a piece of paper and was sent to me from Oria, but since I know the village and its every corner, the name and address of the sender appear faked. It must be one of those puzzles our clever villagers make.
    Wish me and my violin luck with the performance. See you soon,

Love,
Your grandson, Adam

O ria was a village nestling by a mountain range. The hills around it were covered by plants and flowers. You could hardly say the pastures were green, for they were painted in millions of shades of light and dark green, with many other colors amongst the grasses. A gently-flowing river passed through the village and from its banks a delightful view of trees, flowers and fields could be enjoyed. There were three arched stone bridges spanning the river, their supports sunk into the water and covered by weeds and wild plants.

    Oria was famous for its incredible climate. During the summer, clouds covered the sky and the day would begin with a slight rain, cooling the temperature down by evening.

Equally, clouds were scarce in the winter skies and sunshine warmed the village. So the weather was mild and the people didn't suffer hard conditions at any time of year. All year round, flowers and green trees flourished.

Places like this are very rare. The inhabitants of such areas are the luckiest people in the world, for they live in spring all the year through, to the envy of the people of less well-favored lands.

The livelihood of the villagers depended on farming, notably the large citrus orchards. Because of the climate, the amount of fruits produced by every tree was so great that wooden supports had to be put under the laden branches to prevent them from breaking.

Unlike those in other lands, who believe autumn to be the beginning of nature's death, for the people of Oria the season represented blessings, wealth and happiness. It was in autumn that they could harvest and sell tonnes and tonnes of their crops.

Thankful for all the bounty they had been given, they celebrated the first day of autumn every year. The harvest celebration was an occasion of music, feasting and dance, involving rituals and customs unique to Oria. Indeed, this day was the only time when the people had a chance to listen to live music. Adam Keramat, the single musician in the village, played music in public only on this celebration day. The villagers invited him to the festivities to play and they would dance to his music the whole day.

Adam was rather tall, with a bony nose, big dark eyes and a wide forehead. His soft, long hair fell over his forehead, making it look smaller, so that his eyes seemed bigger and drew the attention. Unlike the other young people of the village, he had soft, smooth hands, for his only occupation was playing and composing music and he didn't have to work on the farm or in the orchards.

He had grown up in the village mayor's house and Oria's folk liked and admired him both as the mayor's grandson and a talented musician. The village mayor's only son, who was believed to be Adam's father, had been a musician, living in Rome as an orchestral conductor and music teacher. He had died with his wife in an accident when travelling to the village to see his father. One-year-old Adam, having survived the crash, had been brought up by his grandfather. He had been trained by music teachers hired by his grandfather, who came weekly from Rome to teach him how to play the violin. And at the age of twenty-two he was sent to The University of Rome to study music.

Adam spent long hours during the summer composing songs and playing the violin in a temple which his grandfather had had made for him where the river ended by the hills. The temple floor was a round platform made of stone, on which six carved marble pillars supported a dome of turquoise tiles. Adam had enjoyed this benefit since the age of sixteen. Every day he left the house, passed the farms and orchards where other young people of his age were laboring, and entered his temple. He played his violin with the sound of water flowing in the background.

Just a week before taking the train from Rome to the village, when Adam had climbed up the subway steps and was walking along the alley where his flat was located, a limousine stopped beside him. The chauffeur got out.

'Sir, if you please, get in the car,' said the chauffeur. 'My employer would like to have a word with you.'

'You must be mistaken,' said Adam, looking with bewilderment at the dark windows of the car, trying to see those inside. 'I'm afraid I have to go. I'm late for work.'

'It won't take long, sir,' said the chauffeur, opening his jacket at his waist to expose a revolver.

Adam got in the car. A man in a dark suit was sitting opposite him on the seat.

'Do not panic, my lad,' said the man, leaning forward. 'We are your friends. And we were once your grandfather's friends.'

'How can I help you?' Adam found his voice.

'You are about to be world-famous. But there will be some challenges in the beginning. I'm just here to tell you, when we approach you, don't run away.'

'I don't understand, sir.'

'You will, my lad; soon you will.' He took an envelope from his inside pocket. 'Will you do me a favor?'

'I hope it's something I can do, sir.' Adam struggled to look confident and to overcome his fear.

'It is. Would you give this to your grandfather?' He handed Adam the envelope.

'And tell him this is from who?'

'From an old friend. He will remember me as soon as he opens it. But to save him some time, you can tell him it is from Dr. Mao.'

'Did you send me those letters?'

'What letters?' The man slid down the window and looked at the chauffeur, who was standing outside.

The chauffeur opened the door.

'Have a good day, sir,' said the chauffeur, looking steadily at Adam.

Adam got out of the car and watched the limo until it had gone from the alley.

Karim Keramat, Oria's mayor, lived in a house which had stone walls and a thatched roof with three chimneys. A detached house, it stood by the middle bridge with two windows facing the river and a small blue arched door.

The house had three rooms and a kitchen and a couple of attic rooms where the mayor kept antique books and other items. In one of the attic rooms there was a wooden cupboard which was always locked and the mayor had forbidden his grandson to open it or even to ask about its contents.

The mayor had a short white beard and wavy hair. He was well built and was rarely seen without a smile on his face. The villagers all loved him for his good temper and caring manner. He spent mornings in his orchards, where many of the villagers worked. Every afternoon he met other farmers in a small council which he had established, taking care of their problems. His bedroom light never went off at night as he stayed up to study. He kept numerous books, in Italian, English, Persian and Arabic, in his library. Adam told his classmates that his grandfather's library had been the best education for him ever.

In the afternoon of one of the last days of summer, when Adam was almost done with his practice, Savio, Oria's school teacher, came to the temple. He rarely visited Adam there, for it was too far from where the villagers lived and worked.

'How enchanting it is, the way you play, my brilliant one,' Mr. Savio said. 'I couldn't help hearing your music. You do have a way with these strings!'

'When I am here, it's not me playing, it's nature itself. I'm just a part of the orchestra.' Adam looked around to check if there was anyone listening and continued in a whisper, 'don't tell anyone! I call it "revelation"!'

'The woods always bear a revelation.'

'Let me guess something, sir. You are not here to hear my music or for a walk, are you?'

'You are right, my dear boy.' Mr. Savio put his hands together in a namaste. 'I came to ask you a favor.'

'Anything, sir! But please don't ask me to start the music class in school again. You know what I am here for. Grandpa always tells you everything about me. I should finish the . . .' He stopped as he saw the look in Mr. Savio's eyes.

'I'm not here to ask you that, but it would be great if you could do so.' Mr. Savio smiled appealingly.

'What can I do for you Mr. Savio?'

'We will get to it later,' Mr. Savio chuckled. 'First tell me, have you heard the voices?' he asked.

'The voices?'

'The Cries. Haven't you heard them?'

'Cries? What cries, sir?'

'They have been heard recently in the village. They come and go now and then.' Glancing at the hills, he whispered, 'From behind the hills.'

'What are these cries like?' Adam asked. 'Where can I hear them?'

'They are like a large flock of birds, I couldn't say what kind, but they sound like crows. They all cry loudly together.'

'Have you heard them yourself? It could be one of those rumors which go around before the celebration every year.'

'Yes, I thought the same way myself, the first time one of the students told me about it. But I can hear them now, often several times a day.'

'It's not such a big deal; they could be a flock of migrating birds.'

'True, but you know what? There is something strange about them.'

'You are just trying to scare me!'

'Just after each time the cries are heard, something happens to one of the villagers.'

'Really? Like what?' Adam wasn't convinced, but his curiosity was aroused.

'They disappear!' said Savio.

'You're kidding!' Now Adam did feel scared.

'I wasn't interested in hearing the stories, for I believe they are just coincidences. If you want to know, you can ask your grandfather. The villagers always tell him about their ups and downs. But I must confess that I'm a little worried about this particular case.'

'So that's why he comes home so late these days from the council,' Adam said.

CHAPTER 2

Adam lay on his bed, idly thinking as a preparation for sleep. He was trying to review the poem that Mr. Savio had given him to make a song with and perform with the students on the celebration day.

> *Dawny, dawny, wait tonight,*
> *bliss and miracles comin' along;*
> *nighty, nighty, sing with us,*
> *joy and wealth which comes to us;*
> *rainy, rainy, stop your downpour*
> *the shiny sailor won't be cool . . .*

But there was one thought which preoccupied him and wouldn't let him sleep a wink. It was the message he had received in town.

'Snowfall, solo, sailor. The birds are coming!'

He had seen the word 'sailor' in the song, according to Mr. Savio, representing the comet that was about to be seen after fifty years in the sky of the village and he had heard the strange story of the birds from Mr. Savio. All night he pondered the question. Who had sent him the message? And why? He tried to put these thoughts out of mind and concentrate upon creating something memorable for the celebration, but that was impossible. It couldn't have been a puzzle or some sort of joke, he decided. It had to have been a message.

The next morning, having agreed to the school teacher's request, Adam used his laptop to find the traditional outfit of the area which the villagers used to wear on such occasions. Having printed some of the images, he climbed upstairs to look for something similar to wear for the celebration.

But before he could begin his search for clothes which would suit him both as a musician and as a teacher, he was taken aback by the sight which greeted him. He almost forgot what he had entered the attic room for in the first place. His grandfather's cupboard had been unlocked and its contents were spread around the room. None of the villagers had ever dared even to come close to the attic rooms, Adam reflected. Grandpa was always careful about locking the cupboard. What had happened in the house that morning? Did Grandpa know about it? Had anything happened to him? The blood froze in his veins. Without his grandfather anywhere to be seen, he was at his wits' end.

The floor was covered with jewels, antique books, cloaks and assorted wind instruments. Finding the mess in the attic and his grandfather's secret cupboard unlocked had disturbed him beyond belief. Adam started to search in his grandfather's stuff. An old piece of newspaper caught his attention. On its first page there was a photo of his grandfather, in a white medical uniform, shaking hand with a lady. He read the title:

'The future of the historical genius, in this man's hands.'

Adam tried to find out more about the news but the article below the photo had been cut. On the light part of the photo a sentence could be seen:

> 'In der Knust ist das beste gut genug.'
> Johann Wolfgang Goethe

There was a knock at the door. He ran down the stairs as fast as he could, hoping to see the mayor at the door. But his momentary hope turned into fear again when he remembered that his grandfather never left home without his keys. He opened the door, repressing the nightmare in his mind.

'There you are!' said Mr. Savio.

'For god's sake, is he with you?' Adam asked, looking around to see if the mayor was with his teacher.

'Your grandfather is all right. He has just given me this message for you.' Savio spoke quickly. 'He is on a short trip around the village with a couple of his men in the council.'

'Please tell me if there is anything wrong! Is he ok?'

'They must be having a big breakfast on the hills right now. And he told me, 'Clean up the mess.' What mess does he mean?'

'Dear god, he's ok!' said Adam. 'But why didn't he let me know?'

'Your choir must be waiting for you in the temple, sir!' Mr. Savio said, not answering his question. 'Shall we go?'

'Mr. Savio, I can't make head nor tail of this. Why should he leave in such a hurry?'

'Don't you believe your grandfather is wise enough always to make the right decisions?' Mr. Savio admonished him.

Adam didn't feel reassured. 'It is only a week left to the celebration!' he protested. 'The people expect him to set everything up.' Since I gave him that envelope from the weird visit in Rome, he had been acting oddly, Adam thought.

'I can assure you he will be with us very soon and we will celebrate as happily as we do every year. Especially with your new band this year.'

Adam was silent the whole time on the way to the temple. Seeing the attic in that state and his grandfather's absence troubled him deeply. He was so concentrating on this concern that he didn't remember when he had separated from Mr. Savio. He started murmuring the sailor song to make a melody for it, since the children were expecting him to have something written and ready. But all he could think of was his grandfather's bizarre sudden trip and the message.

Adam and his band had ended a hard day of practicing and had eventually reached a satisfying balance in the group who were to sing the song. The students had left and he was all alone in the temple. He hadn't found a moment to practice for his own performance in college, the one which would be a turning-point in his life. He was so close to achieving the grant which meant he could join the professional company of composers and players. He had to make good use of all the time left if he was to win the Dean's annual grant. Therefore, he decided to stay as long as possible in the temple and play his own pieces.

Later, at his grandfather's house, the door was locked and there was no sign that he had returned. Opening the door with his key, Adam spotted a letter lying on the ground.

My dear grandson, he read,

> *I am really sorry if I have worried you by this sudden trip of mine. I am afraid that I need to take care of a matter of great importance with the council and we won't be in the village on the evening of the celebration.*
>
> *This is the first time that I have had to be away from this joyous gathering. I want you and Mr. Savio to take care of everything this year. He will tell you everything you should do in preparation.*
>
> *I am quite sure that you won't let the villagers feel any disappointment because of my absence.*
>
> *And if you ever hear from Dr. Mao again, just run away from him and his people.*

> *With love,*
> *Grandpa*

Dr. Mao, Adam thought. Who was this Mao? How was Grandpa connected to him?

Adam did not hesitate. He ran to Mr. Savio's place and asked him the question that so troubled his mind.

'Mr. Savio, who is this Dr. Mao?' asked Adam immediately Savio opened the door. 'Do you know him?'

'Come in, boy,' said Savio, 'come in.'

'I can't stop worrying about Grandfather. He mentioned this man's name in his letter. Plus, I had a very weird meeting with him in Rome. I thought he was trying to kidnap me at first. And now Grandfather writes that I should stay away from this man and his people. What's going on?'

'Honestly, I am not in possession of any information about the way Mr. Keramat is connected to Dr. Mao. But I'm not surprised that he wants you to be far from Mao.'

'Why? You have met him, too?'

'No, and, so far as I know, I don't think your grandfather has,' said Savio. 'Mao is an embryology scientist. About twenty years ago, he created an organization in Paris named Human Enchantment.'

'Human Enchantment,' repeated Adam. 'I have heard it before. Isn't it the notion of creating superhumans by genetic engineering?'

'Something like that,' said Savio. 'Anyway, for any couple trying to conceive a baby, it has always been the desire to have a child with good looks and high intelligence. Every parent wishes to ensure these two features for their children before they are born.'

'So?'

'Human Enchantment gathered one hundred supermodels together in Paris. They also gathered a hundred wealthy couples from different countries, people who were eager to pay for their baby to have a supermodel's DNA. Mao developed a technique to clone the models.'

'You mean the rich couples could buy a clone of supermodels?'

'The rich mother could give birth to the clone. Human Enchantment bought the cell from the models and injected it into an unfertilized egg. After the embryo was formed, it was transplanted into the surrogate mother. After nine months the mother would give birth to a baby who looked like their donor supermodel.'

'And was it a successful project?'

'It was. All hundred babies were born completely healthy in Human Enchantment's secret clinic and went back home to whatever country they had come from. The parents had to take the baby to the Paris clinic once a year for a checkup and medical advice. This went on for five years. And then . . .'

'What happened?'

'The parents complained that their babies could not recognize colors.'

'All of them?'

'All of the clones were color blind. Dr. Mao said that it could be treated by gene therapy.'

'But how could all of them have the same problem?'

'This was the question he never answered. Human Enchantment provided the couples with accommodation and money until they could cure the five-year-olds' vision problem.'

'Were they cured?'

'Nobody knows.'

'I don't understand.'

'One night, all the clones, their parents and the scientist disappeared. Nobody has heard from or seen them since.'

Adam's heart thumped rapidly. How could hundreds of people disappear overnight? And what worried him was the fact that the man behind this, Dr. Mao, had engineered a meeting with him a few days before.

CHAPTER 3

O n the other side of the green hill beside Oria's water springs, a camp was set. Soldiers rushed out of their tents, hearing the commander's call on loudspeakers. In less than a minute, six hundred armed WMST men were lined up before the commander. The colonel was standing on the third step of a helicopter, holding a megaphone. Behind him were a hundred-and-fifty military choppers, waiting to fly the commandos to the battlefield. They were armed with air-ground missiles and machine-guns.

'Are we the soldiers of peace?' the colonel cried out.

'Yes, sir,' the commandos responded as one.

'Are we fighting for the safety of the children?'

'We are!' the army cried out again.

'Do we let fear into our homes?'

'We don't.'

'We are leaving the camp at ten hundred tomorrow.'

'Yes, sir.'

'Released.'

The soldiers spread around the camp to eat their last lunch in the beautiful valley and prepare for a savage battle.

A sergeant approached the colonel as he was descending the chopper's steps.

'Sir,' said the sergeant, 'what do we do with the captive villagers?'

'We can't risk releasing them now. We have no choice but to take them with us,' said the colonel. 'We will let them go after the attack.'

'We just received a message from headquarters,' said the sergeant. 'They want us to stay until the fifth regiment joins us.'

'The fifth regiment?' the colonel said, agitated. 'Where the hell did that come from?'

'We have no further details, sir.'

'We leave at the designated time. I will announce the new camp's location before the flight.'

'Yes, sir.' The sergeant got to his feet.

'Sergeant!' The colonel called him again. 'What's going on in Oria?'

'Sir, the villagers are getting worried about the missing ones.'

'Did you contact the mayor?'

'We couldn't find him, sir. He seems not to be in the village.'

At lunchtime the smell of animal flesh burning on fires aggravated thousands of migrating crows which had flown to the safety of the hill's ash trees, hiding there behind the leaves. One after another, the ravenous birds started to squawk loudly. The valley was filled with the echo of the hungry and furious birds' protest and the campsite fell silent, the men listening to them, appalled.

CHAPTER 4

On the dawn of the first day of autumn, when Oria was filled with the festive spirit of the harvest celebration, the villagers put on their traditional clothes and made their way to the field for the ceremony. The women's costume was a light blue robe, which was covered by a cloak of the same color for single ladies. Men were supposed to wear white cotton suits with dark brown belts and shoes.

There was a stone stage by the river which was set every year for the mayor's speech starting the harvest celebrations. Since he was not in the village, Mr. Savio had to perform the task instead. He climbed on the stage, dressed in a purple suit, and waved to the people. They all waved back cheerfully.

'Petals of purple and white! Spirits of this wonderful land of God's blessing. People of Oria!' shouted Mr. Savio. '*Felice Raccolta!*'

'*Felice Raccolta!*' the people shouted back all together.

'We are grateful to God for this joyful occasion he has bestowed upon us. Dear God! Never deprive us of your touch!'

'Amen!' the people shouted together.

'Now let's play 'touch the couple'!'

All the villagers stood up at the table and put on masks made of wood, which had been crafted by the women of the village.

'Six men!' said Mr. Savio. 'Six young men who haven't done military service are needed to start the game. One of them should dress like a bride and one like a groom. Two of them should dress like soldiers and two should be dressed in black. The couple will run around the field and you must run after them in groups of five and try to touch them. The soldiers will run with the couple to protect them from your hands. The other two lads carry pails of black paints and they will pour it on those who succeed in touching the couple. At the end of the game, those whose clothes are black will be announced the winners.'

Six young men dressed as required climbed on the stage and then joined and raised their hands.

'Let the game begin!' said Mr. Savio.

Adam climbed on to the stage as well and started to play the celebration's opening song. The six young men began to dance on the platform. A spirit of joy and festivity began to spread through the field. People applauded the performers, clapping and waving their hands with the music.

There was no priority as to who was to be selected in the first group to run after the couple and groups were chosen at random by Mr. Savio. Adam wouldn't play during the game, for his music would not be heard among the people's excited cheers. Nor would he be seen among all the joyous movements of the villagers. Therefore, he would rather, he thought, join them in the folk dance.

The first five runners started the game when their names were called. After hours of enjoying the thrill of the game by the river, the villagers stopped to sit at the tables and start the celebratory meal. Every family had brought produce from their farms and a special lunch. While eating, the villagers offered their food to each other, making the most of the one day of a gathering of the people.

The game continued in the afternoon, when all the villagers put on their masks and started to dance by the river. Adam walked towards the crowd. He was delighted by the cheers of happiness from the people and the children's laughter and feeling the festive spirit of autumn. He was masked and dressed as every one else was.

At the end of the day all the villagers climbed the hill to wait for darkness and observe the comet. Adam started to play the sailor song and his band sang it several times until the light faded. Everyone was looking for a shiny spot and its tail in the sky. The stars appeared one after another and the crescent moon blazed in the middle like a commander guarded by his army. Twilight had almost gone, giving way to night. There was still no trace of the shiny sailor in the sky.

Everywhere fell silent, for the people were gradually becoming despondent. There was no comet to be seen in the night sky. This was the first time in the history of the village that the comet had not been seen on the evening of the first day of autumn, fifty years after its previous passing across the sky above the village. Joy turned into bemusement. The mystery of the comet's absence had confused everyone and they all stayed up till the morning, for they were heroes of the land of hopefulness and they believed the sailor would finally show up.

Dawn came and the comet was not seen anywhere in the dark sky. Disappointed, the villagers sat on the celebration field, watching the sun rising from behind the mountain. Soon the blaze of sun brought renewed life to the orchards. People started to leave the field, one after another.

The villagers were bewildered by the incident and the unexpected shadows of that melancholy morning. They had been deprived of a part of the celebration's rituals the night before and there was an unwanted prediction of an unsatisfactory farming year in their minds. It had been among their traditional beliefs that the village owed its matchless weather conditions to the shiny sailor. The darkness of the night had dashed all hopes of a bountiful harvest.

Adam picked up his instrument and walked toward his temple. He felt different from the other villagers. The mayor had appointed him to be in charge of their happiness and his mission had ended with dread and disappointment. He had done his best but he felt guilty, for he hadn't been able to fulfill the one desire that his grandfather had for his people.

There was no spirit of community in the place any more. The people were scattered on the river's bank. Suddenly a dreadful but familiar sound turned every eye to the mountain. The swallows stopped their morning song in the trees. Mothers held their babies tightly. The appalled faces of the villagers increased the fear sweeping through their number.

THE CRIES. THE BIRDS' CRIES.

It went on for minutes, becoming louder and louder. It seemed as though the mountain was about to stand up and attack the village. A dark mist appeared on the top of the mountain and it grew larger and larger, while the cries became louder and louder.

Finally they were seen: crows flying towards the village from behind the mountain; thousands and thousands of them, all flying in the same direction. All consumed by savagery. Their red eyes moved in search of flesh and blood. The massive flock of the birds reached the sky above the village. Their dark feathers covered every single spot of blue sky, blotting out the sun. Night arrived for the second time and the whole sky went dark. The birds were flying everywhere. The villagers started to flee to their shelters. They were so scared and baffled that they didn't even know where to run.

Adam stood still and made no movement during the whole terrifying episode. There was just one thought in his mind, the message he had received:

'The birds are coming.'

He had been warned of the terror weeks ago. Besides being horrified by the frantic scene, he felt guilty and responsible for the villagers. He had been alerted to this happening, but he had not taken any action to prevent it. He had not believed the message. He had not even attempted to prepare the people to face its warning. How he wished that all he was seeing was a nightmare. But the more he waited to wake up, the more he recognized the reality of the birds; the more his ears were filled by their cries of fear, the more terrifying the vision of the darkness which they had created.

The nightmare of the birds went on for about twenty minutes. Twenty minutes of an eclipse which was both natural and supernatural. Twenty minutes of an ill-fated morning that the birds had brought to the village.

And then a new sound was heard all over the village: a sound which had the birds flying away in alarm. And the source of the sound appeared in the sky. Over a hundred military helicopters appeared in the sky over the village, flying from behind the mountain. They were so low that the letters written on them could be read: **WMST.**

'What are they, sir?' asked Adam.

'They are called the saviors of mankind from itself.' Said Savio 'WMST stands for Weapons of Mass Destruction Strike Team.'

'They are going to bombard somewhere?'

'This military was formed by the UN to fight against nuclear weapons.'

'With these choppers?'

'They possess their own Air Force, Navy and Ground Forces.'

CHAPTER 5

Adam waited desperately to see his grandfather. He had many questions to ask. He was sure that the mayor and his council had been aware of the coming disaster and their disappearance could have been for no other reason but to prevent whatever had taken place on the night of the celebration. They had gone to protect the village, but Adam was not certain whether they had managed to save it or not.

He dropped by home to see if his grandfather was there or had sent him a letter but, as he had expected, there was no news from the council, no news from the mayor.

He didn't linger and started to make his way to the temple. As he drew close he saw a figure moving within his temple. He started to run. A man with a masked face put something on the stone seat inside the temple. Spotting Adam, he ran away.

The object was a box wrapped like a present. Adam picked it up to see if he could find any note written on the box. He examined it closely, but he could find nothing to identify the sender.

Opening the box, he found a violin covered by a shield made of silver. On its back was written:

'It should be only with a firm instrument and colors of life that a musician can play among the shadows.
THE SILVER ORCHESTRA

CHAPTER 6

Miles away from Adam's music temple, in a cottage which had been secretly built in the Blue Forest by the order of the village's mayor, the council was discussing the catastrophe which was about to hit the village and its people. There were green hills between the forest and the village through which people rarely passed, for they had no business in the forest. Therefore, the mayor gathered his council there to talk over any matters which threatened the village every now and then. This time the council was convened for an emergency meeting to discuss the offer which had both intrigued and scared them.

The council's meeting chamber was a cottage in the middle of a spinney of bent ash trees. The trees met at their tops, above the cottage's roof. From a distance it looked like an impenetrable dome made of trees.

'I have been regarded as the elder of these people for many years and there has never been a crisis that I have not been able to handle and supervise, with your support,' said the mayor, stroking his fair beard. 'But this one has exceedingly mystified me.'

'It is not going to be a painless matter to the people of the village,' said a council member.

'On the one hand we do not know how to inform them of this horrible news; on the other, we do not know how to help them deal with it,' said another.

'I have the final report that I requested from the World Meteorological Organization.' Keramit flipped through the pages of a file.

'What does it say, Mayor?' asked a councilman.

'We have a year of drought and a cold spell ahead of us in Oria,' Keramat said unhappily. 'That means that the water supply to the orchards will be a major problem, plus the sudden cold weather will almost halt the citrus growth.'

'Gentlemen,' said a councilor,' I know it's hard for all of us, but I guess we need to consider the offer.'

'The offer, though intriguing, doesn't sound sensible,' said Keramat.

'She will arrive any minute to present the propositions that may be the only way to save us,' the deputy mayor said.

'Do we have more information on this lady?' Keramat tried to hide his agitation.

Soon a car could be heard approaching the cottage. Then the sound of car doors being opened and slammed. The cottage's door shook as it was knocked. Not waiting for the hosts to open the door, a huge man in a black suit entered the room. He cast a searching look around the room and then another man of similar size joined him. They stood on opposite sides of the room, not saying a word to the councilors.

Through the open door, Keramat could see a couple of soldiers, holding machine guns, standing each side of the dwelling. A tall middle-aged woman wearing a long white silk raincoat emerged from the car and walked into the cottage.

'Ms Heimlich.' The councilor who had introduced the offer rose from his chair. 'I was just talking about you.'

'Good evening, gentlemen,' she said. 'Please accept my apologies for my abrupt entrance to your council, but there is a very serious matter we need to discuss.'

'Who exactly are you, Ma'am?' asked Keramat. 'And how did you learn about this council and its location?'

'I'm here on behalf of Lady Adelheid Fester,' the woman said, 'the founder of *Kristal Hochburg*. Have you heard about us, Mr. Keramat?'

Hearing the name, Keramat could feel the blood run cold in his veins. He was so appalled that he could not respond to the question.

'Adelheid sent you here?' he asked in a low voice, unable to hide his fear.

'Yes, Mayor. Can we get to the offer, please?'

They all sat down around the council's table.

'We are listening,' Keramat said.

'As you all know, the project of building *Der Kristal Hochburg* or, as you call it here, The Crystal Citadel, is almost over. And as has been broadcast by the media, Lady Adelheid and her team designed and built this modern city to revive a great historical ideology.'

'By ideology, you mean Nazism?' asked Keramat. Every eye turned towards him.

'We managed to rebuild the great city of Germania, a city Hitler once tried to build on the ruins of Berlin,' she said. 'This time we built it in a modern way, not like a stony cemetery. We built it to spread peace, not to start a massacre.'

What Adelheid is about to do, Keramat thought, will make the world wish she had only acted like Hitler.

'How is this connected to Oria's council, Ma'am?' a councilor asked after a long silence.

'Oria is not so far from the Crystal City. Also, it's surrounded by mountains, hills and forest. This makes the village a great location for the security center we need to build quite near to defend the crystal city.'

'And by "security center" you mean a military base?' Keramat frowned.

'I'm afraid I am not allowed to reveal any further details,' she said. 'You own valuable lands in your orchards, which, because of the forecast bad weather, are likely to suffer huge bankruptcies and breakdown in the coming year. Lady Adelheid will be happy to buy your lands at double the value.'

'Why would she do that?' a councilor asked.

'I believe you have all been informed that in the coming year the cold spell will prevent flowering in your orchards,' she said. 'The trees will be fruitless, the lands will be wasted.'

'Ms Heimlich,' said Keramat, 'we do not intend to turn our village that we have built, working hard over many years, into a military base. And even if we wanted to, we would need two-thirds of the council's vote to accept your offer.'

'Of course,' she said, 'but time is a luxury we can not afford. Why don't you give your votes right now?'

'We need to think about such a matter and do a study. Also, the people of Oria should definitely be in the picture.'

Ms Heimlich looked down at the men's faces for a minute, saying nothing, then rose and stalked out of the cottage. The councilors watched the woman and her security team getting in the car and driving away.

Finally the silence was broken by an unfamiliar noise coming from the village. It grew louder and louder. The councilors all left the cottage to see what it was.

The birds flew over the trees of the Blue Forest, making the sky dark with their black feathers. They were flying to the north. *En masse*, they seemed like a dark demon spreading his shadows across the land and making the earth tremble with his monstrous cries.

'Look at them!' said a councilor. 'They are flying from the village.'

'Do you suppose they have attacked the orchards?' asked another man.

'I hope they have not attacked the people!' said the mayor.

The birds flew past the cottage and following them, the WMST choppers appeared.

'Where are they headed this time?' someone asked.

'It must be Russia,' said the mayor. 'They handled their job in the US well. Their next stop is not going to be more challenging than that.'

The mayor and his colleagues watched the helicopters disappear behind the mountain, one after another.

After a few minutes the sound of the rotor blades could be heard again from the depths of the woods, increasing in volume. Eventually a couple of the machines appeared, flying towards them. They hovered above the cottage and started to descend, landing on the flat area beside the cottage.

Nothing was written on them and there were no identifying flags. The doors of both choppers slid open at the same time and about a dozen armed men jumped out. Their faces were masked. They spread around the councilmen, pointing their guns at them.

'Who are you people?' asked the mayor in alarm.

His question remained unanswered.

A man dressed in a suit climbed out of the helicopter.

'Hello, Dr. Keramat,' he said.

'Mao?' said the mayor. 'What do you want here? I thought we were done.'

'It's so nice to see you, too,' said Mao. 'You have always been kind to me.'

Mao gave one of his men a glance. Immediately, the soldiers opened fire on the councilors and shot them all dead. In a matter of seconds everybody was lying on the ground in pools of blood, except one man. The mayor stood before Mao, his head in his hands.

'I'm sorry that this meeting wasn't so pleasant,' said Mao, returning to the chopper.

A couple of the masked men held Keramat's arms and followed.

Within moments, the chopper took off and clattered away over the forest.

CHAPTER 7

Adam stretched out his hand to the box and picked up the strange new violin. The metal shield added substantial weight to the instrument and the silver layer shone in the sun; it was far heavier than the violin he possessed. The box had not given up its whole burden yet. Something was still shining inside. He took it out and saw that it was a sparkling silver bow. Examining the bizarre present which had been sent from an unknown source, Adam experienced a strange feeling, something which he had never had with his own violin. When he took it by his left hand and held the metal bow in his right, he felt as though he was holding a sword. The silver cover reflected the sun and the violin felt like a weapon in his hand.

As he drew the bow across the strings, trying to play something on the new instrument, the sound was so harsh that he couldn't even complete the note.

'Playing among the shadows,' Adam thought. What would that mean?'

Bewildered by the many questions that had formed in his mind, he went in search of Mr. Savio. He would be the only person who could possibly know how to solve the puzzle of the birds, the mayor's absence and the new violin.

Savio was still sitting in the celebration field, trying to think of a way to reassure the people. He had to inform them of the disaster awaiting them, the drought which was about to hit the village.

The villagers were hiding in their homes. No one was working in the orchards. No children were allowed to play in the fields. No shepherd dared to take his herds to the pastures. No old man or woman was sitting by the river enjoying the melody of the flowing water. They had all locked themselves in to avoid a possible second encounter with the birds. The village had sunk into such silence that it seemed as if it had been deserted for many years. The swallows had stopped twittering in the trees. But the river was still singing and the branches were still dancing in the rain.

The day had almost ended and a full moon was about to shine on the orchards and, as they believed, protect them from the shadows of night. Savio and Adam sat side by side on the platform. Exhausted and confused by recent happenings, Adam had no strength to ponder his next step. He reclined on the platform by Mr. Savio and closed his eyes. In a few minutes he fell asleep like a child. His dreams were blurry and strange.

Adam woke up on the platform. Savio was sitting next to him, just as he had been in the dream. He could not help but pick up the silver violin and try it. Unlike the first time he had played, in the daylight, the violin sounded good.

'Adam?' asked Savio, 'where did you get this violin?'

'It was sent to me,' said Adam, 'along with a message. But there's something weird about it.'

'What is that?'

'I played it in the morning. It sounded really harsh. But now it sounds great.'

'Let me see it.' Savio took the violin, examining it carefully.

'You see this shield on the instrument?'

'Yes, what about it?'

'The silver shield acts like a solar energy absorber,' said Savio. 'You play it under the sun, it produces electricity and takes it to the end part of the violin '

'Let me take another look.' Adam took back the violin. 'I see, and the strings are loosed, so the instrument will be completely out of tune.'

'Exactly.'

Savio pondered a while.

'And I guess it's time to follow the river,' he said.

'What?' Adam was shocked. 'Are you pulling my leg?'

'No, my lad. Actually your grandfather told me if we didn't hear from him in ten days after he had gone, I must ask you to follow the river. That's where you will find him.'

'Follow the river where?'

'I really have no idea. Everybody knows that he had been keeping a secret for a very long time. Maybe now he wants things to be revealed to you.'

Adam picked up the silver violin and started to play. The melody was so soothing that people gathered around the stage, sat on the grass and listened to it.

CHAPTER 8

T he commandos manhandled Keramat out of the helicopter. His eyes were blindfolded. They walked him down the stairs and then guided him to the elevator.

'Which level, sir?' asked one of the guards.

'The secret level,' said Mao. 'Our friend is going to have a hell of a holiday.'

After a few seconds the elevator door opened on to a hall in which there were four closed doors. There they uncovered his eyes.

'Don't hurt Adam,' said Keramat. 'You can't do this to him.'

'If you hadn't taken him away from us, none of this would have happened,' said Mao. 'Don't worry about him; he will soon be where he must be.'

'He doesn't know anything about the project. I kept him away from everything for twenty-seven years. I have protected him from all this.'

'And that was your mistake; you did not protect him.' Mao paused. 'You betrayed him and you betrayed us.' His voice rose. 'Get him out of my sight!' he shouted.

The guards opened one of the doors which led into a small holding room and pushed him inside.

CHAPTER 9

Adam passed through the hills, following the river's direction. Sticking to the river bank wasn't at all easy. The steeper the path, the easier it was for the river to pass through the sand and rocks, and the harder for Adam to follow. He couldn't go down the slopes as the river did and, because he had to find passable paths, he would lose sight of the river. He wondered constantly why there was no road leading to the destination demanded.

Why were no cars or trains going there?

His mind was mixed up with thoughts, most particularly worry about his grandfather. As far as he knew, the mayor must be the only one who could provide answers to all the mystifying questions which had gathered in his mind.

He thought about the university grant that he was missing; about all the pieces he had composed, yet which he had to keep unplayed beside his mute violin, and about the journey he had to make alone. At last he entered the Blue Forest. In the forest the river was easy to follow. There were no flowers. It was all a green landscape, even a green sky, for the sky could hardly be seen through the green leaves of ash and oak trees which where entangled together. The journey through the woods took Adam three days. He stayed at nearby small towns' inns at night and walked during the day.

Walking on the bank of the river, where the air was filled by the seductive odor of lilies, a green mass the in distance caught his eye. It lay in the river's direction, like a dam or a huge green hill blocking the water flow. Coming closer, he discerned some colorful domes on the green mass as well. It wasn't a hill; it was a long, high wall, made of huge brown bricks. The wall was as tall as the trees. It was extensively covered by plants, their thick branches and green leaves spread over the bricks. There was a tunnel where the river narrowed to its opening and ran through the wall. No one could pass through it, for thick metal rails had been put there to prevent passage. The water flow through the tunnel was so massive and wild that Adam doubted he could reach the other side of the wall alive, even if he could get through.

There were towers all along the wall, equidistant from each other, and on top of them were glass structures, like crowns in shape. They were not the crowns of monarchs. Roses of many different colors had been planted in them. In one, a dome of pink and yellow roses, in another one black and red blooms and in another orange and purple. The crowns of flowers sparkled like lighthouses from a distance.

He had to walk along the massive wall to find his way to the river again, while the wall turned to north. He could hear voices from the other side of the structure. He heard the laughter of men, what sounded like a crowd of people talking and car engines. But all he could see was the high wall, covered by vigorously growing branches and their leaves, and the huge crowns of roses on top.

At last he reached an entrance. A huge gate stood wide open. There were no guards standing there. It looked like the entrance to a citadel. Above the gate were white tiles, a bed of roses painted on them. Above the roses was a huge sign, engraved on crystal. The sign read:

K H

K H? That was the motif on the letter he had received in Rome.

On each side of the gate was a crystal statue of a woman about seven meters tall, holding a tilted pot of water on her shoulders, water pouring out of them into small pools of blue tiles decorated with flowers. Adam didn't hesitate; he scooped up the water with both hands and drank. It was cold and fresh.

To pass through the gate, he had to walk under a large glass arch, on which was painted a broken cross in red. The gate was like a ten-meter-long tunnel, its walls covered by glass. As he moved inside, the light shades became lighter, so that the glass shields displayed markings, written in digital ink. The sensors on the characters seemed to react to the objects passing before them and changed their colors so that they could be read. Adam could read on one side of the wall **EIN VOLK** and on the other side **EIN REICH.**

'One people, one nation,' he translated. 'What could that possibly mean?

As he stepped out of the tunnel, an enchanting music caught his ears. A group of girls wearing white shirts and red skirts with black stripes on them were playing a delightful song. Adam stood still and listened to their music with interest. He took out the silver violin and started to play with them. But as he pulled the bow across the strings a horrible harsh noise shattered the air. The girls stopped playing and covered their ears. Adam had forgotten that he could play the silver instrument only at night.

The band put their instruments in their covers and started to leave. He was so ashamed of what he had done. He had played numerous pieces in front of audiences and he hadn't received anything but applause. And now, because of the terrible noise which came out of his instrument, the group had lost their enthusiasm and gone away.

One of the girls walked toward Adam. She had a gentle expression on her face.

'*Wilkommen sie zu Kristall Hochburg,*' she said.

'*Kristall Hochburg?*' asked Adam. '*Ich spreche Deutsch, aber ich verstehe nicht dich.*'

'So let me try it this way,' said the girl. 'Welcome to the Crystal Citadel; or as some call it, the city of the future.'

Adam took a look around. The city of the future? The roses on the wall, the way these girls dressed, the statues. It looked more like a fantasy city.

'I am terribly sorry about what happened with the violin,' said Adam.

'Not every one can play as beautifully as me and these girls, sir.'

'What can I say?'

'Anyway, we were told to come here and play you the welcome song.'

'That was a welcome song for me?' Adam said, shocked. 'You knew I was coming? Who told you?'

'Our lady, Adelheid Fester, has sent us'

Adam did not ask any further questions for he knew there wouldn't be reasonable answers. He had walked through the forest to get here. There was no road or railway to this city. He did not fly in here. How could she possibly know that he was coming, and when he would arrive?

'Why don't you ask her yourself?' The girl took his hand, gazing him with her brown eyes. 'Shall I show you the way to her place?'

'I'm actually looking for the river,' Adam prevaricated.

'You mean you are not willing to play the violin for our lady?'

'She wants me to play for her?'

'Of course! She has been longing for this moment.'

'I guess I will have to, then. What is she like?'

'She is not like anyone. I really doubt if there are enough words in the world to describe her.'

'You just heard what my violin sounds like! Are you really sure your lady wants to hear that!'

'Follow me,' said the girl, winking at him. 'You look tired; you need to rest.'

They walked along the pavement to reach Adelheid's house, passing through a vast garden of roses. All he could see was roses of different colors, on bushes and trees; he never knew that roses in purple and blue existed, but he was walking among them. Maybe this was a future city, developed in the field of agriculture.

They reached a cluster of trees which where tied together at the top. They were full of flowers. Beneath was a temple, surrounded by leaves and roses.

'Has this been made by the people of the mansion, or is it some sort of natural creation?' he asked.

'This is Lady Adelheid's music temple. She calls it the Temple of Roses.'

'Amazing! She has a music temple?'

'I suppose there is a violin in there; don't you want to practice a bit before playing in front of her?'

'Do you know how many hours I have spent practicing?'

'No offense, but you may not be familiar with Lady Adelheid's instrument.'

'You mean I'd better not play my own instrument?'

'Maybe your instrument does not belong here. You saw what happened today!'

They went inside the temple. Adam took Adelheid's violin and started to play a piece. The girl sat next to him and listened intently. When the piece was over, she took his hands for the second time.

'Has anyone ever told you how wonderfully you play?' she asked.

And before Adam could reply she took the violin and started to play the same piece he had just played. She played the melody exactly the same way. Adam thought that he had only done something like that once, and he could never do it again. He had to listen to a piece several times before being able to play it.

Before Adam could think any more about this, all the blossoms in the temple opened into the prettiest petals and a sweet perfume began to overwhelm him. After nearly two hours he woke up, to find himself still lying in the rose temple. The girl was lying next to him, murmuring a gentle song.

Adam stood up and stepped out of the temple. It was almost dark and the stars could be seen. He took the silver instrument out of his satchel to see if it would make a terrible sound again. But it sounded as wonderful as it had the previous night, when he had played his song for the villagers.

The silver instrument 'does not belong here.' Why did she say that? What do these people know about it? How do they really know me? The questions reverberated in his mind.

'Where are we going now?' asked Adam

'To the mansion.' The girl pointed at the huge illuminated building in the near-distance.

They reached a massive construction which had towers on both sides. On top of these were huge glass spheres, colored pink, red and yellow. The light inside them made them shine in the darkness like two great roses on the sides of the mansion. The building was covered with white stones that reflected the whole front garden like a mirror. The entrance gate was in the shape of a huge triangle, made of dark green glass. In front of it was a round pool with a fountain at the center.

As they approached the gate, the doors swung inward. They entered a large hall which had a high glass ceiling, stars shining through it. At every corner were big vases of roses. The girl walked in front to show Adam the way. The floor was covered by glossy grey stones in which he could see his reflection. The high walls of the hall, which were richly ornamented by large colorful oriental paintings, had no windows, for the glass ceiling would let in enough sunlight. The paintings were of beautiful women of different nationalities. One showed a group of Chinese women in full-length dresses of red, white and orange with a light red background. Another depicted blonde women with long ponytails and blue eyes. And another one was of brown-skinned women dressed in red saris sitting in an exotic garden.

They came to the middle of the hall, where the girl stopped. Adam could hear footsteps from the other room as though an army of women in high heels were tapping their way to the main hall. And then they arrived. A dozen women, dressed in white shirts and red skirts, entered the hall. They formed two rows on two sides of the hall and stood still. Everywhere fell silent. Then footsteps were heard again. But this time they sounded like one person, not in high heels.

A woman wearing a long grey dress with very small white dots entered the hall and the girls knelt before her feet. She sat on one of the silk armchairs placed around a large round table. All the other girls took their seats. Adam was sure he had seen the lady before but he couldn't remember where?

'Don't you want to show our dearest guest his seat, darling?' the lady said to Tania in a soft voice.

Tania bowed to Lady Adelheid and showed Adam to his special seat. It was a tall stool with a feather cushion on it, covered in grey velvet.

'This must be such a hard journey for a young man of your age,' Adelheid said.

'Indeed it is; and in many ways I really don't know why I should be going through it,' said Adam.

'I have heard about the magic you do with your instrument.'

'That is very kind of you.'

'You may know how fond I am of music.'

'Yes, my lady. I met your violin as well.'

'You did?' Lady Adelheid glanced at Tania. She opened the box on the table in front her and took out a violin. 'I cannot say how long my girls and I have been waiting for this moment,' she said, handing him the instrument.

Adam took the violin. He was impressed by his hostess's kindness and hospitality. He liked the way she had praised him and his art. He was in a hurry to find the river, but he had decided to accept the interruption to his journey and experience all he had been summoned to do in the mansion.

He played one of his loveliest pieces and received warm applause from the lady and her girls, who seemed to be her students.

'My lady, it is quite an experience to be in your stunning mansion, but would you mind showing me the way to the river? I'm afraid I have important business and I can't stay any longer.'

'Isn't the river a path that takes you to the higher levels of mastery and being known as you truly deserve, young man?' she replied.

'A path?'

'And you're standing on the path now.'

'I am not following you, my lady.'

'You will have whatever you need here to win the fame that you deserve.'

'What are you asking me to do?'

'I want you to stay here and compose your lovely songs for my girls.'

Briefly, he remembered the Temple of Roses. It had all started with a touch of the bow on the strings and ended up with the joy of making love to Tania. There was the same feeling in everything he had observed in the mansion since his arrival. The beauty of the mansion and its inhabitants produced a unique ecstasy which was not to be found in the world beyond its walls.

'What say you?' asked Adelheid, giving him a smile.

'My lady! I have a mission and I am expected to follow it through. My grandfather is waiting for me. He may be in serious trouble at this very moment.'

'Let's not talk about it now. You can rest here tonight and you decide tomorrow.'

Looking at the night sky through the glass ceiling, Adam reached for his satchel and took out the silver violin.

'You were great with my violin,' said Adelheid. 'Why don't you keep your instrument for after dinner?'

'I know I have insulted your girls today with my own very special instrument.' He rested his chin on the silver violin.

'Please!' said Adelheid, standing up. 'The table is set.'

At the long glass table, Adelheid sat at one end, Adam at the other, with the girls standing on either side about two meters away from the table. Dishes of roast lamb and chicken were placed along the table, baskets of cherries and pineapple and jars of mango juice between them. Half-a-dozen flower pots, fixed to the table, stood among the dishes, containing gloriously colored roses.

Adelheid looked at Adam during the dinner, her gentle gaze soothing his heart, which was full of worries for himself, his grandfather and the villagers. Tania was seated next to Adam throughout.

When dinner was almost over, Adelheid said, 'We will not disturb you any more tonight. My girls will show you where you can rest in peace.'

'Thank you, my lady! Thanks for everything!' Adam said.

'Meet me in the temple at midnight,' said Tania, putting her hand on his thigh.

When midnight came, the mansion was completely silent. There was perfect peace in the building. Adam stepped into the garden, eager to meet Tania. He walked quietly to avoid waking anyone. In the darkness, he made his way to the temple. It seemed empty.

'Anyone here?' he whispered.

There was no reply. The scent of roses had intensified at night; a cool breeze spreading the perfume everywhere was enough to seduce any lover. Then he heard footsteps. They were not very loud, but close.

'Don't move!' He heard a whisper behind him.

Tania!

Soft hands covered his eyes from behind. The scent rising from the cool hands drove him wild with desire. He held the hands, moved them down to his lips and kissed them. He turned around. The midnight lover was not Tania.

'Didn't you expect to meet me here?' she asked gently.

'Lady Adelheid!'

Light filled the temple. Girls appeared from every corner, Tania among them. They all walked towards him, Adelheid in front. He stepped backwards until he hit the wall of roses. He hardly felt the thorns on his back; his thoughts were all on pleasure.

'What is going on?' he asked. 'What are you up to, ladies?'

Adelheid moved closer, took both his hands and clung to him.

'Young and strong like a stallion!' she said, leering. 'Don't you want real pleasure tonight?'

Adam lost all capacity to think. All that he could see was beauty at the heart of night, all that he could smell was the scent of roses arising from the bodies as well as the flowers themselves and all he could touch were the smooth skins of the girls moistened by fresh petals.

CHAPTER 10

In the morning Adam and Lady Adelheid had taken a splendid breakfast in the dining-hall of the mansion. She was eyeing him up the entire time.

'I have come up with a surprise for your girls, my lady,' said Adam, smiling.

'Are you trying to return their surprise of last night?' she asked.

'Actually, I have composed a song for them.'

'A song? When did you write it?'

'Just this morning.'

'Amazing! And what did you call it?'

'No title yet. Titles come when the piece is practiced and ready to perform.'

'Perform or market?'

'You tell me.'

'I see a bright future for you'. She smiled. 'By the way, can you do me a favor?'

'Anything, my lady!'

'I can't wait to see you practicing with the girls.'

'My lady! You know that I cannot stay in the city too long, don't you?'

'Yes, you brought it up last night.'

'But I am willing to practice one piece with them before I continue on my journey.'

'Journey.' She sighed. 'We talked about that. Remember?'

'I do, my lady.'

'Do something for me this morning!'

'Of course, my lady!'

'Go to the town and buy some equipment for your new orchestra. My girls will accompany you to the music store.'

Adam's vision started to blur. 'I feel so sleepy,' he said. 'I guess it's because of last night.' He couldn't resist putting his head on the table, where he fell asleep.

'Take him to his room,' Adelheid commanded.

A couple of men took Adam's arms and carried him to his bed.

Adelheid picked up the cup out of which he had drunk tea. Tania watched her.

'We're in the game,' said Adelheid, looking at the cup. 'Watch and learn what my magic can do.'

In the room where Adam lay sleeping, Adelheid, a man dressed in a white uniform and a nurse were standing by his bed. The room was full of electrical medical devices. Several wires were attached to different parts of Adam's head and the man was observing the changing graphs on a monitor.

'Has he heard what we wanted, Doctor?' Adelheid asked.

'I can't say for sure yet,' said the doctor. 'I need to have his brain washed for twenty-four hours.'

Adam was dreaming.

He left the mansion in the company of a group of girls. Tania was walking in front to show him the way. They were all walking fast. They passed the street market laughing and cheering and walked across the bridge over the river which seemed to have been dry for a long time until they reached a street with the dried-up river on one side and beautiful mansions on the other. Dozens of fine houses faced the river, each owned by a wealthy man of the city. They came to the music store, a massive building formed like a white piano. Between the front legs of the piano was a large shop window, displaying every type of instrument he had ever heard about or seen. Among them, one instrument drew his attention. He went inside the shop. A lyre, shining silver and with a mirror on it stood next to the drums. He walked towards it.

'Don't you want to try that piano over there?' asked Tania, pulling at his hand.

'The lyre, the mother of all the instruments,' said Adam. 'How can you take me away from this miraculous piece of primitive craftsmanship?'

And he started to move his fingers on the silver lyre's strings. The melody coming from the instrument was so enchanting that he did not notice the store clerk's eyes on him. He was lost in the instrument's magical tune. When he stopped playing, he couldn't find Tania or any of Adelheid's girls in the store.

Rising from his stool, Adam started to look for the girls. He walked all over the store, but they had all vanished. It seemed as if there was no one except him

*inside the giant white piano; even the store clerks had
left. He had been so immersed in the lyre and its magical
melody that he hadn't noticed what had happened. He
couldn't even recall how long he had been playing.*

*'Why don't you carry on your lovely tune, young
man?' said a voice from upstairs.*

*A man dressed in a fancy white suit walked down
the stairs.*

*'You must be the owner of this place,' said Adam. 'I
was sent here to do some shopping.'*

*'And all of a sudden you found yourself lost in my
music land,' said the man.*

'I have no idea! Where is everybody?'

*'Isn't it just heartbreaking?' said the man, sitting at
his shiny marble desk. 'Your escorts left you in the blink
of an eye.'*

*'They left without telling me because they didn't
want to interrupt my music, that's it,' Adam suggested.*

*'Amazing! Why don't you finish your piece for me,
then? I will be all ears!'*

*'My pleasure, sir. Actually, I don't find leaving this
place that easy! I could stay here and play like this for
ever!'*

*Adam sat on the stool behind the lyre and started to
play. As he touched the strings, a terrible noise came from
the instrument. He tried a second time, thinking that the
man's words might have affected his confidence. But it
sounded even more unpleasant than his previous attempt.
He tried it several times while the man sat before him,
willing to listen to the rest of the piece. But it looked as if
the notes had moved on the instrument, or else he had lost*

his ability to play. He'd had a bad dream like that before, like he was trying to play his violin and couldn't, and so he thought it was just a nightmare and waited for it to end. But the more he waited, the more he recognized the reality of the situation.

'Well done!' The man clapped.

Tania and the girls came downstairs and stood by his side.

'Now play it again,' said the man.

Fearing to fail, Adam lingered for a minute, trying to solve the puzzle before it could cripple his mind. He decided to give it another try.

He moved his hands on the lyre's strings. He found that he could play it as beautifully as the first time. He didn't stop playing as he feared failing to take control over the instrument again and he played the piece till the end. Adelheid's girls all clapped. So did the man.

'I . . . I don't understand,' said Adam, astonished. 'What is going on? Tell me I am dreaming!'

'Some call it dreaming,' said the man, 'but you are not!'

'Then what is it? I have never found myself unable to play an instrument.'

'Let me ask you something.' The man stood up.

'Go on!'

'Was this the first time you played an instrument other than the violin?'

'No, I have played many instruments in college.'

'Was the lyre among them?'

'No, sir, I have never played it before in my life.'

'And do you know that it's a difficult instrument to play?'

'I do.'

'Yet you played it here as masterfully as a pro lyrist.'

'I did? I guess you are right. But how could this happen?'

'And the fact is quite obvious that you managed to do it in Adelheid's girls' presence.'

'And when they left, I couldn't play it at all!'

'Exactly!'

'It's in our presence that you are master of all the instruments,' said Tania.

'Why is that so?' Adam's head spun.

'Follow me,' said the man.

They climbed the curved stairs and entered a room with large mirrors on every wall.

'What color clothes are you wearing?'

'Gray and white.'

'Now look at yourself in that mirror.'

Adam looked and saw himself dressed in red and yellow.

'Look at the other mirror.' The man turned and pointed to his left. 'Now what do you see?'

There he was in blue and purple. He checked himself on all four sides of the room, and in each saw himself in different colored clothes. Then he started to check his reflection for a second time, and again, different colors appeared on different sides.

'If you stay here and turn for the rest of your life they will be changing and changing and changing,' said the man.

'What is the power of these mirrors?'

'They are just simple mirrors.'

'But . . .'

'But we are living in a magical world!'

'How can this happen in a simple mirror? A mirror is supposed to show things as they are! It cannot change them!'

'My mirrors did not change you. In one you're in red, in the other, in blue and in another in yellow.'

'But I'm dressed in white and gray!'

'My mirrors do not change your look.' The man sat down on a stool which was in the middle of the room. 'They just show you the possibilities.'

Adam checked the man's reflection in all the mirrors and saw only the white suit in all of them.

'Possibilities?' he asked the violin man.

'You are dressed in gray and white. This is a fact. But you could have been dressed in many different colors; these are possibilities. The mirrors show us what you could have looked like, not what you actually look like.'

'And you mean Adelheid's girls act like these mirrors? They show me the possibilities?'

'A little more than that.' He grinned. 'There are things that we have gained, things that we could have gained and things that we wish to get.'

'So?'

'Lady Adelheid, her mansion and her girls can give you what you wish. Playing the lyre has probably been a wish of yours, and it was with them that you achieved it. Adelheid's mansion is a place in which you can have what you could have had and what you'd like to have.'

'If they have such a gift, people should flock to the mansion from all around the world. Why are they so lonely?'

'Because nobody is aware of their gift.'

He was invited to the Rose Temple as on the night before and he willingly accepted. Spending the night with the girls in the temple was the only way out of his worries. He didn't have to think about anything but the soft bodies of the girls and their lovely ploys to make him dance with them. The parties went on night after night. He slept during the morning, practiced songs with his band in the afternoon and made love to them. That sounded like a fair arrangement to him.

One night, when he was at the peak of pleasure, he sensed other ideas in his mind once again. Enjoyment was not the only thought in his mind any more. Alongside with all the ecstasy, he could feel something uneasy within, something that started to distract him from the girls.

He woke up before dawn. He went to his room inside the mansion to fetch the silver violin. He walked far from the building to avoid waking anybody. Then he walked to the music store and sat on the entrance steps and started to play. He played for a long time, picturing the mid-autumn celebration and the evergreen pastures. He could hear the villagers' laughter and the children's chorus.

He played until daybreak. He had passed the night in indecision and doubt. He had stumbled into a life filled with a new type of joy and connections from which he had always been distanced. Living in a residential college, far from any family or caring people and spending all his time in the music temple during the summer had been his whole life in recent years and now he had found a chance to experience a new way of living. His grandfather had been the only caring person in his life and he did not know where to find him.

He decided to explore the town and he knew that the river was the main target of his search. There were no cabs in the city. Indeed, at that hour, there were no cars or people in the streets. He needed to ask someone how to get back to the entrance to the city as he wanted to find the tunnel through which the river flowed and disappeared. He stood in the street waiting for a guide. Twenty-odd minutes passed without a single passerby.

The houses near the street had tall fences and large gardens; each had a big gate with a surveillance camera above it. He walked towards a traffic light. There was not even a policeman posted at the crossroads. There were four cameras watching the four sides of the junction. The lights went red. For almost half-an-hour he had not met a single person in the city. Suddenly, the silence was broken. He heard motorcycles approaching, the sound growing louder and louder. A couple of motorcycles came into the crossroad. The riders were wearing helmets and dark glasses. He waved at them, but they passed by without noticing him. The lights were still red. Three white BMWs passed the crossroad. They had darkened windows and he couldn't see those inside the cars. It seemed as if a prominent person was being escorted somewhere.

Disappointed at not finding someone to take him to the river, he walked on and at the traffic lights he came upon a phone booth. He went inside. The phone was as odd as everything else in the city. It had no buttons to dial a number. There was a knob on its side which could be set in three positions. One was for the police department, the second the fire department and the third showed numbers. Adam picked up the phone and turned the knob to the figures.

'How can I help you, young man with violin?' said the voice on the phone.

Now Adam was sure that he was being watched. Cameras could be seen in every street and they must have been watching him since he had left the mansion at midnight.

'Who am I talking to?' he asked.

'Let's imagine it's the Tourist Information Office.'

'Ok, then how can I find the tunnel through which the river flows?'

'And why would you want to go there?'

'I would like to take a picture there,' he lied.

'Why don't you just hang on for a minute where you are and we will send a guide to pick you up and take you where you want.'

'That would be great. You know where I am, right?'

'Yes, we do and we will be right there with you. We just need you to stay put till we get there.'

Adam waited by the phone booth, drawn into the silence of the city. A car arrived and stopped in front of him. There was no sign on its door to indicate that it was from The Tourist Center and the license plate was that of a normal car. A chubby man got out of the vehicle. He removed his cap and stepped towards Adam to shake his hand.

'Are you the one who called for a guide?' asked the man.

'Yes, I did.' Adam nodded.

'My name is Dmitry. I was told to pick you up and show you the sights.'

'I would appreciate that. Would you mind taking me to the river, please?'

'River?' asked the man. 'There is no river in the city.'

'There is. It flows through a tunnel somewhere near the entrance to the city.'

'What makes you so interested in that tunnel?'

'No offense, but do you mind if we leave these questions for later and you take me there now?'

'No, young man. Let me take your stuff in the car.'

The man approached him, reached in his pocket and took out something like a black shiny stick. Then he raised his hand and rapidly hit Adam on the head. Everywhere went dark and Adam fell on the ground.

When he opened his eyes, he was sitting on a chair with his hands cuffed. He was in a room surrounded by opaque glass shields; it looked like some kind of interrogation room. Dmitry entered the room, accompanied by two other men. One of them unlocked the handcuffs.

'I thought you were a tourist guide,' said Adam wearily. 'Where am I? Police station?'

'Sort of,' said Dmitry.

'Who are you people? What do you want from me?'

'I guess there was a misunderstanding. We are here now to apologize and take you back to your home.'

'To apologize?' raved Adam. 'You hit me on the head, knocked me unconscious and now you want to apologize? Why don't you tell me what the hell is going on? And what do you mean by my home?'

'Lady Adelheid is here. We understand that you have been her guest and you were lost in the city.'

'Where is she now?'

'I am here to take you to her.' Dmitry stretched his hand toward Adam. 'Give me your hand now.'

'What is it? You want to make me unconscious first?'

'No, sir, I explained that was just a misunderstanding.'

'Explained? No one explains anything in this city.'

They went through a long passage which had a number of vacant cells on both sides and arrived at a room where Adelheid and a man were sitting.

'Oh, darling!' said Adelheid. 'What happened to you?'

'I really don't know why I am here' said Adam, his voice tense. 'I just called to ask for directions. There was nobody in the street and then the BMWs passed and I picked up the phone. That's all.'

'Oh dear! You just dialed the wrong number. It was just a misunderstanding. It's good that it is over now.'

'It is not over yet!' yelled Adam. 'I don't want to be in this city any more. I need to find the river now.'

'Ok, ok, calm down,' said Adelheid. 'The head of the department and I will take you where you want to go, right now.'

'I'm afraid I have something to take care of here,' said the man. 'Dmitri will go with you.'

'No surprise this time,' chuckled Dmitri. 'I promise.'

They stepped out of the building. Adam turned back to see where he had been held. The five-storey building did not look like a police station and it had no sign outside. It had very small windows covered by wooden shutters. As he had not noticed any stairs, he thought that he must have been on the ground floor. There were no guards at the door but the entrance was watched by several cameras.

Adelheid's convertible was parked in front of the building. She led Adam to the car. They set off with Dmitri and an official following in another car. Adelheid drove past parts of the city new to Adam. The houses here looked like villas owned by wealthy people. Every house had a big yard, with middle-sized trees which didn't seem to be very old. As Adam had been brought up with trees, pastures and nature, it was easy for him to estimate the age of the trees in the yards; they could not be more than fifteen years old. The glamorous façade of the buildings could be seen at the far end of the yards. It was obvious that all the houses had been designed and built following the same municipal and architectural codes. They had not more than three floors and the proportion of the area dedicated to the building and yard was equal in all the houses. The only differences between them were the colors, forms and materials which had been used on the facades, together with the varied ethnic symbols on them. One building had Japanese-style roofs and windows, another had French windows and another carvings on the walls. One feature was common to all the buildings and that was the extensive use of glass on the façade. Adam surmised that the owners must have had access to construction materials from many different countries and that the whole city must be owned by prominent people who were probably from different nations or at least interested in the art and architecture of different countries. Passing all these elegant palaces, they arrived in the suburbs of the city.

The road was surrounded by tall trees on both sides. Eventually they reached the gate. It was a huge arch, maybe fifty meters tall, all covered by glass and crystal. It looked like the *Arc de Triomphe* in Paris which he had always fancied walking under one day. On the top of the arch a sign hung, displaying a gigantic broken cross. The car passed through the magnificent crystal gate.

Following the road through the woods, they stopped and Adam and his companions climbed out of the car. He could see a large flat area with fences all around it. There were dozens of armed guards patrolling outside the fence. There were no buildings inside the fence; the ground was covered with concrete. Dmitry walked towards the gate and the guard started to search his body. Adelheid passed through the gate without being searched or questioned. She said something to the guards and beckoned Adam, who also went through without a body search.

'Shall we lead your guest to the room, my lady?' asked the guard.

'No, thanks. I will take him there myself.'

The guards, who were armed from head to toe, with military helmets on their heads, treated Adelheid with total respect. She talked to them the way a commander talks to his troops. Dmitry stayed at the gatehouse and Adam and Adelheid were taken to a staircase which led beneath the ground. They went down the stairs and arrived in a large room which had several elevators inside. Adelheid stepped into one in the middle. On the control panel inside the cabin there were no buttons displaying the floors. There was only a knob with three positions, exactly like the phone booth Adam had seen in the street. Adelheid turned the knob to the numbers and the elevator started to move downward.

The elevator door opened on to a vast space under the ground. There were over fifty gigantic concrete containers, with several bulky pipes linking to each of them. At first, Adam thought oil was flowing into the containers and for sure the reserve would be enough for the yearly consumption of a mega-city. There were not many workers, but the whole area was filled with armed personnel. Adelheid and Adam walked for about half-an-hour, passing by the containers. Adam was so astounded that he couldn't ask any questions. They came to a glass room. On the sign above the doorway was written: 'Headquarters.'

Adelheid entered a code into the security lock and the door opened. She walked inside and Adam followed her. He no longer thought about Adelheid as a sexy figure or an elegant woman. All his erotic attraction to the queen of the strange city had been replaced by a new feeling. He was impressed by the fact that she was in command of all that facility. The glass room was quite large, with a conference table in the middle.

'Why don't you take a seat?' Adelheid suggested.

Adam sat down.

'May I make a request?' he asked.

'Go on, darling.'

'Would you please tell me what is going on?'

'Of course. That is why we are down here. If you hadn't run away from my mansion this morning, I would have told you, reducing the shock.'

'I'm all ears now. But just tell me something. We were supposed to go to the river. Where is it?'

'Right here.'

'Here?'

'The containers you saw earlier, they are not for reserving fuel. The river you were following flows right into them.'

'The river flows into this place? Why? What are you saving this amount of water for?'

'Part of it is being purified to be used as clean water in the city. Some of it flows to the other section of this facility, to generate electricity. And a large amount is being reserved here. In the near future we will be selling water to the world.'

'What if the containers are full?'

'Then we let the water flow to where it was headed before we built this city. We let it go to the underground resources.'

'You built this city?'

'Yes.' Adelheid nodded.

'I can see there is secrecy in all these activities, yet you are telling me all this stuff. Why should I know about it? I am just a stranger here. I don't understand why I should know this much about it.'

'I'll tell you. You are not a newcomer any more. Actually, you never have been.'

'What?'

'You were invited here because we wanted you to be a part of it.'

'A part of what?' Adam felt totally confused.

'A part of the orchestra.'

'Wait a minute,' said Adam, staring at her. 'Did you send me that violin?'

'Yes. And welcome to The Silver Orchestra.'

The door opened and a group of men came in, some of them middle-aged and others young. They were all dressed in suits. Adam's first impression was that they were from different nations. They all took their seats immediately, but the chairman's seat was not as yet taken. Everyone was silent. Looking around, Adam realized that he was the youngest in the group.

After a couple of minutes, a man entered the room and everyone stood up, including Adelheid, who was seated next to the chairman. Respecting the group's custom, Adam stood up, too, though he did not know anything about these people. The man sat down in the chairman's place.

'Gentlemen, lady,' he said, 'good morning.'

Adam was the last to sit down. The chair that was left for him was the one opposite the chairman.

'You must be the talented musician,' the man said to him. 'I have been looking forward to meeting you.'

'A pleasure to meet you, sir,' said Adam.

'I am David Steam. As you can see, I am the Head of Finance.'

'I would be lying if I didn't tell you that this place was quite a shock to me, sir.'

'I know. And for your information we are not musicians. Let's break the ice and introduce you to your new friends.'

'I can't wait, sir.'

'This is Yshimo Nakashi, the chairman of Cidur International Group from Japan; Mr Arthur Salvatore, president and major executive officer of G.K Holdings from Italy; Mr. Peter Fretz, chief executive of Yaman Motors from Germany; Mr . . .'

As they were introduced by Steam, all the members proved to be businessmen from different countries. The names of most of the companies they represented were familiar to Adam, for they were world-famous. He had seen the brands in shop windows and the products were frequently advertised on TV. Now he had the chance of meeting the people behind them.

'As you were informed, my dear dignified and fairly elected master of music,' said Steam, 'these people are the most important shareholders of some of the biggest multinational companies in the world. Their companies have been investing in industry, commerce, banking, international trade and the military for over half a century. And now in the new millennium, we needed to gather here and make very serious decisions.'

'Decisions that will remove depression from the world,' said Adelheid.

'Depression?' repeated Adam. 'I am sure you are not shrinks!'

'Of course we are not,' chuckled Steam. 'Depression is a sort of economic term.'

'Let's say Great Depression,' said Adelheid. 'The first era of great depression took place between 1929 and 1940. It was the first time in the history of the modern world that human beings learned how far the economy can fall. It started in the US and its devastating effects hit many countries and millions of lives. We believe this may have been one of the reasons Adolf Hitler could influence his angry and desperate people to start World War II in 1939.

'And this was not the end of the world's depression,' she went on. 'Just at the beginning of the third millennium, when business leaders and politicians are expected to lead the world to nonstop growth, using the science of modern economy, and create welfare for all human beings from any race or nation, provide health and education for all the children of the world and keep nations safe from economic challenges, the world faced one of the greatest crises in its history.'

'The shiny sailor died,' Adam said sorrowfully.

'Excuse me?' said Steam.

'It is a term the people of my village use for your Great Depression.'

'All right,' said Steam. 'You are familiar with the pain and misery which was created by this breakdown. No matter what we name it, it hurt people we love. Many, many of them.'

'It was estimated that around fifty million people lost their jobs; and that means fifty million families were hit directly by the crisis and millions and millions more indirectly,' Adelheid said.

'I hope you do not find it rude of me,' Adam said, 'but are you a business leader, too?'

'Dr. Steam has been more than a business leader to all of us for many years,' said the Chinese man who was sitting next to Adam. 'We have all benefited from his advice.'

'Dr. Steam is not a businessman. He is far beyond business,' said Adelheid.

'He must be an economics advisor, then,' said Adam.

'Professor of Economics and winner of the Nobel Prize for Economics,' Adelheid replied.

'I'm overwhelmed,' said Adam. 'This is quite an honor, meeting you, sir.'

'The honor is mine,' said Steam.

Adam smiled. 'I am really curious about what you are doing in this city that you say you have built. And I am more curious to know that why a person of my age who is not a businessman of your class, or any class, should be involved in your discussions.'

'The people who built this city thirty years ago did not create a large population. They are around seven hundred, give or take,' Steam said. 'They have been summoned here by this council for a very serious purpose.'

'They are all business leaders from different countries; they have employed thousands of people all around the world, first by their intellect and then by their investments,' Adelheid told him.

'Today's world economy must be ruled by prodigies, not those who have caused people to suffer like they do in the twenty-first century,' Steam said. 'We believe this situation could be more terrible than any World War or nuclear attack. This is the moment for the world to grow. Humanity is so developed right now that science, economics, technology and politics should be managed to create better safety, health and welfare for the people of the world but everything is blocked by this crisis, or at least the pace of growth has been considerably slowed down.'

'Wrong economic policies have caused this situation,' said Adelheid, 'and we believe that top economists must take over, find solutions to resolve it and prevent any further sufferings for the world.'

'And what part exactly can I have in this taking over?' asked Adam, mystified.

'We are currently at the propaganda stage,' said Steam, 'and what The Silver Orchestra needs is a young, talented artist, one who can become globally recognized in a short time. He just happens to be the grandson of the former Chief Scientist of The Silver Orchestra's administration.'

'Are you talking about my grandfather?' Adam jumped out of his seat, shocked. 'He has been working with you? Where is he now? I need to see him.'

'I'm afraid that is not going to be possible for a while,' said Steam. 'He is on a serious mission.'

'So you want me to stop my search for my grandfather and stay here and help you with the PR?' Adam asked.

'We can assure you that your grandfather is safe. He will be proud of you if he knows you have agreed to co-operate with us,' said Steam. 'We don't want you to stay here. We want you to travel.'

Knowing that his grandfather was safe and about to join him in what he was doing sparked relief in Adam's mind. He had always been fond of his grandfather. The village mayor was known to be a man of his word; he was known always to do the right thing and because of this, Adam was convinced that if his grandfather had been there, he would have asked him to join the propaganda program.

'You want me to travel. Where?' he asked.

'Around the world,' said Adelheid.

'You will have an accomplished band,' said Steam 'and a high-tech studio to record your first album.'

'Wait a minute: you want me to advertise your plan around the world with my art?' Adam needed to be sure.

'It won't be for us, it will be for peace; for the people of your village and for people around the world,' said Steam. 'You won't be doing this for us.'

'Why don't you ask a celebrity do it?' asked Adam.

'Because each celebrity has a background; and none of them matches what we are looking for.' Steam smiled. 'You are talented, fresh, ambitious and we believe that what we have planned for you will give you the image of a popular musician, worldwide.'

'Just one thought,' said Adam. 'How are you going to give me this image at such short notice?'

Steam picked up the phone which was on his desk. 'Bring in the papers,' he said.

A man entered the room and walked towards Adam. He handed some papers to Adam and left. The title at the top of the first page caught Adam's eye.

'Sama Records!' he said, astounded.

'I see you are familiar with the name,' said Steam.

'That is one of the top five record companies in the world,' said Adam, his excitement increasing. 'If they approve an artist, it means the world will like him.'

'Sama Records belongs to Lady Adelheid,' said Steam.

Adam was so stunned by the news that he couldn't speak for a while. He stared at Adelheid, speechless. He couldn't believe that the woman in whose house he had stayed for many days and nights and to whom he had made love was the owner of the company that he had always desired to publish his album. He had never dreamed that it could happen so soon.

'This is the contract to publish your album,' she said. 'To release and distribute your album all around the world, along with videos which will be filmed here, advertisements of your album on international TV channels and, last but not least, a two-month tour around the world to perform live in our target countries.'

'Concerts!' exclaimed Adam. He could not believe that he was awake. 'I'm gonna give concerts? World tour? I . . . I don't really know what to say!'

'Nothing. Just sign the document and get started,' said Adelheid.

'Less than a week after you sign this contract, my team will arrive here from LA and you know what comes next.'

Adam took the offered pen.

CHAPTER 11

In five days the team arrived in the town. The band consisted of a pianist, a lyrist, percussionist and a drummer. There were three other men in the team: a sound engineer who arrived at the mansion with a van carrying his equipment; Nicolay Imninsky, the famous Russian composer who had won two Oscars for his music for movies. Adam had read his biography and interviews in *Art Times* magazine; he could hardly believe that Imninsky was going to be his special advisor for his album and his part in the great Silver Orchestra project. The other man was Michel Ripasol, the French music video director, world-famous for his Madonna and Michael Jackson videos and for directing the live Paris Symphony coverage on the Tribune de France channel every Sunday.

Adelheid provided a large studio in her mansion for the band's rehearsals. They played, composed, recomposed and recorded music for two months. Adam devoted all his talent and his remarkable compositions to the project. In the meantime, Adelheid, Steam and the rest of the group, or as they called it, The Silver Orchestra, were following the world events intended to resolve the economic crisis.

Huge automotive companies were increasingly facing bankruptcy. Well-known companies were embroiled in financial meltdown and more and more people were losing their jobs every day. National leaders were busy with world summits: the G20 in London, G8 in Beijing and the World Economic Forum in Davos, as well as many other meetings. The resolutions coming out of them seemed too ambitious to achieve. People no longer believed politicians' promises. Stimulus plans did not seem to be working and leaders talked constantly of the need for more money to be injected into the economy. This money could not restore more than a fraction of the damage. It was like a nuclear bomb detonated in a large city, turning all the skyscrapers into rubble and then some people gather and talk about hope of a better future and building a few cottages. They did not know how to clear up the mess they had created. The world was changing.

Having worked hard for about seventy consecutive days, the team came up with an album. Michel Ripasol arranged a concert to be sponsored by the Silver Orchestra International Business Foundation in Theater de la Ville. Adam's performance in front of his college's dean had been canceled and he would instead be performing in Paris with a band of world-famous musicians and the largest economic support ever received from business leaders. He was not worried about his future career in music any more.

At the private airport of the crystal city where a private jet stood waiting, Steam bade Adam farewell.

'Everything is arranged in Paris,' said Steam. 'Lady Adelheid and I will join you there shortly.'

Having arrived at Charles De Gaulle Airport, Adam was met by the limousine which was to take him to his hotel. At that moment he was not thinking about imminent fame, the concert, or visiting the Louvre or the Eiffel Tower. All he thought about was his amazing entry into an artists' paradise.

In due course Sama Records released the album and advertisements went on TV channels in Europe, America and Central Asia. If there was anyone in the world who could make a talented young musician world-famous in such a short space of time, it was Adelheid. The Paris concert was being held by her Association and that was enough to create massive attention and Michel Ripasol's part in it drew large audiences to the theater.

The concert went extremely well. The band gathered at the lobby of the theater when it was all done to talk to the press and audience. People came to congratulate Adam on his first great musical achievement, which was somehow a historical event, too: a young musician, barely known to the public, being supported by the topmost promoters in the world.

The concert over, Adam's heart filled with satisfaction. He stood in the theater's lobby, giving autographs to his first fans. Among the throng, a small man dressed in a white suit walked towards Adam to have his picture taken with him. After that, he clasped Adam's hand in his own. He then disappeared into the crowd, leaving a tiny envelope in Adam's hand.

Adam opened the envelope.

What he saw sent a chill down his spine.

'The message read:

'If there are two threats to the world, one of them is
Adelheid Fester.
Blood will be spilt by her malice.
We will meet soon.'

Adam stood motionless among the crowd, frozen with shock. It had to be a joke, he thought.

Adelheid walked towards him, smiling.

'Here is my hero!' she said. 'You were excellent on the stage. Everyone is amazed.'

'I'm glad the project is working,' Adam said, his voice trembling.

'You look pale, sweetie!' said Adelheid. 'What is it?'

'I'm just tired. I'll be ok.' He put the note in his pocket.

Adelheid came to Adam's room later to give him her special bonus for seventy days of hard work and his confidence on the stage. As before, he liked the way Adelheid treated him in bed. But when he was asleep she reached in his pocket and took out the crumpled paper.

'Son of a bitch!' she said, putting the note back in his pocket.

They had concerts in Rome, Milan, London, Lisbon, Rio de Janeiro, Los Angeles, New York, Tokyo, Beijing, Tehran, Isfahan and Dubai. At all the concerts Adelheid's spokesman talked about the economic crisis and how a part of the profit from the concert would be given to charity foundations of the city where they had performed. Adam was not allowed to use the silver violin in concerts; he was told that the reflection of light on the silver shield of the instrument would damage the films. He could hardly find a chance to play it. He did it when he was alone in his hotel rooms, and even then he was so tired that he couldn't play properly and he would fall asleep before finishing a piece.

He had become a professional musician with an international reputation. The more he met crowds of people at the concerts, the more he felt alone. His only personal contact was with Adelheid and each day he became less and less happy to be in her company. When he had first met her, she was in a mansion decorated by roses and works of art and inhabited by girls who would do anything she wished at her command. He had been attracted to her glory, beauty and kindness. But on the tour she meant nothing more to him than an ambitious promoter and he started to be distant with her in an obvious way.

Adam took the note out of his pocket and looked at it again. What did it really mean if it wasn't a joke, he thought. The last time I followed a message, I ended up on a world tour. But I am at the heart of The Silver Orchestra! I am publicizing them. Where did this come from?

CHAPTER 12

At Dubai Airport, Adam caught a glimpse of the small man who had given him the envelope in Paris. As the man vanished into the crowd, Adam jumped out of his seat to look for him. He spotted him again going up the stairs. Adam ran toward him, but lost sight of him once more. He stood on the second floor of the terminal and looked around carefully. He must have been following me for the whole trip, he thought.

Puzzled, Adam went to the restroom to wash his face before returning to the team. He went to one of the toilets and locked the door. He put his head in his hands and started to cry. *I miss Grandpa! I don't want any of this any more! Why don't you come and take me with you, Grandpa! Why don't they show you to me? What are you so busy with? You always told me that if you had one important task to do in your life, it was looking after me! I need you!* he wept. *I need you!*

Adam heard footsteps coming close to him. From beneath the door he saw a pair of shiny black shoes. And then an envelope was slipped under the door and he heard running feet. He got up and opened the door immediately, but nobody was there. He ran to the lounge and spotted the small man running among the crowds. He ran after him toward the staircase. Speeding down the stairs, Adam slipped on one of the steps and fell. His head hurt and he felt dizzy. People gathered around him. He pointed to the running man. 'Stop that man!' he moaned. He took the envelope out of his pocket. He just managed to read the message before everything went dark.

Get away from them!

CHAPTER 13

The tour was over and, because of the incident at Dubai Airport, the team canceled the return trip to Paris and returned to the crystal city. Adam did not know how he had boarded the plane, for he had hardly been conscious at the time of departure. Falling down the stairs, he had hit his head and did not remember how he had been put in a wheelchair and lifted up to the plane. He did not even remember showing his passport to the officers. Opening his eyes once aboard the plane, he could see Adelheid, Steam and his band. The flight did not take more than three hours and they landed at the crystal city's airport. During the trip he recalled the concerts in his mind. He remembered how he had been applauded by large audiences, playing beside the greats of the music world. This was an achievement he had not ever remotely envisaged. For a moment he had a vision of his grandfather's shining face.

Watching the jet's flaps open on the wings, he heard the note of the engine change. Just as they were about to land, he remembered the small man he had followed in the airport and the unexpected message he had been given. He reached in his pockets to look at the message one more time, but he could not find it. He turned around to ask if anybody had seen the envelope, but everyone had sunk into their seats, with their eyes closed, waiting for the plane's wheels to touch the runway. He changed his mind about interrupting their fears and decided to join them and concentrate on landing.

Leaving the plane, the team and guards headed for Adelheid's mansion. After weeks of performing and travelling, Adam felt he needed a break and to prepare for the rest of the assignment, which had yet to be announced by The Silver Orchestra's leaders.

After a couple of days of staying indoors in the mansion, the team gathered to rehearse the music they had played on the tour. They were also working on new ideas to add to their repertoire in expectation of a possible second tour.

Tania was the vocalist in one of the new pieces. At one rehearsal Adam noticed a strange expression in her eyes. She looked pale and couldn't concentrate on the words of the song. They restarted the piece several times and she kept making a mess in the middle. Finally they stopped rehearsing and Adam announced a one-day recess. He needed the break even more than the vocalist and other tired members of the band. He had made up his mind. His art was being led by those who were called the experts and his own creations were being extensively modified to match—as Ripasol and Imninsky said: the market's psychological demands from art; in fact, from music.

He asked Tania to stay behind and explain why she had ruined the whole rehearsal. In fact, this was something of a ruse. In reality, he wanted to talk about the thoughts which were troubling his mind. He was finding it difficult to make decisions. His mind felt like a flat with two separate rooms. He was in one room and his worries in the other. They accompanied him every hour and everywhere, until he no longer knew what they really were. He lived with them in the same dwelling but the recent huge changes had made a thick wall which separated him from a part of his thoughts.

Tania looked unwell. He needed to talk to her and ask her what was wrong. And she would say, 'You look kind of troubled, too! What's wrong with you?' and he would start talking. He would talk for so long that he could enter that protected room of his flat, drag out the thoughts and worries and deal with them. He was looking forward to someone asking the right questions and helping him get to the bottom of the forgotten inhabitants of that sealed room. But before he could ask Tania the planned question, she said, sobbing, 'I need to see you tonight! It's important and nobody must know.'

'What's happened?' asked Adam, instantly forgetting about the hidden room.

'Just meet me at midnight. Keep this a secret,' she said, trying to stop crying. 'I'll see you in the temple.'

'You are really freaking me out! Tell me what it is about,' Adam pressed her.

'It's about a message I received at Dubai airport when you slipped down the stairs. A man gave me something. Oh my god, I can't believe it!' She started sobbing again. 'How stupid I was!'

'Did he give you a note?'

'No. I will show it to you tonight. It's not safe here.'

Adam stayed in his room the whole afternoon, letting everyone assume that he was composing or working on a piece.

I wish I had not taken these messages seriously in the first place, he thought. I wish I had moved back to college in order to perform for the Dean. I could have got the grant. I would be doing music research and composing this album in college, on my own, not with these people. They freak me out. This is not my time to go on world tours. I should be researching, tutoring and composing in college now. Grandpa knows what he is doing. He has never needed my aid and support. He knows how to protect himself and the village. I shouldn't have followed any message, any constellation and any advisor, except my own thoughts in the temple of music by the river.

He went to the temple longing for Tania to reveal the secret of the small man and what he had given her. The temple was brightly lit. As he stepped inside, he saw Tania lying on the ground. But she couldn't be sleeping. She had talked so frenziedly about what she was about to reveal that she couldn't have slept well for nights.

'Tania!' said Adam shaking her shoulder.

She did not reply. He touched her cheek. It was cold. Very cold, and her face looked ashen. He touched her neck to check her pulse. It was very weak, the merest fluttering.

She half-opened her eyes.

'They are murderers,' she said in a faint voice, scarcely able to breathe. 'Dmitri, Dmitri.'

'Dmitri what?' Adam asked, desperate for an answer.

'The secret gar . . .' she struggled for breath, ' . . . gar . . . garden.'

And she closed her eyes. Adam checked her pulse again. There was nothing. She was dead.

Adam ran toward the mansion, calling for help. In less than two minutes, Adelheid, the girls and guards ran to the temple, thinking that perhaps Adam had had a nightmare. But it wasn't a nightmare and Tania was dead. A doctor came to examine the body. He surmised that an overdose of ecstasy had caused a cardiac arrest. Adelheid said that Tania had been suffering from a serious depression and she had been on medication for a while. She had started having hallucinations. She said Tania had come to her several times at nights, woken her up and claimed that some hunters were hiding behind the roses, trying to shoot her. Adam had not observed any of these symptoms in her since his arrival in the city; as far as he was concerned, she was a talented musician and singer.

How could she possibly have been out of her mind? Adam asked himself. She was Adelheid's personal assistant. She was in charge the other girls. She had been educating them before he had arrived. Why did she use ecstasy on the very night that she intended to reveal a secret to him? A secret that was obviously bothering her. Was this all a figment of her imagination? Did he know anything about what really led to her sudden death? How would he know? She talked about the small man in Dubai airport. That had nothing to do with her state of mind. He had seen the man, too. He had chased him and got knocked unconscious. Could he live with it if he didn't tell anyone that she had been murdered to pay for what she knew?

All rehearsals were canceled for a week to let the team get over the shock of Tania's death. Adam went to Adelheid and told her about his meeting with Tania that never took place. She kept telling the same stories over and over about her. She said she had heard the small man and Tania had made up the story about receiving messages from him.

CHAPTER 14

D mitri was always among Adelheid's guards at the mansion. He had been brought up to do whatever he was told by his superiors. As a schoolboy, when his father said he should not be marked lower than B+ in his reports, he tried not to disappoint him; when his mother said he should turn in before ten at night, he obeyed her. When his teacher said he was not allowed to eat and drink in class, he never did so. When told that lying was wrong, he never spoke anything but the truth, even if a lie would protect the innocent. He was raised as a good child. Good children never lie, they never take risks, they never experiment; they never make mistakes; they do not believe in trial and error for whatever they need to know comes from those who have knowledge. They never learn from experience.

Dmitri was a good child. A good child always makes a great bodyguard for a suspicious rich lady, the nature of whose business is a mystery to the world. He is told to be a good bodyguard and he tries his best, no matter who the client is and what he or she does. But Adelheid had made a big mistake taking her loyal bodyguard on the tour. As a child, Dmitri had wished to become a pianist.

He had watched pianists play in concerts or on TV. He watched their tapes for hours every day. He tapped on his desk while he was supposedly doing homework, imagining himself sitting at a piano on a concert platform. Once he thought that maybe he could attend evening classes in music. He spoke to his father about this, but his father said, 'I don't want my boy among entertainers. I want him to live with more honor.' Dmitri, as a good child, listened to his father.

It all came to a head during the tour. When Adam was on stage performing, Dmitri felt the desk under his fingertips once more. He thought, all these years of looking for honor have passed and I am standing here right now, guarding the stage. Why aren't I on it?'

During the days following, he thought constantly about this, regretting terribly mistakes that he hadn't made. And when the plane landed, just at the moment when his companions were thinking about a possible air crash and a terrible death, agent Dmitri was thinking about a change. And that was the instant at which he decided to stop being a good child. That was the moment at which Adelheid lost one of her most loyal employees.

Adam decided to speak with Dmitri after a meeting at The Silver Orchestra headquarters in the underground compound. He told him about his suspicions regarding Tania's death and the weird messages he had received in Paris and Dubai. But Dmitri did not show any sign of being compromised. He simply advised Adam to relax and get the melancholy suspicions out of his mind. He still pretended to be a good child.

Rehearsals were due to start the following day. Adam made no attempt to resist his advisors. His bewilderment caused him to be submissive. He did whatever he was told. He played the melodies exactly as Imnisky told him to. No argument; no struggle. He did not say a word. He just played the notes; his own notes which had been revised by Imninsky.

He remained silent the whole day and went to bed early. His thoughts shifted too quickly in his mind, so that he no longer knew which one to focus on, resolve and then go to next. They were all in his head at the same time and the demands on his brain made him frustrated. He wanted nothing else but to sleep. He wished for nothing else but a resetting of his mind. Asleep that night, he dreamt that he was walking on a harbor attached to a large luxurious hotel. Suddenly he noticed a plane approaching the harbor, smoke rising from its wings. The engines were making a terrible noise. It was coming directly toward the hotel, below which he was standing. Its right wing hit the building and the plane ploughed forward, scoring a straight line into the hotel's façade. All the windows and the red awnings along that line were smashed and their fragments floated in the air. He had no chance to see the panic on people's faces or observe casualties, for his subconscious mind shifted to a different setting immediately after the crash. He was in a reception hall. Then the walls disappeared and he found himself on a hill. Then he saw a cradle in which a baby was standing, rocking himself and crying madly. Two of the guard rails of the cradle were broken and he was in danger of falling out through the hold. The baby seemed to be frightened by the threat.

Hearing the stairs creaking, Adam woke up. He sensed feet behind his door. He tip-toed to the door, reached for the handle and opened the door swiftly. There was a figure standing in the darkness.

The figure did not move back. It did not freak out. Its face was not exposed as it was standing with its back to the flickering light of the staircase.

Is this here to murder me, too?

The figure walked closer until its face was revealed.

'How could this be?' said Adam, terrified. 'You were . . . You were dead.'

'I have to take you underground,' said Tania.

Adam felt that he was about to faint. *I am certain that she is dead. How is this happening? Am I about to die, too? I always envisaged that death would be the most peaceful moment of my life. She has scared the hell out of me. How come my body is shaking?*

'The second level,' said Tania. 'Below the containers.'

Adam woke with a start. He was breathing rapidly and sweat covered his face.

The second level. There must be another level underground.

He jumped out of bed, put on his clothes and rushed towards Adelheid's room. Dmitri opened his door and came out to the passage.

'What the hell is wrong with you?' he asked.

'I know that Tania was murdered. I know there is something under that compound. I know about the second level underground.'

'Are you out of your mind? You want to be murdered, too? How do you know about that?'

'I know it.' Adam closed his mouth firmly. He wasn't going to tell Dmitri about the dream.

'And where exactly are you running to now?'

'Take me there,' Adam demanded. 'I know that you can pass that gate. Nobody questions you.'

'I am not supposed even to talk about it to you.'

Dmitri did not mean what he had just said. It was time to stop saying what he was supposed to say. It was time to build up his mental courage and do the right thing. It was time to refer to his conscience, not his superior, and break the rules. Tania's blood had been spilt, unjustly, when she had no chance of defending herself. His heart was telling him that he should join with Adam and take action. It would not be without fear. Nor would it be without danger. But he had to do it, for his heart and mind were sure about that.

'Take me there,' Adam repeated. 'You know that something strange is going on there.'

It was past midnight. Adam hid inside the trunk of Dmitri's car and they drove toward the compound. At the gate Dmitri was let in without his car being searched. He was the head of security for the whole city and nobody dared to search him. It would not seem strange if he wanted to check the compound at midnight.

Inside the elevator, Dmitri turned the dial to the required numbers. He connected the socket below the dial to his cell phone and entered a code. The elevator started to move downward. They passed the first level and reached the second underground level. *Thank you, Tania! But why did you have to die for telling me this?*

The elevator's door opened on to a quite large room with curved walls and an oval desk in the middle. A curved red desk lamp stood above a monitor. The chair behind the desk was empty. It looked like a secretary's desk. But there had to be another door in the room to open into the main part. The room they were standing in felt like a waiting room. Behind the desk, hanging on the wall, were two pictures; each looked like a duplicate of the other. The painting was of a landscape of the land near the city, the land through which Adam had walked to find his grandfather: the Blue Forest. In the foreground of the painting was the portrait of a child.

'I really doubt Adelheid knows about here,' Adam said.

'Why is that?'

'The paintings.' Adam glanced towards them. 'I have seen how she uses sculptures and paintings in her rooms. Each of her paintings represents a woman of a particular nationality. Each room is painted in a color specific to the mood which is desired in it. Nothing is repeated. Nothing is double.'

'Nothing is double here either!' said Dmitri.

'A round room with two significant elements which are these paintings; and they are the same?'

'They are of the same place and the same child, but they are not the same. They just share similar parts and properties.'

'I don't think I am in the right mood to argue with you about this,' Adam said.

'You wanted to be on the underground level and I brought you here,' Dmitri said, looking sulky.

'No offense, but are painting and philosophy something we should be discussing down here?' Adam sought to placate him.

'Exactly!'

'Then I'm sorry! Go on.'

'Look at the expression on the child's face in both paintings. What do you see?'

Adam looked closely at the picture. 'He is thinking.'

'Look at his eyes. Tell me more: what is he thinking about?'

'No idea! About his missing grandfather or the river or maybe waiting for the night to observe the constellations and messages from possible other worlds or a friend who was murdered because of her attempt to reveal a secret or missing the chance of winning a valuable grant.'

'He may be thinking about these things, granted. He may be thinking about millions of other issues as well. The boys in these two pictures may each have things in mind which are different from the matters in the other one's thoughts.'

'So?'

'If we are what we think and these two boys are thinking about different matters then . . .'

'Then they are two different people.'

'And these are two different paintings. And they are not displayed here just as a luxury. They are an introduction to the activities in this underground facility.'

'You mean, they murder the citizens to run isomorphic analysis on them?'

'A lot more complicated than that. Imagine there is a machine that takes the child in the first picture and duplicates this child with some desired differences. For instance, the copy may have different abilities and opinions from the original.'

'I don't believe such a machine exists in the world.' This was getting beyond the realms of reality.

'It does, my lad,' Dmitri said with sorrow, 'and it is used in this facility. It is not exactly a machine. It is a long and complicated genetic process. It is called human cloning.'

'Human cloning?' said Adam, his eyes wide. 'They are running secret research on human cloning here?'

'They have gone a lot further than research. They have cloned human beings successfully here. The Silver Orchestra is a wealthy organization which has been secretly supporting clandestine research on human cloning.'

'Going by what you said about the pictures of the child, don't tell me that they reproduce designer humans to order.'

'Unfortunately, that's exactly what they do.' Dmitri paused for a while to let Adam absorb the shock of this information. 'Let me take you inside; you will see more about this.'

Dmitri entered a code using the computer on the oval desk. The walls started to slide. It wasn't just the walls moving, the whole room was turning and a glass door appeared just behind the desk. Dmitri put his thumb on the security device by the door, and the glass gateway to the hidden laboratories opened. They entered another round room, significantly larger than the first one. There were some tables and chairs around the room. It looked like a restaurant or bar. Some people were sitting at the tables. They were silent and unmoving.

'Are these guys the pictures to be reproduced in a form similar to but different from them?'

'No, these are actually the pictured ones. These are the clones.'

'But they don't seem healthy,' Adam said. 'They don't talk. They don't move. They didn't even notice us entering here.'

'These pictured types have properties different from the original pictures and still they are similar to them. The clones have eyes, but they don't see. They have ears, but they don't hear. They have brains, but they don't think.'

'So these are a type of human which is deaf, blind and brainless?' Adam wondered what the point was in creating them.

'Not precisely. They can see, but only certain things. Their vision gene is manipulated in order to make their eyes responsive to specific visual qualities. They are like robots that see only what they are programmed to see.'

'And what qualities would they be able to see?'

'It varies. But as far as I know, their vision is connected to their physiological and psychological needs. In some of them food is the first and only thing they notice. In some others, sexual attraction and in some, weapons. They follow what they are programmed to follow. Each of them has been tested and they have all been declared successful products.

Putting all the results from these experimental clones together, the scientists here, are working on producing a type that will follow certain visual stimuli, certain sounds and even certain philosophies, but only those that they are programmed to follow. And they do not understand ideas or thoughts, they just follow their programmer. They are just robots, but the final products will be processed so masterfully that one could not possibly tell they are not human. One cannot scare the residents of this room, for they do not understand fear. One cannot delight them, for they do not understand happiness. One cannot approach them through kindness and care, for their hearts are like stone.'

You don't need to tell secrets in an encoded language in their presence, for they are like the dead, and nobody minds about telling secrets in a cemetery. The dead do not hear. They cannot be guided, taught, healed or be hopeful. They can learn to a very limited extent, just sufficient to carry out their personal affairs. But they will never change. They will never be free from what they are programmed to be. They will never be free from this prison.'

'I suppose Prison of Wills would be a fitting name for this place,' Adam said. 'So what exactly are they programmed to be?'

'This is a secret from me, too. There are levels below this one that even I do not have access to.'

'You quote something earlier. Who said that?'

'It was an old man who used to be an important member of the Silver Orchestra scientists' team, but later on, they put him into captivity.'

It must be Grandpa, Adam realized. He worked these things out and they threw him out of their association.

'What is he like?' Adam asked.

'I have not met him more than twice. He was already in prison when I was transferred to this city.'

'Do you know where he is now? Can you take me to him?'

'He is in custody. In one of the rooms on the same level that we are on now. What makes you so interested in him?'

'I think the man you are talking about could be my grandfather.'

'Wait a minute!' said Dmitri, startled and furious. 'Did you know that he was being held here? You tricked me to get to him?'

'No, no, no! I swear to god, I knew nothing about this. I was told that he was working with them and he was on an important mission.'

'Oh. It must be true.' Dmitri gave a sigh of relief.

'How come?'

'Adelheid had asked me to tell you the same story about your grandfather if you asked me about him.'

'She is one hell of a liar! But a clever one. I don't really know how come I never got suspicious of her. I believed whatever she said and whatever she did.'

'Me, too.'

'Was any part of what they told me the truth?'

'I have no idea. I still believe they are all extraordinary scientific and economic geniuses. And something tells me they are doing all this secret stuff for good reasons.'

'And what exactly is telling you that?'

'Let's look at it this way: do you know why I, the head of Adelheid's security for this compound, the person who has been trusted more than anyone by Adelheid, turned against her and this facility?'

'Because they killed Tania?'

'It started long before that.' Dmitri sat at one of the tables holding his head in his hands. 'When I saw these robot-like humans coming into existence, I started to doubt everything and everyone in this place.'

'You said they are not human! Why should you doubt, then?'

'Because ever since I can remember, I have been living like them. As a child I obeyed whatever my father said; in the army I obeyed whatever my commanders said; and in this job I have obeyed whatever Adelheid said. These products would do the same thing. Maybe that's what they are made for: to obey the Silver Orchestra, without knowing what they are really following.'

'Can you please tell me what my grandpa is doing here?'

'I told you earlier. I don't know much about him. But if he is being kept at this facility it means that he knows many things about it; perhaps he knows more than I do. And that's why he is not allowed to leave this place. And I can assure you that he does not approve of what they are doing here.'

'I don't know what to do next. If I go back to Adelheid and continue working with her team, I will be trapped in their dangerous activities. I know it's dangerous because I was the one who found Tania's body. Maybe it was a warning to me, too. Whoever murdered her knew that she was about to reveal some secrets to me and they knew that I would find her dead. And if I run away from this city, I may never see my grandfather again. I have come all this way to take him back and help him save the village and its people. I just don't know what to do, Dmitri.'

'I know how you are feeling, for I have been there. The surveillance system will not send the frames of our entry to this level to Adelheid's computer for the next hour, because I switched the transponder off and nobody has seen you arriving here. Plus, the guards will not get suspicious of me for being here, because I often do spontaneous security checks.'

'So?'

'You can get out of here the way you entered. Go back to your room and if any one asks where you have been, you will say you couldn't sleep and you went for a walk. If they ask me about this I will tell them the same thing.'

'And then?'

'In the morning you will go to your rehearsals with the team. You will need to be undercover for a while till we find out what is going on here. And if you want to know about me, that's what I have been doing here for a while. We will work together and we will find a way to get your grandfather out of custody and leave here.'

'Can I see him now? Will you take me to him?'

'I am afraid that will have to wait,' said Dmitri. 'I have not access to the code that switches off the surveillance in his room.'

'Who has?'

'As far as I know, only Adelheid and Dr. Mao.'

'Dr. Mao?' Adam was appalled.

'You know him?' asked Dmitri.

'I met him once in Rome. He is scary.'

'If you can endure some days of acting undercover, I will be able to hand your grandfather a message. I'll let him know that you are here. And you should know we are not alone in this.'

'What do mean, we are not alone? There are others aware of the stuff going on down here?'

'Actually, yes. And you are one of them now. You must be extra careful. I don't need to tell you that one tiny mistake can jeopardize everything and put all our lives at risk.'

'I understand. Who else is with us?'

'I can't tell you more at the moment. I have a head of command. I should contact him first and get instructions. But I can assure you that you will be in the loop from now on.'

'I would like to meet your head of command,' Adam said.

'Soon, but as I just told you, I'm gonna need to talk to him first.'

CHAPTER 15

Next morning, during the recess between rehearsals, Adam and Dmitri met. They set the time for the midnight trip to the safe location, where Dmitri's head of command and his team stayed.

At just past midnight Adam left the mansion pretending that he wanted to take a walk. He walked to the music store and sat on the stairs at the entrance. It was the third time he had found himself in front of the piano castle. The porch light went on. Dmitri appeared, but this time from inside the building, beckoning Adam to come inside. They both entered the building quickly and Dmitry led Adam upstairs. It was not the first time Adam had visited the mirrors room.

'Ok, what is going to be revealed here tonight?' he asked.

'The truth about *Der Kristall Hochburg*,' said Dmitri. 'Shall we take the stairs?'

They walked down the stairs and reached the basement of the store. Dmitri took out his flashlight to guide Adam through the rest of the route to where his head of command lived. The basement was filled with parts of musical instruments and broken furniture. There was a large area at one side of the basement which was filled with carpentry tools; it seemed like a workshop for making music instruments. On the floor were dusty wooden components, waiting to be made up into a piano. On a table lay strings and the carved parts of violins, guitars and banjos. In another corner of the basement, not more than twelve or so meters away from the workshop, lay a rusty old freezer, in which were kept the small parts and joints of damaged instruments.

'I'm gonna need a hand here with this freezer,' said Dmitri.

Adam raised his eyebrows. What on earth had this freezer to do with Dmitri's commander?

'Don't you want to help me with this?' asked Dmitri, pushing the weighty freezer.

They shoved the freezer along the floor. Behind the rusty chest was a round metal lid. Dmitri lifted this and a manhole with a ladder going downward appeared.

'This is the second time you have taken me underground,' Adam said.

'Yeah.' Dmitri grinned. 'But this time from below a freezer!'

They walked to the shaft and climbed down the ladder. After about a minute they reached a tunnel. Everywhere was totally dark.

'The lights,' said Dmitri on his radio.

The light came on. They were in a long tunnel; its walls were covered with concrete and the floor was paved. They walked down the tunnel and arrived at a metal door.

'We are at the door,' said Dmitri into his radio.

The door slid upwards and they were entered a large area that looked like a war museum. Old machine guns, models of World War II airplane and pictures showing scenes of battle hung on the walls. Adam couldn't stop himself looking at the images.

One picture showed an Iraqi child crying with a bombed-out hospital in the background; another was of Cambodian rebels being taken by the army; and another showed journalists lying in the street with soldiers shooting each other just above their heads from either side of the street. There was a Vietnamese farm with dozens of choppers flying at a very low level above it.

But there was one photograph which caught Adam's attention and tore at his heart. It depicted an alley with concrete single-storey houses on both sides; the pavement was nothing but soil. Bodies lay on the ground, in the stillness of death: a child, beside him a cat and, about five meters away a woman; all silent, all at peace, all dead.

'In this picture you can see three dead,' said a voice from behind him, 'but the number of victims was over a hundred thousand.'

Adam looked back in the direction of the voice. The speaker was a man in his fifties. He looked of military stature, with dyed brown hair and mustache. There were scars on his cheeks and forehead, but he didn't look at all terrifying. He seemed like those tough men with so many scars on their soul that the facial wounds seem diminished and they look at ease. His csountenance was that of a man who had found an inner peace. He was wearing a ring a big turquoise stone. Adam remembered his grandfather wearing the same type of ring.

'My name is Colonel Ahmad Beig,' he introduced himself. 'Here in The Silver Orchestra they know me as Colonel Donovan, a name that was given to me when I was trained in Scotland.'

'Mr. Donovan,' said Adam, 'I was told that you are directing anti—Silver Orchestra activities. Is that so?'

'Though Donovan means The Great Warrior in Gaelic and I am known by this name, I would rather you called me by my real ethnic name, as your grandfather does.'

Adam felt a surge of hope. 'Are you a friend my grandfather, sir?'

'We are friends and allies in many ways. And I am the director of the WMST branch in Europe.' The Colonel studied Adam from head to toe. 'I expect you have a lot of questions in mind to ask.'

'Indeed. Please tell me about Adelheid and her people. Who are they?'

'My dear lad, the organization you were campaigning for and the people who made you world-famous are not a humanitarian group as they claimed to you. I understand that Agent Dmitri has familiarized you with some of their secret activities. And unfortunately we have recently suffered the loss of one of our best sources in Adelheid's organization, someone who had got very close to her.'

'Tania? She was working with you?' Adam asked.

'Yes, and I cannot express the extent of my grief for her.'

'She was a great friend of mine, too, ever since I arrived in this mysterious town. Her death came as quite a shock to me.' Adam sighed. 'Colonel, I was an artist, with my instrument and my temple. I was a man of feelings and creativity. These recent happenings have been driving me mad. I was introduced to a group who called themselves saviors of the world economy, the guardians of the next generation of innocent people coming to this world, with no intention of allowing more suffering in such turbulent times. I became world-famous with them, they took me somewhere beyond my wildest dreams, and then I realized that this was just a cover for their subversive activities and now I am talking to a colonel and his agent. Colonel, I am overwhelmed with questions and I would like to get answers to them.'

'One of the war pictures you were looking at earlier was of the Halabche chemical attack.' The Colonel sank into silence for a while, resting his forehead on the photo. 'My wife and my two children were among the victims.'

'I am so sorry, sir.' It seemed inadequate, but there was nothing else he could say.

'It was after the war that I received messages through a contact. The messages were signed by an organization named WMST. I was invited to Scotland where high ranking army people from all over the world were gathered. We were all operating under the cover of a multinational industrial firm. Our real target was to observe all the organizations which were trying to gain access to chemical and biological weapons across the globe. Our assembly was totally private and no government was aware of our activities. I had personally observed where human greed can go when there is access to such weapons. My country has been the victim of these weapons. Thousands of my countrymen were killed or are still suffering from the effects of the chemical weapons which were used by Saddam during the Iran-Iraq war, including my own family. I could not be silent against those who support and produce these weapons. I joined WMST and for nearly nine years I have been directing an intelligence operation to observe Adelheid's activities.

'But she has nothing to do with weapons; I guess she is just sponsoring prohibited research which may be useful for man some day.'

'How did she even get involved in such a thing?' asked Adam.

'When I was introduced to WMST, Adelheid was the head of the group of multinationals who were financially supporting our activities. She was one of the first people who helped to form this group. But then we got intel that she was about to run secret biological research to use human cloning technology for military purposes. She supported us because she wanted to use our resources.'

'She supported me, too. And I still don't really know why,' mumbled Adam. 'And what happened then?'

'She chose to live under the cover of what she had told you about this town and her humanitarian services to the economy.'

'Human cloning for military purposes? That sounds too far-fetched! How could clones possibly be used in the military? Is Adelheid about to create an army of clones?'

'We do not have a precise answer for that. And that's what we are trying to find out.'

'She may be just supporting a new era of science,' Adam suggested.

'It's not that simple. For some years, those living and working in her enclosure have disappeared or died in suspicious ways. Billions have been invested in her secret projects by multinational manufacturers, and recently your music has made The Silver Orchestra a world-famous association and, unfortunately, a popular one.'

'And I am the only public figure in this group!' The idea seemed preposterous.

'Nothing is your fault. You have been used; like many others.'

'I can't believe the whole thing was just a game! No one was supporting my talent.'

'Games! You are still a long way from that, my lad!' said the Colonel. He turned to one of the images in which there was a pile of corpses; dozens of naked men. 'When I was a trainee, my commander put me in a class called 'prisoners' dilemma'. We were supposedly two prisoners held in two separate cells. The commander came to me, suggesting three options. One, betraying the other prisoner; if he remained silent about me, I would be released and he had to do ten years. Two, we each betray the other and both receive a five-year jail sentence. And three, we both remain silent and are released after six months.'

'Which one did you choose?'

'We both chose the third option. And guess what? We were both detained for making that choice. The commander said, 'In a real game you should choose your moves according to the moves that your opponent may pick. And in the game of war, you can never take risks.'

'Game of war?' said Adam sadly. 'Is that really a game?'

'If only it was a game!' said Colonel Beig. 'Wars are disasters of creation, the most shameful dimension of mankind's capabilities. Human beings kill when it comes to race, wealth and even ideology. But I believe most wars today are based on economics. I remember once an American Army Major said, "I spent thirty-three years and four months in active military service and during that period I spent most of my time as a high-class muscle man for big business, for Wall Street and the bankers. In short, I was a racketeer, a gangster for capitalism, while simultaneously the highest ranking and most decorated United States Marine, including two Medals of Honor.[1]"

'I cannot tell you how shocked I am,' Adam said. 'All these activities going on beneath this town! And I will not say any more that these matters do not concern a musician, for I find myself now in the middle of a highly complicated challenge.'

'And by challenge you mean what?'

'War.'

'This is the challenge which has never been resolved throughout history, not by politicians, men of power, philosophers or economists, and it will not be resolved in the near future.'

'And it won't be right now by a musician assisting a determined military man. I think we both know that. Tell me, Colonel, what is it precisely that you want from me?'

'First, you tell me, how did you get to my base, here underneath this town? What risks did you take?'

'I chose to take huge risks the moment I left the village.'

'My dear Adam, I respectfully disagree,' Beig said. 'The fact that you started this journey is in itself a significant sign of your being prepared for a big change.'

'Do you believe that my moves were being manipulated ever since I left the village? Please don't tell me I was the hero, chosen to set out on this quest.'

'Chosen, manipulated, no. Watched, yes.'

---

[1]   Major General Smedley Darlingon, From Common Sense magazine

'By whom?'

'Us and them.'

'Colonel, what exactly is your game now? I am in the middle of a terribly complicated situation. I need to find my grandfather and I was told that he is held by Adelheid. Can you break into that underground facility and release him from captivity?'

'I could have done that long ago. But I changed my mind when you arrived here.'

'I don't understand.'

'Your grandfather is the only person in possession of crucial intelligence about Adelheid's project and that's why she is keeping him in jail. We need that intelligence and if we besiege the facility, Adelheid's people will continue her project somewhere else and we will be no wiser. Arresting her will not stop her and it will achieve exactly nothing. On top of that, in this part of the world, we have no legal warrant to enter her property using force. We need to send you back to Adelheid along with Dmitri and wait until you can get to your grandfather, obtain that information and then we will attack.'

'You want me to work for you undercover?'

'I'm afraid that is our only option.'

'Colonel, you know that I'm a man of sensitivity. I belong to the world of art. I'm not familiar with or even interested in the world of games.'

'The beauties of human life and the whole of nature are affected by the dirty doings of human beings. Bringing back the sensitivity and humanity to life is exactly what I am talking about.'

'Interesting!' Adam said. 'Adelheid talked me into joining her activities with the same concept; just it was said in different words.'

'And you believe murder is a part of bringing back beauty to the world? You are really under the impression that she is telling the truth?'

'Not at all. What I am saying is, warfare would not suit me.'

'What if I tell you that Adelheid has your DNA and they're cloning your double?'

'What the hell?' This was beyond belief.

'The scientists in her association have developed something called Agnet biotechnology.'

'And what might that be?'

'Having obtained your DNA, they grow your embryo in the laboratory situation to your present age in less than six months. It means they can have your double exactly in the same form and age that you are now in under half a year.'

'And how accurate is your information about this?'

'We are a hundred per cent sure that they have your embryo in their lab as we speak.'

'Will the double have my talents and skills as well?'

'Of course not. But the double has the same genome that brought this brilliant creativity to your life. With intensive training by musical experts they have in the city with whom you have worked, they will have an Adam, probably in the near future.'

'But with all due respect, Colonel, this doesn't make sense! They are doing all this just to have my double?'

'Not exactly, son. You are just a part of the project.'

The room became silent, Adam was starting to believe what he had just heard and the very notion appalled him. He went numb and his vision started to blur.

'You have been brought into this because we believe you can help to stop these criminals,' Dmitri said.

Adam collected his wits and took a deep breath. 'I am still not convinced that they are criminals,' he said, 'but considering their efforts to use me in this way, I shall willingly join with you.'

Adam returned to Adelheid's mansion in Dmitri's company. He found himself in a completely unlooked for and bizarre situation. With little warning, the nature of his business in the town had changed. He was surrounded by experts and musicians who were unaware of the real nature of Adelheid's organization, while working to increase its popularity.

'*Popularity is what Adelheid is seeking,*' Adam remembered the colonel saying, '*and this really concerns us. An organization with an attractive face and terrifying intentions, alongside a multi-billion-dollar fund and guided by brilliant people, using ingenious scientists from all over the world who have been brought to this town. This is what we call neo-terrorism. It can be more dangerous than Nazism.*'

Adam went to the rehearsal hall as usual. He couldn't help feeling pity for the rest of the musicians and technicians and scientists who he had never met. Nobody knew what was going on just beneath their feet. Nobody knew that the whole thing was about to be blown apart by Colonel Beig and his people.

CHAPTER 16

The only light came from a small dormer window protected by steel bars joined to the metal structure of the walls. The window was about five meters above Adam's head. Looking from the best angle upward to the window, the only thing he could see outside was the top of one of the two rose towers by Adelheid's mansion. When he opened his eyes he could see through the window the illuminated glass rose, shining like a colorful sun in *Der Kristall Hochburg*. He stood up, using the concrete wall for support and, searching for a doorway, found one, a bulky steel door which had no handle from the inside of the tiny room.

Finding himself imprisoned inside the cramped basement, Adam sat in a corner, trying to remember what had led him to this jail. He did not even know in whose jail he was. He did not know if there was anybody out there to worry about him or if there was someone out there whom he should care about. And he was away from his violin. This was one of the first times in his life that he had felt lonely. He was in total solitude, in desperate need of his instrument to keep him company. He wished that one of those fairy-tale fairies could fly in through the window and ask him to make a wish. He knew without question that he would wish to have his instrument.

And then, against all probability, his wish was granted. The door creaked open and a huge figure appeared in the dark. He was holding a box which shone silver in the swelling darkness.

'The lady has sent this to you,' the man said. 'She said you could use some refreshment down here.'

'Down here?' Adam repeated. 'Where am I now?'

'In a cell, below the lady's mansion.'

The man put the box on the floor and left. Adam reached out for the shiny box and opened its lid. The silver violin! Immediately, he put his chin on the chin rest and moved the bow on the strings. With the first movement of his right hand, he was transported to his altar by the river. The flowers, purple, blue and pink, were dancing with the melody coming from his instrument and the river was singing at the side. He had found an escape from all the dirty tricks played by the people in *Der Kristall Hochburg*. At that moment he had no intention of even finding out which side was telling the truth. He had no interest in the cloning industry. He did not care about bio-tech weapons. He simply let all his feelings flow in the calm stream of his music. After a while he stood up again, trying to see the constellations through the window, but the sky could not be seen from that depth of the rose mansion and the only thing he could see was the illuminated glass rose.

FOUR DAYS EARLIER

Adam left the rehearsal hall, remembering what Colonel Ahmad Beig had told him about his Agnet in the secret lab. If Adelheid is seeking to make my double, he thought, I must be the first to know this. If they are hiding something like this from me, then the whole propaganda thing is just a game. And I don't like games. I'm going to put an end to this game.

Looking to see if there were any more wonders in Adelheid's mansion, he started to wander in the corridors and halls of the building. Adelheid was out of the city that day. She had given no reason. It was just after he passed through her private quarters that he found himself in front of mirrored doors. There were over a thousand pieces of mirror in different sizes, shapes and colors on the surface of the two doors. On the top of the door was written *Der Image Zimmer*. A broken cross hung above the door. What did the Germans have to do with this room?

There was no handle on the door. Only a small red light blinked behind one of the small pieces of glass on the door. Beside the lamp there was something like a small hidden camera. But it couldn't be hidden with the blinking lamp beside it. He leaned towards the light look at it more closely. Above it was a small LCD. Three shapes appeared on it. He realized that it must have been activated because the electric eye which looked like a hidden camera had scanned him. The shapes changed to photos. He recognized one of them. It was Beethoven's portrait. The other two, he didn't know. He touched the Beethoven image and some shapes appeared on the small screen. From the left, there was a snowflake, a violin, and three birds. Adam shivered.

Snowfall, solo, comet, the birds are coming. This was so familiar, the message he had received in college from the unknown sender. And the symbols had turned into real events. But where was the symbol for the shiny sailor? Why was there no comet shape?

A virtual keyboard appeared on the screen and Adam typed as he saw the shapes: snowfall, solo, the birds are coming. The doors hissed and opened inwards. Behind the doors was a large hall. Unlike the outer surface of the door, on the inside there were no mirrors. Hanging on the wall opposite was a portrait of the intense-looking Beethoven with a pencil and a music note-book in his hand. The background was covered with green leaves from bottom to top. The man had longish wavy hair. In the bottom left corner of the canvas was the signature of the artist: Joseph Karl Steiler, 1820.

In a corner of the room was a very old wooden piano. It looked more like an L-shaped coffin rather than a piano. It was like the one Adam had seen in *Beethoven Haus* in the composer's birthplace, Bonn. On it was written: *das duplikat Klavier von Ludwig van Beethoven.*

He heard a movement from outside the mirrored doors and then the doors opened again. The visitor would enter the room before he could hide behind the piano, Adam realized, beginning to panic. But then he saw that there was no reason to panic. It was Dmitri.

'I saw you in the surveillance cameras,' he said. 'How did you get in here?'

'I just entered the code.' Adam laughed.

'How did you get the code?'

'Long story,' Adam replied. 'Is there something I should see in here?'

'You never cease to amaze me!' said Dmitri. 'Actually, yes. Follow me.'

Dmitri walked toward the portrait of Beethoven. On the note-book cover in the painting was a small lid. Dmitri removed the lid and a virtual keyboard appeared on the screen behind it.

'This will be the code, which even I don't have. But I can hack into its system. It will take a few moments.'

'Try "comet",' Adam suggested.

'What?'

'"Comet" is the password.'

'How can you be so sure?'

'I'm not.'

'Then . . .'

'For god's sake, enter the word!' yelled Adam.

Dmitri put in the code as he was told. He gave a sigh of relief.

'That was a terrible risk. An incorrect code could trigger the alarms. You wanna go undercover this way, I should prepare for death.'

'I told you before. I'm not a spy and I won't be. I'm a bloody musician.'

The frame moved back and a passage appeared behind it. Adam followed Dmitri into the passage. The walls and the ceiling were covered with a golden reflective shield. Lights were embedded in random places, illuminating the passage. It felt like walking inside a golden tunnel. Rounding a turn, they walked down a staircase and found themselves in front of an opaque glass door.

'This is Adelheid's private recreation center,' said Dmitri, pulling the door open.

They were in a large octagonal area with a splendid oval swimming-pool. The golden roof was supported by four marble pillars around the pool.

'We must use all the time we got,' said Dmitri, rushing toward the pool. 'Adelheid will be back in an hour.'

He shrugged off his backpack and put it on the diving-board by the pool. He took out two oxygen masks and a couple of small air capsules.

Adam stared at him, startled.

'We are going diving?' he asked.

'You may wonder how many surprises you will face in this mansion,' Dmitri said. 'I'm going to harness this capsule to your back and I need you to wear this mask.' He put on his own equipment, instructing Adam to prepare for an underwater journey in Adelheid's private pool.

'There is quite a long water-filled passage beneath this pool, to where we are going,' said Dmitri. 'We shall need air down there.'

'Where are we headed to?' Adam removed his mask to speak.

'To the place where I believe your clone is located.'

Adam replaced the mask, asking no more questions. Dmitri adjusted the air pressure for him and they jumped into the water. Adam followed his instructor and they swam to the deepest part of the pool. It was about twelve meters deep, much deeper than most private pools. Dmitri took a knife from his pocket and started to count the tiles from the wall toward the center of the pool. Locating the tile for which he was looking, he removed it easily with the knife, revealing a knob. He turned it and moved backward. About two meters away from the knob a square-shaped section of the pool bottom started to move upward on four metal posts joined to the corners. Adam swam backwards, fearful of being dragged somewhere by the flow of water. But the area below was filled with water. Dmitri beckoned to Adam and, turning on his underwater projector, swam into the tunnel below the pool. Adam followed him.

After about five minutes they reached an upward curve. Swimming up to the surface, they climbed out of the tunnel and removed their masks. They were in an octagonal room.

'Hurry up!' said Dmitri, running on tiptoe towards the wall.

On a digital panel on the wall was a set of shapes and symbols.

'Is this meant to be another key code?' asked Adam, slightly breathless from the swim.

'You bet it is.'

'Then what are you waiting for? Enter the code. Hack into it.'

'The area we are about to enter has the most sophisticated technology or, let's say, future technology in the world. We believe the knowledge which has been used to develop this project is owned by scientists who do not practice their science in the upper world any more. They are dedicated to the future and are banned from carrying out most of their experiments. That's why they have built this area.'

'Upper world?'

'They have divided the world of science into two major sections: underground section, which we are in now, and the upper world knowledge. That means on the ground, where the content is disclosed to people around the world.'

'Are you telling me that we are about to enter an area of secret science?'

'Secret science of the future. They have developed things here that you will not have seen up there in the world.'

'And my clone is one of them?'

'Yes,' said Dmitri, 'and I believe you are the one who can figure out the key code.'

'This is a set of symbols which I do not even recognize. Who do you think I am? Robert Langdon? Or maybe Dan Brown himself.'

'I don't imagine even Langdon would risk figuring out this code using these symbols. He wouldn't know at what level of science and technology this security system has been designed and what the outcome would be if he entered the wrong code by choosing the wrong shapes or choosing then in the wrong order.'

'So you were aware of this future-science-based security system and you had me dive all this way here?'

'I am telling you that you can figure out the code, looking at these shapes.'

'How do you know that?'

'Your grandfather told me so.'

'And how did he know that?'

'I guess you figured out the code to enter the pool area just by looking at it and I don't know how you managed to do that. Don't you think you can unlock this door the same way?'

'I worked out that code by remembering the message I received back in college.' Much more of this and his brain would burst, Adam thought.

'This is the area where your clone is. It has summoned you and it has given you the codes. I guess you have got to follow through in the same way as you have done so far.' Dmitri looked at Adam strangely. 'Dr. Samuel is the name.'

'What? What name?'

'If anything happens to me I want you to meet this person. According to the intel the colonel provided, he must be on the other side of this door. He is a friend of your grandfather as well. And he is working with us.'

Adam looked at the images. Eleven simple shapes in silver and a blank white square. It looked like a puzzle for children, but the wrong choice could result in death. He pondered for a while, peering at the shapes.

'"It should be only with the craft of form and the colors of life that a musician can live among the shadows",' said Adam. 'That was the second message I received from The Silver Orchestra.'

Dmitri shrugged, as if puzzled. 'So? Which shapes will you pick?' he said.

'These shapes can have different meanings in different cultures and even different meanings in the same culture at different times.'

'And perhaps they can represent a different concept here from the upper world,' Dmitri said.

'I can relate "craft of firm" to the shape which looks like a sword.' Adam stroked his chin thoughtfully.

'Which one? There are three of them.'

'The one that is not widened like the other two; the one in the left column.'

'This is so not the way Robert Langdon would do it.' Dmitri laughed. 'And how about the "colors of life"?'

'I guess the white square. All lights and colors are derived from white. It is the single color that contains all colors of life.'

Adam touched the sword shape and then the white square. The octagonal walls started to turn and a doorway appeared. A recorded voice said, 'Welcome to Project Beethoven.'

Contrary to what Adam was expecting, on the other side of the wall there was no underground lab, nor bio-tech facilities and scientists. The door opened on to a small garden with a square area of grass in the middle and trees on the opposite side. There was a three-storey building on the right with a sloping roof. Vegetation had made its way up the outer wall to cover the building. Next to it was a plaster statue. Adam and Dmitri walked towards it.

'Holy god!' said Adam. 'This is Beethoven. I have been to his house, which is now a museum. This whole garden is like the one in his house. Can we go inside?'

'Based on our intel, there is no one except Dr. Samuel in this section today.'

'Then what are we waiting for? Let's go in and meet him.'

They approached the door and tried the handle. It was locked. There was no puzzle-like key code panel by the door. The whole future science area looked like a European neighborhood of three hundred years ago. A voice coming from the small hut on the left startled them. A middle-aged man dressed in blue shirt and gray pants walked out of the door.

'I knew I would finally meet you here,' the man said in an eastern accent. 'I am Dr. Samuel. I'm a bio-tech scientist and an old friend of your grandfather's.'

'I'm so pleased to meet you, Doctor. 'What is all this stuff with Beethoven here?'

'It is a genetic-psychological and social experiment. As you have been informed, the name of the experiment is "Project Beethoven".'

'Yes, sir. I have just learned the name. I just don't know why they have built a duplicate of Beethoven's house in *Der Kristall Hochburg*.'

'Simply, my lad, because he is about to be reborn here.'

'Reborn?' said Adam, amazed. 'Beethoven?'

'Yes, my lad, a new Beethoven is about to be born,' said Samuel. 'Come inside.'

He stood in front of the locked door and inclined his head to the french door, which had reflective glass, as if checking his appearance. As the door hissed open, Adam realized that Samuel's face had been scanned by a camera inside or behind the glass. Consequently, he was expecting to see a facility inside the building a lot more developed than a three-hundred-year-old German detached house.

'Welcome to Beethoven's house,' said Samuel.

As he entered the building a digital voice said, 'Identified entry. Harry Samuel. Entry number two hundred and twelve.'

Dmitri entered the house next. The voice said, 'Dmitri Ivanoff. Entry number one.'

As Adam entered the voice said, 'The project. Entry number two.'

'And when will we meet Herr Ludwig Beethoven himself?' Adam asked with some amusement.

'Soon my lad, soon. The room we are in now is the duplicate of Beethoven's kitchen, exactly according to the building plan. The equipment has been chosen in accordance with what you may find these days in a modern kitchen. What do you expect to see on the upper floors of the house?'

'The life and death masks of Beethoven and his birth room on the second,' Adam replied. 'That is, in line with the museum. And the first floor, I don't recall. You are not serious about newly-born Beethoven, are you?'

'This is the most serious thing I have ever done in my life.'

'Is it you who is going to perform it? I have heard about the secret human cloning. Is the Beethoven Project a part of that?'

'Actually, not a part of it. Project Beethoven is the whole project.'

'I heard about my DNA and the clone's embryo,' Adam said.

'That is exactly what I am talking about.'

'What?' said Adam, shocked. 'You're telling me that the new Beethoven will be my clone?'

'Indeed.'

'And how would my DNA produce a Beethoven, Dr. Samuel?'

'Simply by producing a child with the same genetic inheritance to develop high musical ability and putting the child in the same environment as Beethoven's.'

'And you are doing this by putting my music skill genome into a duplicated environment to that in which Beethoven grew up?'

'In simple words, yes, my lad.'

As far as Adam remembered from his visit to the composer's house in Bonn, there was no elevator in the original building. The first and second floors were reached by staircases on either side of the house. But in the *Duplikat Beethoven Haus* the building was equipped with an elevator. Dr. Samuel led his guests to it and they rode to the first floor, to the room in which Beethoven's organ was supposed to be. He played it when he was ten years old at the Minerate church In Bonn. He was too small for the instrument, so that his legs didn't touch the floor when he sat at the piano. The organ had been made in 1748. But the room that Samuel showed him didn't hold a three-hundred-year-old organ; instead there was a high-tech Yamaha.

'Is this for the new Beethoven to play?'

'Yes. He will be trained so that he will be able to play it at the age of eleven.'

'And how will he learn how to play? Beethoven's first teacher was his father and then he used several music teachers and masters, including Mozart, when he moved to Vienna. Are you going to duplicate the same level of music masters for the baby as well?'

'Indeed,' said Samuel. 'Let's move up to the birth room. There are things you should see.'

As they arrived on the second floor, four men, dressed in black, their faces covered with black masks, were waiting for them. The commandos aimed their guns at the would-be visitors to the birth room.

'Put your guns down!' yelled Dmitri. 'I am the head of security for the city.'

'So what? You are not allowed to come in here,' said one of the commandos.

The next moment, the four guards attacked Adam and his companions, using some sort of electric shock devices. Adam had passed out before he knew what had happened.

CHAPTER 17

In the darkness of the jail, hearing the sound of high heels approaching the bulky door, Adam put down his instrument. It was not hard to guess who might be coming to visit him. The only woman who could be aware of his presence down there was Adelheid herself. But how could he explain his disloyalty to her? And how could she explain the deception and the lies to him?

The door creaked open. Adam had guessed right about his visitor. Adelheid was standing at the door, two guards beside her.

'How are you, honey?' she said, a charming smile on her face. 'If only you had been more patient! Or you could have just asked me.'

'What the hell is going on here?' said Adam, trying to stand up. He still felt dizzy, so he had to use the wall to avoid falling.

'Come with me, my dear,' said Adelheid. 'It's time to know everything.'

They walked out of the basement. Adelheid led her baffled guest to the pool area, asking her guards to stay away from them. At the pool, she asked Adam to sit on the sun-bed.

'We are not by the pool to relax, are we?' he said.

'It depends. I just want to tell you the truth. And I want you to know that this has always been my intention. But I had to do it at the right time.'

'Where is Dmitri? Where is that doctor?'

'Dmitri is ok. We just have to keep him put for a while. And Dr. Samuel will join us later today.'

'But your guards attacked him. Just like me. I was there.'

'I'm terribly sorry for what happened. But your friend's weak judgment, alongside your impatience, left me no choice. I can't believe how I let him become the head of security in *Der Kristall Hochburg*. The colonel so easily got to him and poisoned his mind.'

'They told me that there is a clone of me somewhere in the city. A clone that is growing in a very special way to become the second Beethoven.'

'And Dmitri took you to the secret garden and told you the rest of the story.'

'Yes. What is this Project Beethoven? And where is this Agnet clone of mine?'

'Agnet clone? This is what they have told you?'

'This is what Dmitri told me. A clone being grown under laboratory conditions. A clone that will be my age in six months.'

'Did you really believe that?'

'Not at first. But it started to make sense to me when they told me about the secret future science. They said I will see things here that I may not find believable in the world outside this city.'

'The future science project is true, honey. But cloning you and giving birth to a clone at your age in a six-month process, that is just a science fiction. An impossible one for at least for the next thirty years. Colonel Beig must be highly influenced by Michael Bay's movie in which scientists clone rich people and keep them in a vegetative state in an underground facility. In the film, the clones are called Agnets, or products. So whenever the original person has a serious problem with a body organ, they take the same organ from their clone and transplant it into their body.'

'So you mean there is no human cloning going on here?'

'I'm telling you there is no such thing here as your Agnet. And there will not be for another generation. Dr. Samuel is just working on this theory. And the replica of Beethoven's house you visited has been built for a different purpose.'

'And what about those people I met in that underground lab? Dmitri told me they were clones whose genes had been processed to make them deaf and stupid.'

'They were clones. They were human clones. And I am not too proud to admit that they are the failures. But we did not do anything to their genes here. They were born that way. They were the first generation of human clones in our labs. And there have been deficiencies in that project.'

'Your computer in the secret garden called me "The Project". How can you tell me that you are not cloning me?'

'Honey, there is no project to clone you and grow it into Beethoven. The project that Samuel told you about is just a backup plan for the major one.'

'So what is this major project?'

'Honey, *you* are Project Beethoven.' Adelheid seemed to be trying to say it as kindly as possible. '*You* are the clone.'

CHAPTER 18

Stunned by what he had just heard, Adam stood up and walked this way and that by the pool.

'No way! No way!' he shouted. 'How can I be? How . . .'

'I'm so sorry, honey! It was never meant to be revealed to you like this. But you were going to hurt yourself. It could have been so dangerous if I hadn't told you myself.'

'Dangerous? How dare you people do this?'

'I understand your indignation. But please calm down.'

'Calm down? How can you possibly understand how I feel? Or are you a double, too?'

'No, honey, I am not and I can imagine how furious you must be. But you are no different from any other human being who has ever lived in this world. You were born and grown in perfect health. It's something that we couldn't achieve in the previous trials.'

'Oh! Thank you, your highness!' said Adam, fury making him sarcastic. 'I'm really grateful for my hands and feet. My sight and my ears. I will dedicate the remainder of my life to you and your secret projects.'

'Say whatever you want, my dear!' said Adelheid soothingly. 'It is your absolute right to be mad.'

'Mad? I wish I was mad. For my whole life I have been a lab rat. My whole life has been a game. You know what? Colonel Beig was right. This is a dirty business you and your people started. Wait a minute!' Adam's face twisted in distress. 'What did you do to my grandfather? Is he my real grandfather?'

'Honey, sit down, please. If you don't pull yourself together I will have to have you drugged and send you back to jail. Please! I don't want to do that again.'

'Oh, don't pretend that you care about me.'

'I am not pretending anything, and you have never been a lab rat. We never fostered you in the secret garden; you lived in your village with total free will. Music was your own choice. We were not even the ones who introduced the world of music.'

'You have played with my whole life, my existence, my identity and you say that you care about me? I will sit down, but you are a liar, a really good one. And I will not be your slave violinist any more. The tour is over. The violinist has died.'

'I'm sure if you realize whose clone you are and how you are free as you have always been and what a marvelous future is awaiting you, you will stop over-reacting this way.'

'Surprise me! Whose duplicate am I?'

Adelheid took her cell phone from her bag.

'Do you recognize this young man?' She showed Adam a picture on the screen, a painting of a young man in his twenties. He looked liked Adam, but dressed in a classic European style.

'It's me. Or maybe my original me.'

'This painting was made in 1798 in Vienna.'

'How can this be possible?' said Adam, aghast.

'Oh, dear. We made it possible. Yes, the man in the painting is Ludwig Van Beethoven.'

'And I'm his clone?' Adam could barely take it in.

'Absolutely.' Adelheid took his hands in her own. 'You are Ludwig van Beethoven's clone.'

CHAPTER 19

Adam woke in his new oval suite in Adelheid's mansion. He was lying on a four-poster bed which was located just opposite a big window covered by luxurious golden curtains. He got out of bed and walked into the small kitchen. Unlike his previous days in the mansion, there was no message on his phone inviting him to breakfast.

The parties are over, he thought. They have no more reason to treat me like a guest and fascinate me with fancy dining-tables and sexy girls. I know what I am now. The choice was made for me years ago and I can do nothing but give in to it. He took another look around the suite. It's not that bad, he told himself. I'm gonna be Beethoven the Second.

He opened the fridge which was filled with all he could possibly desire for breakfast. Ludwig never had all these choices for breakfast, that was for sure. He took the tray to the marble dining—table which was by the window, picked up the remote control and pressed the button to open the curtains. A view of the secret garden lay before him. He sat at the table, examining his reflection in the glass top of the marble table.

'*Guten appétit, Herr Beethoven!*' He grinned at his reflection.

There was a knock on the door.

'*Guten morgen*, Herr Ludwig,' said Adelheid. 'Are you enjoying your new place?'

'Good morning. Actually, I like the independence I feel in here. And the view outside.' He turned to the window. 'It feels like home.'

'I'm glad to hear it,' said Adelheid, smiling, 'but you'd better enjoy this privacy, for people are not going to leave you alone after next week's event.'

'Next week's event? What would that be?'

'You are going to have a concert.' She stood beside him looking out at the garden. 'But it is going to be a little controversial.'

'Why is that?'

'We are going to announce to the world who you really are.'

Adam turned back to Adelheid, staring at her in astonishment. 'Where is this going to happen?'

'The concert will be held in *Beethoven Halle*.'

'*Beethoven Halle* in Bonn?'

'Yes, his birthplace. And at the end of the concert, just when our very special guests will have been amazed by the magic you do with your violin, we will announce your identity.' She sat at the table. 'That will be the moment of Project Beethoven's victory. The moment I have been waiting for, for twenty-eight years.'

'And who will be your special guests?'

'That's going to be a surprise for you. The last time we announced the project you were two years old. We brought a

TV to one of our secret labs. It was a historical day. And the day we announce that you have turned out to be a musical genius like Beethoven, that will be a hell of a historical day.'

'Did they believe you? I mean, when I was two, what proof did you have that I was the clone?'

'It seems you haven't opened this yet,' said Adelheid, touching the hard-covered book on the table.

'I have only just woken up,' Adam protested. He slid the book toward him on the table. Nothing was printed on the front or back covers. He opened it. Newspaper headlines and articles were pasted on to the pages. He went through the titles.

Second Clone Baby Born
The second clone baby, fifteen months after birth
Baby clone in healthy state
Revealed by The Silver Orchestra: Clone's DNA donor is Beethoven

The book was full of these titles, alongside pictures of himself in infancy. One picture caught his eye. The caption read: from left: Dr. Mao, Dr. Shamil, Lady Adelheid, Dr. Keramat

In the picture Adelheid was holding the baby and his grandfather was standing next to her. They were all in their twenties. The light of ambition sparkled in their eyes.

'Scientists came here from the Beethoven Study Center in California,' said Adelheid. 'They had a lock of Beethoven's hair and also a piece of bone from his skull. They ran a DNA test on you. Your DNA and that of the bone matched and they announced it in the press.'

'There is a bone of Beethoven's?'

Adelheid gave him a penetrating look. 'Where do you think you came from?'

'My DNA came from a piece of bone?'

'A very precious piece of bone that was sought for about one hundred years.'

'So how did it end up here?'

Adelheid shrugged. 'The point is, it did end up here, to be turned into a brilliant musician like you.'

Why is it the first time I have seen these pictures? Adam asked himself. My grandfather is a scientist? How come he never told me that?

He said, 'Why isn't my grandpa coming with us to Bonn? According to these headlines and newspaper pictures, isn't he one of the principal scientists of Project Beethoven?'

'Honey! He always has been. But I'm afraid his sensitivity messes up everything. That's why we're protecting him.'

'Protecting him? In a jail? From what?'

'From himself. His emotional vulnerability has made him lose his enthusiasm for this project. We decided to keep him away from it till complete victory is achieved. He is not in custody. He is just somewhere safe. We will make all the effort and when we pass the victory line, the trophy be certainly be shared with him.'

'The trophy?'

'Bringing a genius of the past to the future and benefiting mankind; this is what he had been looking forward to achieving. And now that it's almost done, his sentimental attachments to human beings is holding him back.'

'By "sentimental attachment", you mean he was not willing to hurt people?'

'That is exactly what he once said to me! I mean unreasonably giving up something that can bring comfort to a future generation. I believe this sensitivity is his weakness. Our goal is an extraordinary one. We needed stronger men than he is to achieve it.'

'Somehow, I always knew my grandfather was a man of great knowledge, but I never knew why he was only a village mayor.'

'You could not possibly have imagined him to be a world-class geneticist.'

'No. I never did. He always seemed like a wise and respected mayor to the villagers and a caring grandfather to me. But a scientist working at this level, that never crossed my mind.'

'Your band is awaiting you. We have a magnificent and historical concert to perform.'

Adam swallowed. 'Actually, I have not decided yet to be with you in Bonn.'

'Honey, this is not a good time for pulling my leg.' Adelheid tapped his arm with mock annoyance.

'I'm not joking. I will be there, but I need to see my grandfather first.'

'I'm leaving now, honey,' she said, ignoring his words. 'Your guards will show you the way to rehearsal.'

After a couple minutes two well-built men in their thirties came into the room.

'Sir,' said one, 'we are here to show you the way to your band.'

'I told Lady Adelheid, I'm not rehearsing.'

'I understand you would like to meet Dr. Keramat.' He leaned towards Adam. 'If you really want to see your grandfather alive again, you will come with us to rehearsal and you will perform in Bonn.' The guard stepped back.

'Let me put on some clothes,' said Adam, defeated. 'I will be with you shortly.'

Dmitri is exposed, he thought, and god knows what they have done to him. How do I contact Colonel Beig and tell him who I really am?

CHAPTER 20

'That's my boy!' said his grandfather. 'Now you may open your eyes.'

Adam took his hands away from his face and saw himself in the mirror with its carved wooden frame, wearing a blue jacket and pants and a cap on his head. On the cap was written, We Love School.

'And here is your birthday present, my boy!' said his grandfather. 'You are seven now and you will go to school in two weeks.'

'I like this cap, Grandpa!' said Adam. 'Is everyone going to wear caps in school?'

'Yes, my boy! Everyone.'

On the first day of school, Keramat took his grandson's hand, took the path between the colorful orchards along by the river and accompanied him to the school. Unlike for the other children, the first day of school was not a frightening one to Adam. He liked being in a community, though he did not know what this word meant. His lonely days at the village mayor's home were over and now he had a chance to spend time with others of his age at the village school. The school ran elementary and secondary programs. The boys and girls had to complete all their studies in the same school until they were seventeen, but the classes were not mixed.

On the first day, Mr.Savio taught them the rules about right and left, like when they crossed the street in town they should look to their left first or when they wanted to enter the school they had to make a line on the right side of the entrance. After his grandfather, Mr. Savio was the first person to teach him, although school was not the first place that Adam had met his teacher. Mr. Savio and his grandfather were good friends and he had come to their home many times. Usually, when Adam had gone to bed, Savio would come to their home and talking with the mayor in his library for a long time. Adam always wondered why Savio didn't call his grandfather 'Mayor' and kept calling him 'Master'. But later he realized that his grandfather has been teaching Savio. Whenever Adam asked his grandfather what he was teaching Savio, he smiled and answered, 'I'm practicing with him to ask questions, starting with how and why.' And when Adam was a teenager, he learned that his grandfather had been teaching Savio philosophy and on those nights they had been having debates on philosophical subjects and metaphysics.

Every day after school, Keramat picked Adam up and asked him how his day had been at school. Adam would tell him everything he had done since morning, even the games he had played with the other children. Then the mayor would say, 'How about a race, my boy?'

'You got it!' Adam would reply.

'On my count,' said his grandfather. 'One, two, three.'

And they would laugh and run by the river toward the council chamber. They would have their lunch there where the mayor met the villagers and talked to them about their orchards and customers and helped them with their accounts. Adam would fall asleep after lunch and the mayor would visit the greenhouses and check the equipment. In the evening they would return home and he would help Adam do his homework and then Mr. Savio would come and the lessons and debates would start. Sometimes, when Adam couldn't sleep, he would join the philosophy class. His grandfather and teacher never told him to leave the room. They would change their language to a style more suitable for a child so that Adam wouldn't be bored.

One night they were talking about metaphysics. The subject was modality and possible worlds. It was one of those nights when Adam couldn't sleep or, rather, couldn't fall asleep in solitude. He went to his grandfather's library where the modality discussion was going on.

'So, you are joining us tonight, boy?' asked his grandfather.

'May I, Grandpa?'

'Of course you may!' I hope Mr. Savio doesn't mind,' said Dr. Keramat.

'How about if we talk about apples from now on?' said Mr. Savio.

'Hmm, apples!' said the mayor with a smile. 'What a delicious subject!'

'Let's do that,' Adam said.

'Come and sit here, boy!' said his grandfather.

'What do we need to start, sir?' asked Mr. Savio.

'Three baskets and some apples,' said the mayor. 'I'll be back in a minute.'

'No, Grandpa!' said Adam. 'Let me get them.' And he ran out of the room.

The mayor and Savio looked at each other and laughed. After making a bit of a noise in the kitchen, Adam came back to the library with three straw baskets and some red, yellow and green apples.

'Ok, then!' said the mayor, 'here we go. Now, give me the red apples.'

He put the red apples in one basket, while the other two baskets on the table remained empty.

'How many full baskets do we have, Mr. Savio?'

'One, sir,' said Savio. 'I see five red apples in one of them.'

'Right! Now I let the baskets share these fresh red apples,' said the mayor, putting red apples in all the baskets. 'How many full baskets do we have now, my boy?'

'Three,' answered Adam.

Dr. Keramat emptied two baskets and filled one with the red apples.

'And now we have only one full basket again. That is a fact. But the truth is, we have different possibilities as well. These apples could have been placed in any of the other baskets. And we call these possibilities. Possible facts that could have happened and which may happen in the future. Now imagine the universe as these baskets. Imagine there are possible parallel worlds to the one we are living in. We see the fact and that is the earth with its population. But the possible truth is that there could be people living somewhere in outer space which is not yet known to us, but we have no evidence to reject it either.'

'Like the baskets which are not full?' Adam said.

'Just like them, boy!' said his grandfather, 'but they could have been filled and they may be in future. And imagine there are baskets in very far parts of the universe that we cannot see. And they are full right now. So we call them the possible worlds. Spirits may live in one of these worlds. Not the dead ones. Even ours. And right now as we are talking, our spirits may be in the same debate in that world.'

'We have no proof to see that the possible worlds do not exist!' said Savio.

'No, we don't,' said the mayor.

When Adam turned ten, his grandfather invited all the children of the village to his birthday. The party was held on the ground in front of the mayor's house. Among the children was a red-headed girl with brown eyes. Her name was Rose. In all the games they played, Rose tried to be next to Adam. When they were cutting the cake she was the one who served the cake to all the guests. The day after the birthday party, Adam and Rose fell in love. They were both ten. They arranged meetings every day in different places in the village. Every morning before leaving home for school, he told his grandfather that he would come home on his own and the mayor needn't bother leaving the council to pick him up. Of course, the mayor realized what was going on the first time Adam said this and he said, 'You are becoming a man, my boy.'

There was a valley behind the hills that the villagers called The Spring Valley. They called it this because there was a spring rising from it all through the year and the valley was all over covered by grass. Adam and Rose walked to the valley every weekend. Their day would pass with telling and listening to stories and running on the pasture-land. When they grew tired after the games, they lay down by each other and remained silent until they fell asleep with the soft wind of the valley blowing on their faces. They wanted to stay there one summer night and talk about the constellations, but the mayor didn't approve of their request. He believed that the two innocent companions could learn what friendship and love really meant, for their relationship was not an impure one. Rose lived with a foster family. Her foster-parents were very fond of her and would do anything to see her happy. She had been brought to them by Dr. Keramat, her real parents having died in an earthquake. The foster-parents believed that the mayor's idea about the two children was right and that they shouldn't try to keep them apart.

Mr. Savio arranged seminars in school in which students had a chance to speak about different subjects. These classes were held for students of fifteen and above and they were mixed. Adam and Rose had reached the right age for taking part in the seminars. Rose was enthusiastic, but Adam always tried to talk her out of it. He thought Mr. Savio would talk about the same matters as were discussed with the mayor and the subjects and opinions would be repetitious for him.

But just ten minutes after the beginning of the first seminar, he changed his mind. There were no questions about philosophy. Mr. Savio asked them to make up a story about a person who had grown up in the wild, on their own, with no parents and no education. He asked them to make up one line of the story each and the next student had to continue it. At some points Savio interrupted the story-line and asked them what they thought about the character's actions and feelings. The children were free to take the story to wherever they wished.

'How does this person learn stuff about making his livelihood?' asked one student.

'Maybe she learns things in dreams,' said a girl.

'Yeah!' said Adam, 'they can learn things in dreams from the parallel worlds.'

'What would that be?' asked a classmate.

'A possible world which exists and we don't see,' said Adam. 'Our spirits live there.'

'If our spirits are there, how come we are alive?' asked the boy.

'Can't you imagine that the spirit lives with us and also in that possible world?' asked Rose, annoyed.

'Somebody is getting backup here, guys!' said one of the kids. 'Who do you think he is?'

'What makes you two so interested in ghost stories?' asked another boy. 'Has The Spring Valley been haunted lately?'

Everyone burst into laughter. Rose looked angrily at Mr. Savio to tell him that he should stop the kids mocking her and she and Adam left the seminar.

They agreed that they had to stop supporting one other when among the other students. Clearly, it irritated the others. Rose attributed their aggression to jealousy.

On the first day of summer, which was the day after the school examinations had ended, Adam and Rose went to Spring Valley. They were sitting on the grass under an ash tree while the scorching sun struck the leaves and so they were well protected from the heat of the direct rays. Suddenly they noticed a sound from beneath the ground, as if the earth itself was grumbling. And then they heard the leaves of the trees shaking above their heads. Before long, the earth started to shake. Shocked by the shaking, they watched the branches above them trembling strongly and the tree started sink beneath the ground. Scrambling to their feet, they started to run downhill to get away from the tree. When they reached the bottom of the hill, they looked back to see if the tree was still there. It wasn't. At the same spot on the hill where they had been sitting, a very large hole had appeared, its diameter big enough to hold about sixty trees.

'What is that?' asked Rose.

'I have no idea!' said Adam. 'Run! We should let Grandpa know!'

In the village nobody had heard the rumbling from the earth and nobody was talking about the earthquake. But when they were told about it, everyone went to Spring Valley to see the hole. They did not dare to get close to it at first, for it could become bigger and take them down. After about three hours some of the men went nearer to it. They reported the depth of the hole to be so great that they could not see the bottom and it disappeared into darkness. The next day they went back to the valley to see if anything had changed, but nothing seemed to have happened. Geologists were asked by the mayor to find out how the massive hole had been created. After hours of searching every part of the hole and several meetings they did not come up with any clear reason, though they said the cause might be underground water streams undermining the soil for thousands of years, and on that day the surface had collapsed.

Adam and Rose were not as fond of Spring Valley as they had been and their visits to the region of the hole diminished. Rose talked about a trip she had to make to the town with her foster-mother. She had to have surgery on her eye. In five years Adam had not been far from her for a single day. The trip to town did not please him. He was not the kind of person who was willing to taste half-a-dozen oranges. If he went to the funfair, he would take just one of the horses on the merry-go-round, the green one, and if he couldn't have that, he preferred not to go on the ride; he never tried a different horse. With Rose he had the entire world; without her, he would be left without any friends in the village, or perhaps in the world. The intimacy in his soul was shared with just two people: Rose and his grandfather.

The day for the trip arrived and Rose left the village with her parents. They were not expected to return for at least three weeks. Adam passed the first week in solitude and silence. He did not even want to see the merry-go-round. The second week he went to the council with the mayor, but became bored with the farming and trade issues that were discussed there, so would leave the council chamber and sit by the river. He woke up very early every morning and turned in to bed very late at night. He had little appetite and he was reluctant to socialize. On the third week he went to Spring Valley to watch the tourists who came to see the hole. There were those who jumped down the hole using parachutes. They would be dragged up by villagers with the ropes which were tied to them. Flying downward into the hole, they laughed and screamed and the echoes of their pleasure could be heard all around the valley.

Look at these idiots whoooing inside that hole! This new place was a possible world of its own! Did ghosts live in there? Adam laughed at his own idea. But the thought would not leave him alone during the night. Let's put some ghosts in there, he thought. They have been digging this hole for a long time and now they are showing it to us. There must be a reason for this performance. They are sending us a message. Let's assume there is a larger-than-life explanation for its existence.

There was at least one more week before Rose could come back to the village and he was looking for some entertainment to dispel the anxiety caused by being apart from her. Why don't I spend some time with this hole alone, the idea came to him. It could have something to tell him. It would be quite an experience. He would go through its darkness at night, to its deepest part. He would not seek for anything in particular. He would just go there to see if something came for him. He wouldn't tell anyone. They would think he had gone out of my mind, especially now that Rose was not there.

The next morning, Adam got up very early, as he had on the other days since Rose had left. In the dark before dawn, he went to Spring Valley. He thought about using a rope to climb down into the hole. He had to grab the rope and slip down it for 357 meters. When he grabbed it and found himself hanging in the hole, his heart was not filled with fear or anxiety any more. He had just one thought in his mind. A terrific experience! At the bottom, he started to dig a hollow in the wall. He whistled and heard the echo inside the hole. Daylight broke into the hole, but the bottom could not be seen from the top. He hid in the hollow and waited for the first visitor to arrive by parachute. Were they jumping in there for the same reason he had done that morning? The first tourist jumped in. He could see the excitement on the man's face. The man was brave enough to journey to the valley and go through this experience. He would surely appreciate if I, Adam, gave him some more entertainment.

'A visitor from the earth!' whispered Adam. His voice echoed all around the hole.

The man was flying down. Adam could no longer see his face from within his hollow. He had to continue the game he had started with the expectation that the tourist was going to find the whispering pleasantly scary.

'Would you like to have luncheon in our dwelling?' Adam's voice echoed again.

The man did not seem to be too pleased with the welcome he had received.

'Take me up!' he cried. 'Hurry! Take me up!'

It did not take more than half a day before rumors started to spread among the tourists and the villagers. Everyone was talking about the haunted hole. The man had told other tourists that he had heard a strange voice in the hole, welcoming him to the dwelling. Neither the village folk nor the tourists could have imagined that the hole-dweller was a fifteen-year-old boy. They would never have guessed that someone from the village had dared to climb down 300 meters to terrify the tourists. Instead, they started to believe that something unnatural was going on down there, but they could hardly say what it was. Adam was not enjoying frightening people; he had just wanted to share an extraordinary experience with them. The outcome was considerably greater than he had foreseen. With the news of whispers in the hole spreading, the tourists became keener than ever to try jumping in. The number of visitors increased. Very few of them were truly scared and a lot of new visitors made the journey to the village. The area was renamed Lunacy Valley.

The three weeks of separation passed and Rose came back to the village as she had promised. Nobody was aware of the nature of the voice which had been heard in the hole. Even the mayor did not know that his own grandson was the source of the fear. Adam hesitated to tell Rose about the ghost. She had heard about it from her parents but she had no idea that her best friend was behind it. Adam took her to Spring Valley to tell her everything. He was looking for the right moment to reveal the truth, but something prevented him. Rose had brought a box to the valley.

'What's with the box? Lunch for me?' asked Adam.

'You want to guess what I have brought you from the town?' Rose said.

'Will I lose it if I can't?'

'No, you will just have to wait until you get the answer in your dreams.'

'Is it that difficult to guess?'

'No, it is just so real.'

'Do you remember once you were trying to convince all the kids that I had not broken our classroom window in a game?'

'Yes. And I remember that everyone was convinced when I told them that the hurricane which had hit the night before had broken the window.'

'Are you going to tell me what my souvenir is?'

'When I was in town I had a strange dream. We were all sitting in an open amphitheater which was located on a vast pasture, surrounded by mountains. Everyone was sitting on their seats, watching some kind of performance. Suddenly you stood up. You were terrified and you were looking at the mountains. You were trying to say something, but you couldn't. It was like you could not produce any sound. All the villagers had sunk in their seats, silent and still. Nobody could see you, except me. You were trying to scream, but you couldn't. I reached to the empty seat beside me and picked up a musical instrument that was there. I don't really know what it was. I had never seen anything like it. I gave it to you and you started to play it. All at once, everyone rose, hearing the voice of the instrument. We looked at the mountain and saw huge stones flying in the sky. They were coming towards us and they were thrown from behind the mountains. Seeing the flying stones, people started to scream and run. And then I woke up.'

'What a terrible nightmare!' said Adam. 'Do you believe it means something?'

'I don't know what it means! But I am sure if it wasn't for you and that instrument, everyone would die.'

She opened the box and took out a violin. There were some tapes and booklets in the box as well.

'With these tapes you can learn how to play this instrument,' she told him.

The dream sounded so troubling to Adam that he nearly forgot what he was about to reveal to Rose. He had been terrifying people in the hole while she was having the dream.

From that day Adam started to practice and he soon fell in love with the instrument. About eighteen months later he found out that Rose's nightmare had not been the only reason for buying him the violin; her parents had planned to move to the town where their daughter could study and become a physician. And finally, when she graduated from the school in village, they moved to town. Rose wanted to prepare Adam for this separation and let him form a deep relationship with the violin so that when she left, he would not be friendless.

Three days before Rose's departure, they went to Spring Valley and Adam played her all the songs he had learnt. He asked her not to say goodbye to him; he said that he could not afford to accept that she was leaving. And Rose did as she was asked. She bade a farewell to everyone in the village but Adam.

He did not do anything crazy such as pretending to be the ghost of the valley any more. His grandfather stood by him even more than he had done previously. He did not try to draw his grandson into farming and trade business in his council, for he knew that Adam was in love with music and creativity. He hired a music teacher from Rome who visited Adam weekly and taught him how to play every song he heard.

One morning he missed Rose even more than ever. His heart was filled with fear and he went to the valley. He walked towards the hole. He took the rope and climbed down to the bottom. He found his hollow in the same shape as it had been before. There were people in the valley taking photos and some were preparing to jump inside. He did not intend to whisper or give the visitors any strange experience.

He took out his violin from his satchel and started to play. The music echoed in the hole. An enchanting melody filled the whole valley. The visitors were charmed by the music. Everyone in the valley stopped whatever they were doing and sat on the grass to listen to the music. When it was over, they crowded around the hole and applauded Adam. This time nobody assumed any extraordinary creature lurked in the hole. The stunning music told them that a well-trained musician was down there.

Back at the top, Adam found his heart filled with a new and wonderful feeling, a blissful sensation created by seeing people calm and at peace in the valley. And it was he who had created this spirit among them by his craft.

He started to spend more time with his grandfather. He wanted to see what it was like to be in the council for many hours every day, taking care of the villagers' affairs, visiting them in the orchards and discussing their businesses with people from towns near and far. He even asked the mayor to let him participate in his classes with Savio and he was allowed into a few of the sessions. He went on some of the mayor's business trips. The meetings were held in hotels and the subject discussed was the exporting of oranges, lemons and flowers to the Netherlands and Germany. The mayor associated with many export and packing companies which belonging to government officials. The village had benefited from his influence and an airport had been built ten kilometers from the village, specifically for exporting the produce abroad.

Chapter 21

*B*eethoven Halle was located on the bank of the Rhine, between *Theater Strasse* and *Wachsbleiche*. It was a huge semi-oval amphitheatre with two circles on the left and in the middle of the upper floor and stalls on the ground floor, with a total capacity of two thousand people. On the east of the building was the river and on the west a parking lot. The edifice, which had been reconstructed three times in a hundred years, was used mainly for formal ceremonies, important speeches or symphony concerts.

The Silver Orchestra's concert was about to begin. In the front row of the stalls, the mayor of Bonn, the chairman of the Music Society of Bonn, the director of the Beethoven Study Center and several art psychoanalysts were sitting. The circle seats were taken by bio-technology, neurology and genetics students. An email had been sent to all the bio-tech and music faculties of the best universities of the world inviting academics to watch the live feed of the event on an internet link and also to wait for the historical moment of the announcement of the project.

Adam started the performance by playing a solo piece. He was supposed to end the concert with another solo, *The*

Seed for The Future. The announcement of the success of Project Beethoven was to be made by Adelheid just before the final piece.

The concert went as had been planned. Everyone was amazed by the magic the twenty-seven-year-old musician was weaving on the stage.

In an Audi parked outside the building, Colonel Ahmad Beig and Oberst Fitzgard, director of the Bonn branch of The German Intelligence Service, were watching the event on a laptop screen.

'Colonel, you have provided us with vital intelligence about what The Silver Orchestra is going to announce tonight,' said Fitzgard. 'My people and my government will be grateful to you for not letting these criminals distort the face of our historical genius.'

'Director Fitzgard,' said the colonel, 'I have been looking forward to turning this mad group over to justice, but they never let me find hard evidence against them. If I had engaged in any operation against them they would have destroyed all the evidence that could convict them. I wonder if you could give me just another week. There is much more about them that needs to be revealed.'

'As you were informed the Chancellor has directly ordered me to arrest them before they can announce the success of Project Beethoven. So I'm sorry if we have to act in a way that will put an end to your investigations.'

'I do understand the Chancellor's concern, especially now that she is only two weeks away from winning the election. If she allows the Beethoven clone to be introduced to the world in this country, she will definitely be defeated in the election.'

'On behalf of the Chancellor, I appreciate your understanding, Colonel. My team are all in position. We can engage in the operation any minute.'

'*Sich in position begeben*,' said Fitzgard on the radio. '*Warten von meine anweisung.*'

In the *Beethoven Halle*, two men dressed in suits walked towards Adelheid's seat. Her bodyguards moved towards them, blocking their way.

'German Intelligence,' said one of the men, showing his badge. 'We need to talk to your employer.'

Seeing this, Adelheid rose from her seat and rushed towards the stage to make the announcement as soon as Adam had finished the piece he was playing, while her guards stalled the agents. Adam realized that the Germans were so angry about this project that they did not even want it to be announced. Dozens of undercover agents among the audience rose from their seats and spread around the amphitheatre. Adelheid walked towards the nearest exit door, accompanied by her bodyguards. In the lobby she was handcuffed by the intelligence agents, as were those who had joined her in hosting the concert.

The concert was almost over, with only one piece left to be played. Adam had observed the quiet pursuit of Adelheid and her people by the agents during the performance. Knowing that no announcement could be made because of the apprehension of Adelheid and her people, Adam started to play the final piece, *The Seed of The Future* right away.

The concert was over. Responding to the warm applause of his audience, Adam walked to the backstage area. A couple of agents were waiting for him.

'Mr. Adam Keramat, let me congratulate you first on your amazing achievement,' said one. 'As you may have observed, your promoters have been taken into custody during your performance. We need to take you to *Bundensnachrichtedienst* to ask you some questions.'

'Take me where?'

'The Federal Intelligence Service of Germany. This bureau is under the control of the German Chancellor.'

Adam was taken to one of three BMWs with dark glass windows that were parked on the east side of the building. Three agents were with him in the car: the driver, one on the back seat beside him and the third on the front seat.

As they drew close to the bridge across the Rhine, the agent sitting beside Adam took a small black device out of his inside pocket. He put this on the back of the agent sitting in the front seat and pushed the bottom. The agent slumped sideways, unconscious. He then put the device on the driver's head and he, too, lost consciousness. He jumped into the front seat, grabbed the steering wheel and pushed the driver aside.

'Beneath your seat,' he said to Adam.

'What's going on? What's beneath my seat?'

'The air capsule and the diving mask. Put them on. Come on, we don't have much time.'

'What? You don't want to . . . .'

'We need to go diving. I know you have done this before. Just put them on.' The agent was trying to keep his eyes both on the road and Adam.

'But who are you?'

'You will thank me for this. Just hurry up.'

Adam reached beneath his seat and took out a couple of small packages containing diving equipment. He handed one to the agent and put on his own mask.

'Good boy,' said the agent. 'We will jump into the Rhine from the back door.'

The three BMWs turned on to the bridge, Adam's in the middle. Without warning, the car lurched into the rails at the side of the bridge and plunged into the river. Just as it hit the water, the agent opened the tailgate. As it began to sink, they both jumped out.

The agent dived in front of Adam, leading the way under the water for about five minutes before ascending to the surface. Emerging from the river, Adam saw a 207 parked at the roadside.

'To the car!' said the agent. 'Run! Run!'

They both got into the car.

'Where are we going now?' asked Adam.

'I work with Colonel Ahmad Beig,' said the agent. 'I'm taking you to a safe house.'

'And what am I supposed to do next? I have escaped from the intelligence forces' custody. Do you have any idea what will happen if they capture me?'

'They won't capture you. Because you will leave the country before they can catch you.'

'What do you mean, leave the country? Diving out? Or through an underground tunnel this time?'

'Now that Adelheid is in custody, her people are going to change the location of your grandfather's prison. You need to get to him before they do. He is the only one who knows the truth about The Silver Orchestra and we need to find him.'

'By "we", you mean you and colonel's team?' Adam asked.

'Also the German Chancellor. She ordered a covert operation to let you escape, leave the country and find all the evidence against Adelheid with the help of Colonel Ahmad Beig.'

'So why didn't the Chancellor abort the operation to arrest them in *Beethoven Halle*?'

'Because that operation was her order, too.'

'Wow! So are we going to meet the colonel now?'

'Not exactly.'

'I don't understand.'

'You will soon. We are almost there.'

He drove into the parking lot of a five-storey residential building. They took the elevator, travelling up to the penthouse. The agent pushed the doorbell. They heard the footsteps of someone walking in high-heeled shoes coming close to the door from the other side.

Adam was stunned. Before him was a young woman in her late twenties, red-headed with pretty green eyes. She hadn't changed much since the last time they had met in Spring Valley.

'Rose!' Adam exclaimed. 'Unbelievable!'

Rose stepped forward and hugged Adam without saying a word. Tears rolled down her cheeks. They had always thought such an encounter would be impossible. But it had happened.

'You're growing old,' said Rose, smiling.

'And you just look like a doll.'

'You mean an ugly one or a Barbie doll?'

'You know what I mean,' Adam said.

'Thank you. Your compliments always were different from everyone else's.'

'I know.' Adam raised an eyebrow. 'It's really great to see you after all these years. I've really missed you. I didn't think I would meet you again.'

They hugged again and this time didn't let one another go for several minutes.

'What are you doing here? Are you working for the German government?'

'It was a joint operation to rescue you. I'm a researcher in Genetic Engineering. I was brought into this case by Colonel Ahmad Beig.'

'So you know about Project Beethoven.'

'Actually, I do. But not as much as your grandfather does.'

'I heard he was a scientist. Did you know that?'

'I learned that recently. He is a world-class embryologist.'

'And what is that exactly?'

'In this instance, it means he has the knowledge to perform human cloning.'

'And clearly he has done it and grown the clone as his grandson. How long have you been involved in this?' Adam asked.

'I have only known about this group for about a month. Technically I have been involved since The Spring Valley.'

'What do you mean?'

'Remember I went to Rome with my parents and brought you back a souvenir?'

'The first violin I ever had. How can I forget it?'

'Was that the only unforgettable part?'

'Of course not. Among all the violins I have ever had, I always took good care of that one because you gave it to me.'

'When I was in Rome, Adelheid gave me the violin and asked me to give it to you.'

'What!' Adam said, shocked. 'And the story of that dream? Was that made up?'

'I was just a teenage girl, and she knew how to play the game. I had no idea what I was doing.'

'Oh, my god!'

'I'm sorry for all that happened to you. I met her in the lobby of the hotel we were staying in. We talked for hours. She said if I gave you the instrument and spun you that story, you would never forget me.'

'They were watching me even in Spring Valley, then.'

'And perhaps for some considerable time before that,' Rose said.

'The whole thing is just too complicated.' Adam passed a hand over his forehead. 'Sometimes I lose patience dealing with it.'

'I understand. But you need to be strong. We have work to do.'

'I still don't get it. What are you doing here? What did Colonel Beig bring you into this for?'

'When he first heard about Project Beethoven, he did not totally believe it. He asked me to study this project from a scientific point of view.'

'Why you? How did he even know you?'

'Because Dr. Keramat told him I was a genetic scientist and he could trust me. The colonel believes The Silver

Orchestra is using this project to get credibility for their other projects.'

'Other projects? You mean producing bio-tech weapons?'

'He believes your grandfather is in possession of vital information that will reveal everything. Also, the Chancellor is trying her best to find out everything about this group.'

'And why is this the Chancellor's concern?'

'Because one of their projects is producing an army of unthinking clones.'

'Unthinking clones,' Adam repeated. 'I have seen them; just under the city.'

So you need no further proof of how dangerous The Silver Orchestra is.'

'What should we do now?'

'The colonel is trying to find Dr. Keramat. And I am on my way to Vienna to start my research into Project Beethoven.'

'If my grandfather knows everything, what should we be looking for in Vienna?'

'If Adelheid doesn't tell them where Dr. Keramat is, we may never find him. Plus her people may . . .' She couldn't finish the sentence.

'Her people may what? Get to him before us and kill him?'

'Unfortunately, this is a possible scenario. That's why we need to act fast and find him before Adelheid can contact her people outside. Dr. Keramat has been in contact with the people we are going to meet throughout Project Beethoven.'

'And I guess Vienna is where I am going, too. Am I right?'

'The Chancellor has given us a jet. It takes off in two hours. And your ticket is booked.'

'What I learned here today was that Ahmad Beig hasn't confirmed that I am Beethoven's clone. Right?'

'Nothing has been said about Beethoven's clone for twenty-six years. And now, all of a sudden, they are maneuvering over this project and it is going to be their winning card. The colonel believes something is missing. And we need to find the missing parts.'

'*So, gehen wir an Vienna!*'

CHAPTER 22

T he jet flew over the green European countryside. There was nowhere which was sparsely vegetated. Everywhere was green, covered with fields and farms. Adam and Rose were sitting on opposite seats, gazing at one another and, occasionally, at Europe below them.

'So,' said Rose. 'Mr. Beethoven, the Second.'

'I really wish I weren't that.'

'The interesting point is that he had a childhood somewhat similar to yours. I have been studying Beethoven's life lately,' said Rose. 'He was born into a family where both his grandfather and father were musicians.'

'Actually his first teacher was his father. He made him stand at the keyboard and play. Beethoven's first concert posters were pasted all around the town when he was only seven.'

'Born in Bonn, yet he became famous in Vienna. Why did he move?'

'Mozart, who was known as a prominent music master, lived in Vienna at the time. But Beethoven never got the chance to be his student.'

At Schwechat International Airport a couple of agents were awaiting them. A car stood on the tarmac.

'Mr. Adam Keramat, Fraulein. My name is Peter Koch. By the order of the German Chancellor, I will be your companion while you are in Austria.'

'Nice to meet you, Peter,' said Adam. 'I guess we need to find an address.'

'Anything. Where would you like to go, sir?'

'The School of Music and Performing Arts,' Adam said.

'Sure. Please get in the car and enjoy the sights of Vienna. We will take you there.'

'*Wo gehen wir?*' asked the driver.

'*Anton-Von-Weben Platz, der Musik Universität.*'

Leaving the airport, they entered a highway which had buildings with sloping roofs on one side and farms on the other.

'So,' said Rose, 'the person from whose DNA you are supposedly cloned from moved to this city once. Do you feel in any way like him?'

'It feels great to be in the city where Mozart, Schubert and Beethoven lived. But to be honest, I can't wait to figure out how the DNA of a person who died around two centuries ago has been turned into another human being.'

'I'd like to know the answer to that question, too,' Rose said.

'Who are we meeting first?'

'Professor Rael. He teaches theory of music and has published several papers about Beethoven's symphonies. He wrote a book psychoanalyzing the symphonies and showing how they were connected to his personal life.'

'You mean *Beethoven's Magic*? I read that back in the college in Rome. I never thought I would get so deep into it one day.'

'We never know what's awaiting us, do we?' Rose looked Adam in the eye. 'Could you possibly imagine we would meet after all these years?'

'No, I couldn't,' said Adam quietly. 'That's why it seems like a miracle.'

At the university they went to the Department of Music, where Dr. Rael's office was located.

'What if he is not in town?' asked Adam.

'He is already expecting us, sir,' said the agent.

Rose knocked on the door. A tall man in his sixties wearing a brown velvet jacket opened the door.

'Dr. Rael, I'm Dr. Rose Illiano and this is Adam Keramat. I believe we have an appointment.'

'*Guten Tag, Fraulein Doktor, Herr Keramat. Wie geht es ihnen?*'

'*Guten Tag*,' said Adam. '*Danke, und ihnen?*'

'I was told you are Italian, sir,' said Rose.

'*Naturlich. Ich bin. Aber kann ich nicht spreche mit Beethoven klon Italish!*'

'He is just joking,' said Adam to Rose. 'He says that although he is Italian, he cannot speak to Beethoven's clone in a language other than German.'

Rael laughed. 'I was contacted by the Chancellor herself. She asked me for my full co-operation with you and the young lady.'

'Sir,' said Adam, 'we need to find out the truth about the possibility of Beethoven's DNA existing.'

'Why don't you sit down and I'll bring you some interesting . . .' Rael went to his desk and searched among the papers spread on it.

'You didn't tell me you were a doctor,' whispered Adam.

'You didn't tell me you were known in the University of Vienna,' Rose whispered back, suppressing a laugh.

'I'm famous and wanted.'

'Sure you are.' Rose winked. 'You are so wanted.'

Rael came back with a picture frame containing an old paper.

'Take a look.' He gave the frame to Adam.

'Is this Beethoven's handwriting?'

'This is his letter to his beloved, Contessa Giulietta.'

'She was one of his students, am I right?' asked Rose.

'Yes, she was a seventeen-year-old girl when Beethoven fell in love with her.'

'The handwriting is in German,' said Rose. 'What does it say?'

'It says:

"My angel, my all,
my self—only a few
words today, and indeed with pencil
only tomorrow is my lodging positively fixed
what a worthless waste
of time on such—why
this deep grief, where
necessity speaks—
can our love exist
but by sacrifices,
by not demanding everything,

can you change it, that you are
not completely mine. I am not
completely yours—Oh God!"

Rael translated the letter without looking at the handwriting.

'Amazing,' Rose breathed.

'I will give you a translation of this poem, young lady,' Rael said. 'The sounds of the world started to fade away from this wonderful man in his mid-twenties.'

'His deafness was a real tragedy,' said Adam. 'A musician of his stature becoming deaf. That's really sad.'

'Did they ever find out the cause of his deafness?' asked Rose.

'Not when he was alive. He also suffered from a fever from his early twenties. His doctor never figured out the cause.'

'Did he become completely deaf?' Rose asked.

'Yes. At the age of forty-one he stopped performing in concerts, which was his main livelihood, because of his deafness. It was in the Ninth Symphony concert that he couldn't hear the audience applauding him and tears rolled down his face.'

'What a sad story!' said Rose. 'How could he cope with such pain?'

'Indeed. It was sad. And at the age of fifty-seven he couldn't handle it any more.'

'He didn't commit suicide, did he?' asked Rose.

'No, not at all,' said Rael. 'He died of a fever.'

'All we are looking for starts from the moment of his death,' said Adam. 'What happened to his skull? Is it right that the DNA was obtained from the skull?'

'The day after his death, a local physician, Doctor Johann Wagner, and Beethoven's private doctor performed an autopsy to discover the cause of his deafness and also the cause of his death,' Rael answered. 'Dr. Wagner sawed out the two temporal bones, one on each side of the skull, and made another cut across the top of the skull so that he could remove it like a cap. This caused considerable fragmentation of the skull bones. Beethoven was buried the day after, when thousands of Viennese were present at the funeral.'

'So?' Adam asked. 'What then?'

'It was also customary at that time, when a famous person died, for locks of his hair to be cut and given to certain people. We are pretty sure that this happened with Beethoven's hair.'

'I don't get it? What happened to the skull?'

'In 1863 the board of directors of the Society of The Friends of Music in Vienna voted to exhume the bodies of Beethoven and fellow composer Franz Schubert, allow medical examinations of the remains, and then rebury them at a new, more elaborately honored location,' Rael said. 'Present at the examination were Carl von Patruban, a professor of anatomy, Dr. Standthartner, a physician and the director of the board of the music society, and Gerhard von Breuning, a physician whose family had been close to Beethoven since his Bonn days and who, as a teenager, had personally known the composer. These three observers found that the skull membrane had fallen apart, that the skull was in nine fragments, and that besides the temporal bones, some other bones, such as part of the crown, were missing. The committee in charge of the exhumations wanted to rebury the rest of the skeletons but to keep the two skulls for study and spiritual inspiration. The committee members were heavily influenced by the current popularity of phrenology, the study of the skull based on the belief that it indicates mental faculties and character. They also hoped that Beethoven's temporal bones might reappear and be reattached to the skull. The committee therefore placed Beethoven's skull temporarily into Breuning's hands for safe-keeping. But the committee members were overruled by the music society's administrators, who, at an October 15 meeting, decided to rebury the entire skeletons, including the skulls. Consequently, on October 23 both complete bodies were reburied in new vaults at the Währing Cemetery.'[2]

'And the missing parts of skull?' said Rose. 'What happened to them?'

'They never made it back to Beethoven's grave,' Rael said. 'Dr.Henry Lehmann' was the chief professor of medical history at the time. He possessed a collection of skulls that he kept for scientific study.'

'I guess I'm losing you,' said Adam. 'What happened to the missing fragments?'

'Breuning did have possession of them. He did openly state his belief that the skull should be preserved for study,' Rael said. 'He secretly gave Lehmann two of the nine large skull fragments discovered at the 1863 examination plus eight small pieces that broke off during handling. Those bones have remained in the Lehmann family to the present day.'

'And where are the fragments now?' asked Adam.

---

[2]   from The History of Beethoven's Skull Fragments, by William Meredith

'Robert Wright, Lehmann's heir, who lived in California in the1990s, had them.'

'Had? So what happened to them?'

'About forty miles away from where Robert and his family lived, in San Jose State University, The Beethoven Study Center had been established. In 1994 some members of this center bought a lock of Beethoven's hair at an auction in London and took it back to study it and find out the cause of Beethoven's unknown illness and also the cause of his deafness.'

'You're telling me that at that time skull fragments and the lock of hair were both possessed by San Jose University?' Adam looked for confirmation.

'Indeed,' said Rael.

'It was in 2003 that Mut-Art, the first human cloning organization, announced that they had successfully cloned a human being for the first time from a frozen cell,' Rose put in. 'The baby's name was Eirene and she was born in an underground lab.'

'And just a year after that The Silver Orchestra announced the news of the birth of the second human clone—who happened to be Ludwig Van Beethoven's clone,' Rael said.

'So,' said Adam, almost amused. 'Adam and Eirene; the first human clones.'

'The authenticity of The Silver Orchestra's claim was proved by DNA tests. 'The clone's DNA matched with the skull's and that matched with the lock of hair.'

'Everything points to the fact that I am that clone,' Adam said.

'We don't know it for sure yet,' said Rose. 'We need to talk to the center and get proper proof.'

'And how do we find Grandpa?'

'They will lead us to him.'

'You mean we walk into San Jose University and I say, 'Hi, I am Beethoven's clone'?'

'Is there anything better we can do?' Rose asked. 'The faster we get the answers, the sooner we can save Dr. Keramat's life.'

'If the DNA was obtained from the center,' said Adam, 'it means that they were behind the project.'

'He is right,' said Rael. 'It is not safe just to walk in there. You need to do it under cover.'

'A visiting professor could be a good idea,' Rose suggested.

Chapter 23

In the Munich headquarters of *Bundesnachrichtendienst*, Adelheid and Dr. Mao were being processed out. The agency had no hard evidence proving any threat from The Silver Orchestra.

Once released from custody, Adelheid and her team flew back to *Der Kristall Hochburg*. The first person Adelheid wanted to meet was, without question, Dr. Keramat. Getting off the plane, Adelheid asked her security men to take her to the underground energy facility beneath which he was being held.

At the lowest and secret level, the elevator doors hissed open to a hall in which there were four closed doors.

'Keramat's cell,' said Adelheid, giving the guard a key card. 'Open it.'

The guard pushed the card into the security device by the cell door. Then Adelheid put five fingers on the scanner. The lock clicked and the door opened. The room was empty.

'Where the hell is he?' asked Adelheid, flustered. 'How could he possibly escape?'

A guard came rushing into the cell.

'Lady Adelheid,' he said, 'Dmitri is gone, too.'

CHAPTER 24

The jet flew over San Francisco Bay and landed at San Jose International Airport after an eight-hour flight from Vienna. Adam, Rose and the two German agents drove to Cahill Street, where a detached house had been rented for them. The house faced Sunny Hills Park in the eastern part of the city.

The next morning the agents drove them in a rented Camry to San Jose State University in the city center. The driver toured around the university. They passed by the Aquatic Center and then drove north until they reached the Martin Luther King Library.

'We will be waiting for you in the car,' said the agent. 'Don't forget that you should sound like research scientists. If they get suspicious, you won't get anywhere.'

'Here is your letter of recommendation from Vienna University.' The other agent gave Adam an envelope. 'You will be under the name of Christian Salvatore.'

'Don't worry. I won't blow my cover. I am used to living like this. And I still don't know if I'm a real human or not,' Adam said. 'Where should we go now? This university looks as big as a town.'

'We need to find the Martin Luther King Library,' said Rose. 'The Beethoven Center is on the fifth floor.'

At the corner of San Fernando 4th and 5th they stood facing an eight-storey building. The library had entrance gates from both the campus and San Fernando Street. The elevator took Adam and Rose straight to the eighth floor. Rose walked to the director's office, where she was told that Dr. Meyer, the center's director, was at the museum, giving some visitors a tour.

Entering the museum, Adam noticed a middle-aged man watching him. The man was standing at a vending machine pretending to have some problem with getting his coffee. But Adam could tell that there was nothing wrong with the machine and the whole scene was just an act. He had seen the man downstairs on the ground floor. He was casually dressed with wavy hair and a beard. He looked like a MIT nerd.

If he is just working in this university, why is he making himself so obvious, Adam wondered. Maybe he wants me to see him. Maybe he is looking for an opportunity to get to me.

'It is a real pleasure to meet you at last, Dr. Meyer,' said Rose, discreetly nudging Adam's shoulder to let him know of their host's presence. 'I'm Doctor Illiano and this is my assistant, Mr.Salvatore.'

'My pleasure,' said Meyer. 'Oh my! Such a busy day! Come on, guys, let's not keep you waiting any longer. You wrote that you are doing a study on Beethoven's lock of hair. Right?'

'Yes, I am,' said Rose. 'We followed its journey from Vienna to here.'

'Sounds great! Why don't we take a look at the items in the museum? The lock of hair is here, too.'

They passed by the two keyboards owned by Beethoven, first editions of his music, microfilms and photocopies of his sketches and autographs owned by other libraries, including the complete collection of the composer's manuscripts kept at the *Staatsbibliothek zu Berlin*. There were also Beethoven memorabilia on sale, including medallions and coins, plaques, plates and glass objects, bookends, clocks, and other commercial merchandise. They stopped by the original portraits of Beethoven, paintings and works of art that had been made by artists inspired by Beethoven's music.

And finally they reached the window behind which they could see the lock of hair.

'This lock of hair was bought by our center at an auction in London in 1980,' said Meyer. 'The lock contains 422 hairs with three clearly observable colors: grey, white, and brown. The hairs range in length from seven to fifteen centimetres. Given that hair grows at an average rate of one-half inch per month, the hair cut from Beethoven's head on his death bed represents hair grown during the last six to twelve months of his life.'

'Have you run scientific tests on these hairs?' asked Rose.

'Of course. There were three tests. First we wanted to know if Beethoven had used morphine as painkiller during the last months of his life. We used three strands of his hair to do the test.'

'And the result?' asked Adam.

'Negative,' said Meyer. 'The second test was a trace metal analysis in which we found a high lead concentration in his hair. Some scientists believe lead poisoning was the cause of his deafness, life-long illnesses and even his death.'

'Was it?'

'It's a theory, but this amount of lead can be found in any fifty—year-old man's bone or hair.'

'We didn't see the bone fragments in the museum,' said Rose. 'Do you keep those in a safer place?'

'The bone fragments were temporarily donated to our center for study by the Wright family. After the tests we gave them back to the Wrights.'

Adam and Rose glanced at one another, but Adam immediately asked his next question, pretending not to be surprised that the bone fragments were no longer in the center.

'How about the third test?' he asked.

'It was a DNA analysis that would help us match the other existing hair strands with the ones we owned.'

'Does it mean that you captured the DNA?' Curious, Adam's heartbeats quickened.

'We did. But the DNA was damaged.'

'It was damaged?' He hadn't expected that. If the DNA was damaged, how could they possibly have used it for cloning?

'Yes, it was damaged. In the sense that it had disappeared.'

After lunch in the university's cafeteria, Adam and Rose said goodbye to their host.

Confused by the new information, Adam went to the rest room. He was alone. He took off his mask, washed his face and looked at himself in the mirror. Why did he look like the great man?

Suddenly he saw the man with wavy hair and beard in the mirror. The man stood at the sink beside Adam and started to wash his hands.

'Other strands of hair exist,' the man said, without looking up.

'Excuse me?' said Adam. 'Do I know you?'

'Meet me tonight at this address.' The man put a business card in Adam's pocket. 'And put your mask back on, Mr. Keramat.' He turned sharply and walked out of the room.

Adam examined the business card.

Benjamin Saeidi
Embryologist
2077 San Fernando, San Jose

When he returned to the cafeteria he found Rose busy with her laptop. Leaving the cafeteria, they went to the university campus. Some students stood in groups, chatting and laughing, while others were walking fast to get to their classes. Adam remembered his days at university. How small had been his world. How simple had been his life and how few had been his concerns. He wished he was an ordinary student again, walking in the campus with his childhood soulmate, talking to her about his future plans. He wished he had not been on a world tour. He wished he was not a clone. He wished for a simple life.

'Rose,' said Adam, his voice trembling, 'do you miss it, too?'

'Spring Valley?' Rose knew at once what he was talking about. 'So much. I miss the pastures and the innocent life we had there.'

'Do you remember one day we walked for such a long time that it got dark and we didn't dare to go back to the village?'

'We didn't notice how the time had passed and suddenly we found ourselves in front of your grandfather's forest house,' she said.

'I can't forget the way Grandpa looked at me when I saw him in the morning, rocking in his chair by the fireplace.'

'And I can't forget the sound of his rocking chair waking me up.' Rose laughed.

They walked for about two hours. They checked out every corner of the campus and just when they were entering the Department of Linguistics, Adam's phone rang.

'Herr Keramat,' the German agent was on the phone, '*sie mussen aus gehen. Ich bin hinter Busbahnhof, zu der auto.*'

'Our German friends are getting impatient,' Adam said.

In the car Adam told his companions about the strange meeting he'd had with the man who had given him his business card.

'He knew exactly who I was and what I was looking for in SJST. He even knew that I had a mask,' he said.

'*Wir trefen ihm nacht,*' said the agent, '*Aber wir mussen sehr behutsam vorgegangen . . .*'

'What did he say?' asked Rose.

'He says, we will make the visit tonight but we should take a very cautious approach.'

At nightfall, the agents drove Adam and Rose to San Fernando Street where the stranger's office was located.

It was after nine and the town's streets were deserted, presumably because many people were enjoying the night life in San Jose's hectic clubs and bars. San Fernando was the same street in which the Beethoven Center was located. They finally reached No.2077, a five-storey building with no sign above the entrance. It seemed like a residential block. The entrance door was open and as they entered a guard asked them whose flat they were looking for.

'You need to go to the penthouse, guys,' said the guard. 'That's where Professor Saeidi lives.'

At the top floor, Adam rang the bell and the man with the beard opened the door.

'Come on in,' he said. 'You haven't been followed, have you?'

'No, sir,' said the German agent.

'As you know I'm Benjamin. Nice to meet you at last.'

'And you know I'm Adam. This is Dr. Illiano. How long have you known about me?'

They entered the penthouse while one of the agents stood guard at the door.

'Since before your birth, Mr. Keramat,' said Benjamin, guiding his guests to the living-room.' I'm a friend of your grandfather's and I owe him a lot.'

'Really?' said Adam. 'He has never mentioned your name.'

'Adam,' said Benjamin. 'I know what you are looking for in San Jose. You have no idea what these people are capable of.'

'What people? The Center?'

'No. The Silver Orchestra.'

'Have they contacted you?'

177

'Not yet. But they will. And I need to tell you something before that happens.'

'Go on,' said Adam. 'You are scaring me.'

'I have a message from your grandfather.'

'My grandfather? You know where he is?'

'Actually, I don't. But I'm keeping a precious possession of his. He gave it to me long ago and asked me to give it to you in case you came to the Beethoven Center.'

Benjamin went to one of the rooms and soon after came back to his guests with an envelope in his hand.

'This is now yours,' said Benjamin, giving Adam the sealed envelope.

The seal belonged to Dr. Keramat and dated back to five years earlier. Adam tore open the envelope. He took out a flash drive.

There was a sound from the door, as if someone had bumped into it.

'Are you expecting someone, Mr. Saiedi?' asked the German.

Benjamin shook his head.

'I'll go check, then.'

Opening the door, the agent found his colleague lying on the floor with his face covered in blood. There was a hole in his forehead.

'He has been shot. On the floor! Now!' The agent slammed the door shut.

Benjamin ran to his room. But this time he came out with a shotgun.

'What's going on here?' Rose demanded.

'Go behind the kitchen bar.'

Crouched down behind the bar, Adam and Rose heard a window breaking, swiftly followed by three masked men dressed in black running into the room. Benjamin and the German agent started to shoot at them and the intruders returned fire. After a minute or two, the penthouse floor was slippery with blood. Nobody had survived. The exchange of bullets had put an end to the lives of the masked men and also of Benjamin and the German agent.

Adam and Rose, shocked by what they had just witnessed, left the apartment. They walked cautiously by the agent's body where it lay in his blood in the corridor. The floor numbers on the elevator's indicator were moving upward.

'Someone is coming up,' said Adam. 'We'd better take the stairs.'

On the ground floor they found the doorman dead at his desk. He had also been shot in the forehead.

'We can't leave the building,' Rose said. 'They must be waiting for us outside.'

'To the parking lot,' Adam said, breathing rapidly. 'Down the stairs.'

They ran down the stairs and hid behind an old Cadillac. The car's wheels rested on wooden panels. It seemed like an antique car that had not moved for years.

'I should call him,' Rose said.

'Call who?'

'The colonel. He gave me a number in case I needed to contact him in an emergency.' Rose took out her mobile and pressed the digits.

'Colonel, we are being attacked. We need your help. Please do something,' she begged when he answered.

'Rose?' said the Colonel, 'where are you? Calm down and tell me where you are.'

'It's me and Adam,' she panted. 'They are after us. San Fernando 2077. We are in the parking lot.'

'Where are the German escorts?'

'Dead.'

'Oh god! Leave your cell on. And stay where you are. I'll have my agents track you. They will get you out of there.'

'Just hurry up, Col.' She broke off. The cold metal of a revolver pressed against her head.

Adam and Rose were surrounded by masked men, pointing guns at them. They were taken, blindfolded, to a SUV. There was nobody outside the building at that hour to help them.

'Are you working for The Silver Orchestra?' asked Adam as the vehicle gathered speed.

He got no answer.

The car was moving on the deserted streets of San Jose. It was the second time that day that Adam wished he had a simple life; just him and Rose and no agents and armed men around them.

They sat in the back of the SUV with a masked man holding an Uzi beside them. The driver honked the horn to make the truck in front move, the lights having turned green. But the truck started to reverse, hitting the SUV. Adam saw the lights of another truck approaching fast from the street on their right straight towards them. In a few seconds the lights had disappeared as the truck hit the side of the SUV and the car spun with the force of the collision. The noise of the crash echoed so wildly inside the vehicle that Adam and Rose hardly took in how they were hurled from one side of the car to the other. Gunshots resounded from outside and after a few moments they heard footsteps nearing the car. The masked man beside them had his gun pointed at the back door to shoot the assailant on sight. But he was not quick enough and was shot in the chest before he could fire his weapon.

'Mr. Keramat, Madam,' said the man who had opened the door. 'I'm Robert. I'm working with Colonel Beig. Sorry to hit your car.'

'You almost killed us,' said Rose, trying to control her shaking.

'Please accept my apology. It's late and there is no police patrol. But I'm not a drink-driver.' Robert grinned.

'Robert,' said Adam, 'I appreciate your sense of humor, but can you take us somewhere safe, please?'

'Of course. A plane is waiting for you. It won't be safe for you in San Jose any more.'

'Where are we going?' asked Adam.

'We will find out during the flight.'

Once in the air, Rose's cell phone rang.

'Hello?' she said. 'Colonel, thank you so much for saving us.'

'I'm glad you are both safe now,' the colonel said. 'Just tell me what you were doing in Benjamin's place.'

'Long story, but we got a flash drive. He said it contains a message from Dr. Keramat. I'm going to check it out now.'

Adam, Rose and Robert gathered around the laptop that had somehow survived all the day's adventures in Rose's satchel.

Rose linked the memory stick to the computer and clicked on the only file that it contained.

An image of a cat lying on a couch appeared on the screen, accompanied by strange music.

'Does that ring any bell, Adam?' Rose asked, puzzled.

'We never had a cat in Grandpa's home.' Adam leaned forward, gazing at the screen. 'What is he trying to say?'

'And the music?' asked Robert 'Have you heard it before?'

'This is not music. It's just a beginner, playing some scrambled notes on a cello.'

'So you're telling me we are in the middle of nowhere and we have to find our flight destination with the picture of a cat and some cello music?' Robert grimaced.

'That's all I can tell you,' said Adam.

'Wait a minute!' Robert slapped his forehead. 'How could I be so stupid? This is not a simple image and an amateur musician. This is an encrypted message.'

'Can you decrypt it?'

'I don't have the software here. But I'll give it a shot. Do you have Photoshop on your laptop?'

'Grandpa used to tell me stories about writing on the shaved heads of soldiers in ancient times,' Adam said, 'and after the hair had grown back, they were sent to a far region to carry a message.'

'That's exactly what I'm talking about,' said Robert. 'This image is the head covered with hair and the message is hidden somewhere beneath the hair. Digital pictures, which contain large amounts of data, are used to hide messages. For example: a 24-bit bitmap image will have eight bits representing each of the three color values, red, green and blue at each pixel. If we consider just the blue there will be 2^8 different values of blue. The difference between 11111111 and 11111110 in the value for blue intensity is likely to be undetectable by the human eye. Therefore, the least significant bit can be used for something else other than color information. If we do it with the green and the red as well, we can get one letter of ASCII text for every three pixels.'

'I got it,' said Robert after about half-an-hour. 'I removed all but the two least significant bits of red, green and blue. It became a relatively black image. Then I made it seventy times brighter. And I got this.'

Adam studied the numbers on the white screen. 'Amazing!' he said.

301239766

'What do these numbers tell us?' asked Rose.

'They are another code,' said Robert.

'And how do we break it?'

'I guess the key is in the music,' said Robert. 'Can you tell me the frequency of each note in the sound file?'

Adam took a pen and notepad from his pocket. Listening to the file several times, he wrote down the frequencies.

A= 5   E=5   C=5   G=7   B=1   D=0   F=2   FLAT   F=3

'Great job,' said Robert. 'Now could you write down the notes as you hear them on the file?'

Adam listened again and wrote:

EGB flat D EC flat F DD F

'Ok. Now, if we put back the frequencies of the first notes, we will have this.' Robert wrote down the numbers:

5716553002

He scratched his head. 'If we put the two sets of numbers by each other we will have:

301239766

5716553002

'I think I know what they mean,' said Rose. 'They are the co-ordinates of a location.'

'Exactly,' said Robert.

	Degrees	minutes	seconds
Latitude	30	1	23.9766
Longitude	57	16	55.3002

'Let's Google that now.' Rose entered the co-ordinates on the search engine. 'Oh! We don't have a connection here.'

'I'll go ask the pilot,' said Robert, getting out of his seat.

'Where do you think this is, Adam?' Rose asked.

'I don't really know,' said Adam, 'but I'm sure Grandpa didn't leave this message just for me, because he would know I could never break it on my own.'

'Maybe he knew Colonel Beig would be helping you when you acquire the message,' Rose suggested.

'I guess he did,' said Adam.

Robert came back from the cockpit.

'We have the location,' he said. 'It's in Iran. Mahan, a small town near Kerman.'

'Kerman?' Adam repeated. 'Grandpa was born and raised there.'

'It's a public place,' said Robert. '*Baghe Shazde.*'

'He showed me videos of it,' said Adam. 'A magnificent historical garden at the heart of the desert.'

'Are we going there now?' asked Rose.

'The jet is not allowed to land in Iran,' said Robert. 'We need to go to Istanbul first.'

CHAPTER 25

Adam and Rose stood at the entrance gate of Shazde Garden. The rectangular garden was spread along the steep rise of the hill. Standing at the huge wooden gate, they were amazed by the magnificent view of the garden which was a huge contrast with the barren area outside its walls.

'It's really awesome,' said Rose.

'Grandpa has taken me through this place with his videos. I know every corner of this garden.' Adam smiled, remembering.

'How old is it?'

'It was built about a hundred-and-fifty years ago by the Prince of Kerman and Sistan province. Look at the tiles above the entrance.' Adam pointed at the arch above the gate. 'Do you see that?'

'One tile is missing,' said Rose.

'The tiler stopped putting the last tile on the wall the moment he heard the news of the prince's death.'

Buying tickets, they passed through the gate and found themselves in front of the picturesque twelve levels of waterfalls.

'The water flows down the garden through the main axis. You can see the stream of water divides the garden into two symmetrical parts. Everything you see on the right can be found on the left. The heights of the trees and the kind of fruits are identical, with the same number on both sides of the water. The only unsymmetrical point can be found among the inner trees by the eastern wall of the garden. They were chosen to be taller to protect the garden against the eastern winds and storms.'

Climbing up the steps between the tall trees, Rose checked the co-ordinates on her cell phone to find the exact location. They climbed up the twelve levels of the garden and reached the main building, exactly where the two axes of the garden met.

'It's not in the building,' said Rose checking the GPS. 'We need to go further.'

'It must be in the back garden, then,' Adam said.

They entered the smaller garden that was located behind the main building.

'You see that dead tree over there?' asked Adam. 'This tree is exactly located above the main axis of the garden. If we look at it from the entrance, we will see it as a tall tree standing over the line of water stages, dividing the garden into two symmetrical parts.'

They walked towards the tree.

'And I have news for you, sir,' said Rose. 'The tree is our co-ordinates.'

'Really? But what can be inside this tree?'

'Inside it, or maybe beneath it.'

'We need to wait until dark. The garden will be closed to tourists at ten. And then we will be able to start digging.'

'There are rooms available for tourists to rent. Let's get one and stay there till midnight,' Rose said.

Soon the tourists began to leave the garden one after another. Guards were patrolling around the place to make sure the garden was secure for the night.

Finally, at ten o'clock, the gate to the garden was shut and the main lights were switched off. Adam and Rose came out of their room and tiptoed toward the dead tree. Adam took the separate parts of a small spade out of his satchel and started to assemble them.

'Watch the path to the main building, Rose,' he whispered, starting to dig the ground beside the dead tree.

Fortunately, it was a misty night and it would be difficult for anyone to see movement at the back of the garden. Adam, the master of sounds, knew how to use the spade without making a noise. But he couldn't muffle the spade when it hit something hard below the tree.

'I think we've got something,' he whispered. 'It's a box. It seems too heavy to lift.'

'It must be a safe,' said Rose. 'Let me give you a hand.'

As they were struggling with the heavy box, they heard footsteps from behind the bushes.

'Someone is coming toward us,' said Rose. 'We must get it out before we are discovered.'

'It's stuck. I can't move it.' Adam tugged at the box again. Still it refused to move.

A large figure was walking out of the mist and they quickly hid behind the dead tree. He was so close to them that he would hear any movement they made. The figure was getting closer and closer, finally stopping above the hole which Adam had dug. He was wearing a cloak and his face could not be seen in the darkness.

'Friends,' said the man, 'you cannot get the box out of the hole. The roots of the tree are tangled around it.'

Adam jumped out from behind the tree.

'Grandpa!' he said. 'Oh, my god!'

'My boy!' Dr. Keramat clasped Adam in his arms, embracing him like a father who hasn't seen his son for years.

Overcome by emotion, Adam couldn't say a word. For a crazy moment he thought that the journey was over and he could go back home with his grandfather.

'I'll open the box,' said Keramat.

'Do you have the code, sir?' Rose asked.

'I was the one who locked it and put it there twenty years ago.' Dr. Keramat opened the box and took out a leather briefcase. 'Let's fill the hole.' He started to put the soil back in the hole. Adam stood still, watching his grandfather in astonishment.

Dr. Keramat took Adam and Rose to his room in the lowest part of the garden. Adam's heart was filled with comfort, but he couldn't conceal his anger with his grandfather for his abrupt disappearance.

'How come you never told me you were a doctor?' he demanded.

'I understand your anger,' said Keramat, 'but it was all done for your safety.'

'That's exactly what Adelheid told me,' Adam objected. He glanced at the briefcase, which was locked and sealed. On the seal was written: Project Beethoven. 'Is there anything inside this about me and Beethoven that I don't already know?'

'There is much more than you can imagine yet to learn,' his grandfather said.

'Like what?'

'Let's start with this: you are not the clone. You are my grandson. And in this briefcase there's compelling evidence to prove that.'

For the second time that night Adam felt relief. And for the second time he wished they could just go back to their life as grandfather and grandson. He wished they were just tourists in the garden, spending the night there and enjoying its natural splendor.

Dr. Keramat opened the briefcase and took out a CD.

'I guess we can use your laptop,' he said to Rose.

'Sure. It's not the first time we've used it for decoding,' she said.

'Oh that! I'm really sorry for the trouble I caused you with getting the address to the garden. I had to use a code language.'

'It's ok, grandfather!' Adam grinned. 'After all I'm your grandson. Smart enough to get your messages.'

'I never doubted that.'

On the screen an mpeg file was being played, showing twenty-seven-year-old footage from one of the surveillance cameras in *Der Kristall Hochburg*. Adelheid and Dr. Keramat could be seen.

'Are you sure about that?' Adelheid asked.
'Unfortunately, yes. I was just talking to the hospital.
The clone is dead,' Dr. Keramat said.

*'The failure of Project Beethoven is going to cost us.
We'll lose a hell of credit,' said Adelheid.*
'His death is in our hands.'
'This is not a great time for sentiment, Dr. Keramat.'
Adelheid's voice was harsh.
*'But it's a time for regret. I'm quitting The Silver
Orchestra.'*

'According to this footage, I'm dead,' said Adam.

CHAPTER 26

Twenty-eight years earlier
Kerman University

Dr. Karim Keramat was walking out of his class, eager students around him, intrigued by the lecture he had given about developing human organs. The students were thrusting themselves forward to ask questions.

'Sir, when will we have the new generation of human clones?' asked one of the girls.

'We already have them.' said Keramat, slowing his pace to be able to answer as many questions as possible. 'Just three years ago, the first human clone was born at the Mut-Art organization.'

'You mean Eirene, sir?'

'Yes. Her healthy status was confirmed after she was taken to the US and examined there.'

'Is Mut-Art a legitimate organization?'

'Of course. They are running stem cell research and also give IVF reproduction services to married couples.'

'But human cloning is banned in every country, isn't it?' the girl persisted.

'It is. And that's why they have cloned this Eirene in a secret lab. Even her birthplace is undisclosed.'

Karim Keramat rushed to the parking lot. It was his wife's birthday and he did not want to be home later than usual. His only son was a music conductor who lived in Rome and was married to an Italian woman. After his son left, Keramat started to feel lonely, but the depression never affected his work in the groundbreaking scientific research that he pursued. He was running a research project into stem cells and developing human organs using stem cell techniques. All through his professional career, even during his first years of teaching in his early twenties, he endeavored to be hardworking and intense and that caused him to be on top all the time. His achievements always took him to a position much higher than his colleagues. He believed the more he taught to those around him, the bigger his spirit would be. He never felt he would lose his distinguished position by giving away his knowledge.

But not everyone in the campus felt that way. Each success made Keramat appear more of a threat to his co-workers. And eventually they could not tolerate him any more and conspired to get rid of him. He decided to release himself from the stresses of the university job arising from the false allegations with which he had been bombarded. His colleagues persuaded a student to file a complaint against him, accusing him of using human subjects for unethical genetic experiments. The allegations were never proved, but he couldn't stand the situation and quit the university. He believed in natural justice and thought that if he hurt a person, he would be hurt back in the same way. Therefore, he abandoned his colleagues, being sure that one day what they had done to him would rebound on them.

He decided to continue his research in the private lab he had built on the second floor of his house. At first he found it difficult to work at home because some of the equipment he needed was only available in the university lab. The President of the University, aware of losing a great mind among his staff, agreed to let him use the university lab at weekends, indeed he offered this facility to him.

Used to the life of a teacher who left home every morning to meet his students and colleagues, he found that the solitary life he now led made him long to socialize with people and see the outside world again. But there was no chance he could return to his previous job. With one possibility left, he made up his mind to dedicate the rest of his life to science and fulfil his social needs through doing a mundane job. And that was the beginning of a new and different life.

His mornings were filled with his new job in a park and in the afternoons he pursued his studies in his private lab. He was able to draw on his bank deposit for funds, while he was seen in public as a gardener. Many of his faculty friends and former students came to his lab and some of his close friends even paid visits to him in the park as he was cutting the weeds and watering the grass.

After a year, his followers started to fade away and eventually he was totally abandoned by his former colleagues. His wife, who had been used to the privileged life of a university professor, couldn't bear the way people now regarded her. She left her husband when he needed her the most. He was making good progress in his research, though, and finally, after two-and-a-half years of endeavor, he was ready to present his findings to the world.

The first gate opened to him was an invitation from The European Society of Human Reproduction and Embryology to an international conference in Rome.

With no friends with whom he could share this news and no money to finance the trip, the outlook seemed bleak, but Kerman University granted him a sabbatical so that he could achieve the best outcome with his research.

Fiera Roma

Dr. Keramat was standing at the gate which would lead him to a bright future: the entrance to a gathering at which he was about to present his findings. The European Society of Human Reproduction and Embryology was hosting about three thousand guests from all over the world. At ten o'clock sharp, the doors to Fiera Roma opened and the guests and visitors where warmly welcomed by the doormen. The entrance corridor was under a roof structure with several peaked slopes. Crowds of people swarmed towards the entrance. Walking for a couple of minutes through the heaving passage, he reached the escalator. At the top was a big sign showing directions to the different sections of the fare. Showing his card to the doorman and inserting it into the machine, Keramat entered the hall. The conference was about to take place in the amphitheater. Among the presenters, Keramat was unusual in feeling no tension at all speaking in the presence of three thousand scientists, all staring at him. He imagined himself on the stage, with his face shining in the spotlight. In the great conference hall were dozens of colorful stands. He studied the displays on which different institutions had posted their findings in embryology and human reproduction.

In an hour he was on the stage, giving his speech to hundreds of top scientists.

> 'During the earliest stages of human development, when the embryo consists of fewer than a dozen cells, the genes inside every cell nucleus have their full potential. These embryonic cells, in the jargon of biologists, are totipotent, for each has the ability to develop into a complete human organ.'

In the evening, among the green hills of Rome's suburbs, a supper party was held. The participants in the fair and the conference speakers were invited to the palace. It was a night filled with Italian music, provided by a small band. Colorful lights reflected on the faces of men who were dressed in tuxedos and ladies in glamorous gowns.

At the dinner table, a woman dressed in green approached Dr. Keramat.

'Great speech, Dr. Keramat!' she said. 'I have been reading your papers on stem cell research and developing human organs. I'm a great fan of your work.'

'That is so kind of you,' said Keramat. 'To whom do I have the pleasure of talking?'

'Media and music people know me as Adelheid,' she said. 'I'm the owner of Sama Records. My company is based in Los Angeles.'

'Nice to meet you, madam. But what you are doing at this conference. Are you looking for a future pop star?'

'Something like that.' She sat down at the table. 'But music is not my only business. My firm has established a research organization.'

'That sounds interesting,' said Keramat.

'It is the best equipped science facility in the field of embryology and cloning in the world,' Adelheid said.

A smartly-dressed man dressed joined them. He held a glass, half—filled with margarita.

'This is Dr. Mao,' said Adelheid. 'My advisor and assistant in the project.'

'Pleasure to meet you, Dr. Mao,' said Keramat. 'What project are we talking about?'

'The project in which we would like your assistance,' said Mao. 'We call it "Project Beethoven".'

'How do you think I can be of help with your project?' Keramat asked.

'Why don't you come to our facility and continue the rest of our discussion there?' suggested Adelheid in her gentle voice. 'I'm quite sure a man of your knowledge would enjoy a visit to our center.'

'That would be a pleasure, but I have to get back to my university. I'm here on their budget.' He needed to think about this.

'Your country will be proud of you when news of the success of Project Beethoven hits the media. You could visit home any time you wish.'

'We will arrange for a jet to take you to our airport,' said Mao.

'Your airport?' This was certainly big stuff.

'You are about to visit the future city. And you will be running one of the most prominent scientific experiments in the history of science there.'

'The future city?' Keramat could hardly take in the idea of such a city. He thought about his lonely days back at home.

'The city has built with the financial support of some the most prominent multinational companies in the world supporting scientific research, but our researches do not seem to have many supporters outside the walls of the future city,' said Mao.

'Because they are dangerous?' asked Keramat.

'That could be one reason,' Adelheid said.

The jet landed on the runway of the future city's airport. Through the window, Keramat could see a BMW waiting to take him to the land of his fantasies. Adelheid and Mao were standing by the car.

Driving through the streets of the city and enjoying the architectural designs from the nations of the world, they arrived at a fenced area that looked like a military compound. The guards led them to an elevator. On the control panel inside the elevator, Adelheid pushed a button with some numbers on its side. Then Mao connected his cell phone to the panel's socket and entered a code.

The elevators door opened on to an area with what looked like huge water containers.

'Welcome to *Der Kristall Hochburg*,' said Adelheid. 'It is to this place that future generations will owe a great deal of their technological and scientific progress. We are three-hundred meters below the earth.' She showed Keramat to the glass room.

'Welcome to Project Beethoven,' said Mao.

'I'm really impressed by this facility,' Keramat said, "and the huge benefit it could give to science and to future generations. But to be honest, I still have no idea what this Project Beethoven is.'

'Dr. Keramat, let me cut the story short,' said Mao. 'We have obtained the complete DNA of the great composer and musician, Ludwig Van Beethoven.'

Keramat could hardly believe his ears. 'Where are you going with this?' he said.

'We would like to clone him,' Adelheid said.

Keramat could hardly speak for shock. He thought, this will be a project far beyond my dreams. My endeavor has taken me to a wild place.

The next morning, he was taken to his new lab.

'This is where Beethoven the Second will be born,' said Adelheid, 'and where you will open new and real gates to the future of what was previously just science fiction.'

On the screen of the LCD hanging on the lab's office wall, a tall woman dressed in a green hospital gown could be seen sitting on the bed. She looked European, slender with her blonde hair tied back.

'Is this her?' asked Keramat.

'Her name is Sheila,' said Adelheid. 'She knows about the entire process but you may want to brief her yourself.'

'I'd rather do so. How old is she?'

'Thirty-one. She's a stewardess with Swissair.'

'Interesting! Does she know the baby is not going to resemble her at all?'

'Not exactly. But she is willing to be the surrogate mother of our Beethoven.

Keramat walked into the room where Sheila was waiting.

'My name is Dr. Karim Keramat,' he introduced himself.

'Sheila,' said the young woman, stretching out her hand. 'Are you the doctor?'

'I am,' said Keramat, seeing the stress in her eyes and anxious breathing. 'How much do you know about the process, Sheila?'

'I know that I'm going to give birth to Beethoven the Second.' She laughed nervously. 'You may not believe it, but a hundred grand is not the only reason I'm doing it.'

'A hundred grand?'

'Yes. That means I won't have to work for the airline any more. But I'm also doing this because it's a chance to do something different.'

'Thank you. We greatly appreciate your offering to help with this project,' Keramat said.

Sheila smiled in acknowledgement. 'I don't know why women refuse to donate eggs for medical use. Why is it wrong if my eggs eventually lead to someone's successful cancer treatment?'

'Some women object to women's bodies being used for research,' Keramat said. 'I guess you have been informed that this process can have its risks and side-effects.'

'I know that,' said Sheila, overcoming her nerves. 'A great lady told me that this project will be using a woman's body for the benefit of both science and nations.'

'Nations?' asked Keramat. He wanted to hear more.

'If using my body to help scientists find a cure for millions of people with terminal disease is wrong, then let them call me a whore.'

'You are truly a great person, Sheila,' said Keramat. 'I'm really impressed.'

Sheila looked down at her lap modestly. 'How should we begin?' she asked.

'I need to run some tests on you. It will take about ten days.'

'I was told there are going to be some injections.'

'Indeed. For the second step we need to stimulate your egg production. You will be given follicle-stimulating hormones to increase the number of mature eggs your body produces.'

'How will this hormone work?'

'FSH injections are similar to the natural hormones your body produces. The FSH is typically injected just under the skin for a period of ten days. Throughout the cycle I will continually monitor you. I will run blood tests and perform ultrasound examinations to determine your reaction to the hormones and the progress of follicle growth.'

'And when will you take my eggs?'

'Once the follicles are mature. Approximately thirty-six hours before retrieval, you will be given one more injection of the hormone HCG to ensure that your eggs are ready to be harvested.'

'Is it a kind of surgery?'

'The egg retrieval is a minimally invasive surgical procedure that requires a light general anesthetic and lasts about twenty to thirty minutes.'

'So it won't be painful?'

'Not at all. I will use a small ultrasound-guided needle inserted through the vagina to aspirate the follicles in both ovaries. Immediately following the surgery, you will rest in the recovery room for an hour or two.'

'Do I have to stay here afterwards?'

'It can take from one day up to a week to fully recover, but generally donors return to normal activities the next day.' Keramat perched himself on a stool. 'In your case you will have to stay in the clinic with us for the next stage of the project.'

'What is that?'

'Once your egg is retrieved, I need to remove its nucleus. Then we will place the cell inside it and fuse it by electric shock. The resulting embryo will grow to about ten cells and it will split three or four times.'

'How about the transplantation?'

'Some of the embryos will be available for transplantation. We will plant them inside your ovary until conception takes place successfully.'

'How long will the pregnancy be?'

'Like a natural one. Nine months. But there is one thing you should know.'

'You are not going to scare me?'

'Absolutely not. Since your egg will be unfertilized, the baby will not resemble you at all.'

'I know. He will look like the twin of his father, Beethoven.'

CHAPTER 27

'I don't suppose I can keep this safe.' Rose removed the CD from her laptop's drive and handed it to Keramat, who put it back in its cover and placed it inside the pocket of the briefcase. Digging inside the briefcase with both hands, he carefully retrieved a small chest. Before opening it, he pulled the curtains to cover the old walnut wooden doors and the whole night view of the garden behind them.

'Are we about to witness another surprise from history?' asked Adam.

'In this vacuum-sealed chest, I have kept what you traveled to San Jose for.' He sat down by Adam. 'It has been buried in this garden for twenty-seven years.'

'I traveled to San Jose to find my true origins,' Adam said.

'You mean the clone's origin,' his grandfather corrected him.

'I don't think I have ever cared for the clone.'

'You have every right to be mad at me,' Keramat said. Opening the chest, he felt carefully among its contents. 'This is where the clone came from.' He took the bone fragment and the lock of hair out of the chest. 'These hair strands in my hand carry the complete DNA of Beethoven.'

'This is what that poor man in San Jose was killed for, isn't it?' Rose asked.

'Unfortunately, yes.' Keramat sighed. 'They kidnapped you to get to this chest.'

'And they are willing to destroy it,' Adam said.

'This is the only existing proof of the death of the clone.' Keramat replaced the bone fragment and the hair in the chest. 'And also a DNA matching test would be proof of Adam's real origin.'

'What should we do now?' Adam asked.

'Once we give the world the truth and this irrefutable evidence, everything will be over.'

'And how will we do that?'

'A contact of mine is arranging a conference at the University of Zurich,' said Keramat. 'There we will put an end to this game.'

'You are going to expose the evidence?'

'Yes, my boy,' said Keramat. 'I should have done it long ago.'

The next morning Keramat, Adam and Rose took a bus to Kerman, a distance of thirty kilometers from the picturesque garden. Kerman was the center of a province which could be traced back to the oldest civilization ever discovered. It produced seventy per cent of the country's annual agricultural exports. In a single day, one could enjoy the four seasons in different parts of the province. The north was desert, with the northwest and west covered by large pistachio farms. These lands were nicknamed the green gold mines. In the southern section was Jiroft, a humid and fertile land covered with acres of citrus and flower orchards.

Fruit and flowers were exported from its airport to Europe. Bam Citadel in the southeast, surrounded by abundant date palms, was two thousand, five hundred years old, and older than this was Meymand, a hobbit-like village in the east, which had its roots in ten thousand years of civilization. Another village nearby was believed to be the residence of dwarf humans in 6000 BC.

'Why do we need to fly to Zurich, Grandpa?' Adam asked. 'To announce that The Silver Orchestra's claim is without foundation?'

'That will be our second mission,' Keramat said.

'Mission?' Rose said angrily. 'What mission?'

'We need to clear Adam's name and detach him from The Silver Orchestra.'

'After I have been with them on a world tour supported by TV Channels?' asked Adam. 'Is that possible?'

'I believe Colonel Ahmad Beig has told you about the evil purpose behind this tour?'

'He said I was being used as a tool to give them a popular face,' Adam said.

'And I am determined to isolate them from you and your art, my boy,' his grandfather said.

'If I stay away from them, my name will be clear. Why should we risk going on this trip?'

'Because one cannot stay away from them for ever. They will hunt you anywhere you hide in the world. We need to destroy them.' Keramat turned his head to the window to look at the desert 'and also . . .'

'Also what?'

'I received a message a couple of days ago.' He reached in his pocket and handed his cell phone to Adam.

Amazing, Adam! How you fooled your grandpa!

'When have I fooled you? Was this supposed to be sent to me?'

'No. the text conveys a message to me.' Keramat turned back to Adam. 'Unfortunately, a terrible one!'

'Encrypted?'

'Capitalized.'

'Let me guess. The capital letters, A, A, H and F.' Adam handed the phone to back Keramat.

'They stand for Agriculture, Animal, Human and Financial.'

'Oh. In what way is that threatening?'

'AAHF is the name of an operation that was planned by The Silver Orchestra many years ago. Now it's activated.'

'What kind of operation?' asked Rose.

'It's a four-pronged attack in Europe,' said Keramat. 'A biological attack on the watersheds used for agriculture and then infecting animals with a biological agent, and then infecting humans.'

'Oh, my god!' Adam said. 'And what is the fourth part?'

'Attacking the financial system.'

There was silence.

'What do you mean by "it's activated"?' asked Adam eventually.

'They are infecting the water used for agriculture with a bio-agent as we speak.'

'Do the European officials know about this?' asked Rose.

'If the colonel knows, most surely they do,' Keramat said, 'but it can happen anywhere in Europe.'

'I have seen the water stores below *Der Kristall Hochburg*,' said Adam. 'Is that the source of the infection?'

'I doubt that,' said Keramat. 'They may start it at one of the dams.'

'Are we capable of stopping them?' It seemed too much to ask, Adam thought.

'No, but WMST can do it. Colonel Beig and his people are working on it.'

CHAPTER 28

Der Kristall Hochburg

The underground recovery room's window opened on to a garden filled with the distorted shapes of trees and plants created by The Silver Orchestra's scientists using genetic engineering. Sheila was lying on the bed, dreaming of the baby she'd had delivered by caesarian section in the No. 2 operating theatre. She forced her eyelids open. Gradually, the blurry images in the room became clearer. A tall figure in green was standing by her bed. She was not quite sure where she was, but from the dark depths of her memory she finally worked it out. She was in the recovery room; the figure must be Doctor Keramat.

Though the blurred images had turned into clear ones, she still couldn't move her head, for the anesthesia drug nauseated her. Hearing the gentle voice of Dr. Keramat, she was sure that she had guessed right.

'You did a great job, Sheila,' said Keramat. 'The baby is fine and, thanks to God, so are you.'

'I already know he's got his father's looks,' Sheila said in a weak voice. She smiled. The only thing she wished to see at that moment was her baby. She wanted to hold the little creature and smell him. And if she did, she would never let him go.

In Operating Theatre No. 2, the physicians had been examining the baby for an hour. He was breathing normally, weighed as much as a normal healthy infant and his skin glowed like the sun.

'Congratulations, Miss Adelheid!' said one of the doctors. 'The baby is in the pink.'

'Are you calling the press in to report this historic moment?' asked Keramat.

'Soon we will,' said Adelheid, shaking Keramat's hands vigorously, 'but not here. We need to let the mother and baby rest and then we will transport them to a hospital.'

'Of course,' said Keramat. 'I totally forgot this place is supposed to be secret.'

'The world will soon be proud of *Der Kristall Hochburg*,' Adelheid said, 'and you will be the scientist who made a long-held dream come true.'

'Indeed, it is a momentous day.' Keramat found it hard to pretend enthusiasm.

'Is something wrong, Doctor? You don't seem well.'

'Actually, I'm glad for the success of project. But I never imagined I would be away from my own family on the day I became a grandfather.'

'What are you talking about?'

'My daughter-in-law delivered her baby yesterday in Rome.' Keramat sat on a stool. 'I couldn't even tell my son why I couldn't be there.'

'Which hospital are they in now?' Adelheid asked.

'It's a children's hospital.' Keramat struggled to remember the Italian name. *'Bambino Gesu.'*

'What a coincidence! That's where we are taking Sheila and her son.'

'You're kidding!'

The trip to Rome was one of the most exiting journeys of Keramat's entire life. Arriving in the city, the first thing he did was to take a cab to *Bambino Gesu*. Standing at the nurses' station to ask which room his daughter-in-law was in, the words would not come out of his mouth properly. He felt as if he had forgotten how to speak and all he wanted was to bypass all this and to hold his grandson.

'Just give me the name of the mother.' The nurse smiled reassuringly.

'Angela! Angela!' He had even forgotten the last name.

'Room Four,' said the nurse, showing him where to go. 'Congratulations!'

In the room, Keramat found Angela lying on the bed with his son sitting beside her holding little Adam in his arms. The family reunion spread a warm feeling in Keramat's heart after such a long time. He felt secure again.

The hospital was filled with journalists from all over the world to report the news of the clone's birth and take his picture. The days passed by with interviews and news conferences.

Keramat's son and daughter-in-law were unaware of his part in Project Beethoven. They figured it out when they saw him on TV. A BBC reporter was introducing him to the viewers.

'This is the man who performed Project Beethoven. A project that has brought the musical genius of the nineteenth century into the present, using the most advanced techniques of biotechnology. Ladies and gentlemen, please welcome Dr. Karim Keramat.'

After the announcement of this remarkable breakthrough, things gradually quietened down. Keramat had to return to *Der Kristall Hochburg* and once again the sorrow of saying goodbye to his family tugged at his heart. But he had no choice, for he believed he no longer belonged to himself. He was dedicated to the future generation and there was still work to be done. Like any other man of his age, he wished for a peaceful retirement spending the days with his children and grandchildren, working in the garden or going on cruises. But Keramat had taken an oath to pursue the long and challenging journey of a scientist who believes in his power to make life better for the people of the world.

Six months later

Keramat tossed on his bed, trying to get some sleep after a hard day in the lab. Whenever a big event was imminent, he could not sleep the night before. He tried to calm himself by listening to the branches moving with the wind. The sounds of nature could help him to sleep and avoid disturbing premonitions for the next day. The curtain danced softly in the breeze blowing in from the secret garden. The window opposite belonged to the replica of *Beethoven Haus*, the building in which the baby was supposed to be raised.

There was a knock at his door, then a frantic hammering.

God help us! Something must be wrong!

He jumped out of bed and rushed towards the door.

'Sheila!' he said. 'What are you doing here?'

'They won't let me see him.' Tears flowed down her face.

'What's happened?'

'It's the baby. Something is wrong with him and the doctors won't let me see him.'

'Where is he now?'

'In the clinic. He has been having these fevers for a week. They said he will be fine. But tonight . . . Tonight they took him.' She wept uncontrollably.

'He is going to be fine, Sheila.' Keramat put his hand on her shoulder. 'Stay here in my room while I go check on him. Ok?'

'Please, just do something!'

Keramat went swiftly towards the clinic. In the passage that led to the clinic's emergency room, he could see most of *Der Kristall Hochburg*'s staff. But for the first time none of them seemed keen to approach him. They all avoided speaking to him and he could see the fear on their faces. At last he got to the room. The first thing he saw was Adelheid's pallor as she stood by the bed. Several physicians stood alongside her. Keramat stepped towards the bed. The baby was lying, his eyes closed and his skin ashen. Seeing Keramat, the physicians moved away, just like those in the passage. The only one who dared to look him in the eye was Adelheid.

'I'm so sorry!' she said, her voice trembling.

Keramat could not believe what she was about to say and looked at one of the physicians.

'He is gone,' said the doctor, shaking his head.

Keramat stood still by the bed and looked at the baby. He did not say a word. Then he sat down on the ground and held his head in his hands.

'Why?'

'The cause of death is still unclear,' said the doctor. 'The baby went into a coma as a result of high fever and died.'

'You couldn't stop the fever?'

'We couldn't stop the cause of the infection. Whatever it was.'

The days passed by for Keramat in grief and sorrow because of the poor creature who had died for no clear reason.

If he was a real human he would be alive now, Keramat thought. How could he have done this to him? How could he have done this to his mother?

He thought of the choices the baby could have had for leading his life. Just like Keramat's own son had when he chose to move to Italy or when he announced his engagement to Angela. Keramat remembered the day he had handed in his resignation, left the university and gone to the park to work as a volunteer gardener. It had not been an easy decision to make. But he had made it.

All that has occurred in my life, he thought, has been the result of either my or God's intentions. Or both. But how about this baby? What choice did he have in being born with an unknown disease? I brought him into this world. I was so selfish that I did not consider the risks of the project. His blood is on my hands.

But how could the poor baby have decided what he wanted for his life? What had happened was the consequence of man's selfishness; a terrible knowledge that Keramat and Sheila would have to live with for the rest of their lives.

CHAPTER 29

The Silver Orchestra had provided Sheila with a modern residence with a huge garden in front. Waking up in the morning, she could order her breakfast through the virtual maid, who was present twenty-four hours a day on every transparent wall of the house. Then she could get into the glass elevator which would take her to the roof, where the swimming pool was located. After a while she realized that her only roommate was the virtual maid with her kind face and gentle voice. She would adjust the room temperature for Sheila, play her favorite rock music while she exercised, classical at lunch time, and even read her stories at night. In that house, she needn't turn the TV on or off or even sit in a certain spot to watch it. Anywhere she wished, she could get her favorite program on the wall, just by giving a voice order to the maid. She had a few visitors as well, the kindest of them being Dr. Keramat.

Throughout his conversations with Adelheid, Keramat had insisted that Sheila needed to spend time grieving for her lost child somewhere far away from The Silver Orchestra. Maybe spending some time with her own family would help her manage her feelings better. Adelheid would agree with him initially, but she did nothing about it. Keramat started to speculate that The Silver Orchestra did not want Sheila to leave her secret underground dwelling. If she left for the outside world, the press would get to her. And that would be a threat to Adelheid's company. An announcement of the clone's death would be a disaster for the organization. In less than a month, Sheila started to complain about her lonely life in the city. And one night, when the maid told her that the entrance gates to the building were locked by order of Adelheid, she realized that the wonderful house with its fantastic features was indeed her prison. She could not use the phone to contact anyone outside *Der Kristall Hochburg*. Her internet access was blocked for sending information; she could only read and download. And even Keramat was not authorized to enter the house any more.

Keramat was living in the same type of house, but he had virtual access to all the prominent libraries and research centers in the world. He spent his days in video conferencing with genetic engineering researchers all over the world, watching his grandson's daily growth on the walls of his bedroom and also worrying about Sheila. One thought never left him alone and that was the crime they had all committed against that little creature who had died at the age of six months.

Receiving an invitation from home one day gave Keramat new hope. Kerman University had arranged a ceremony to honor him. He could not wait to be there again. But what he heard from Adelheid gave him a feeling he had never had before in his life.

'I'm afraid that our airport has had to be closed for a couple of months,' she said.

This meant that he was imprisoned in *Der Kristall Hochburg*, too. Just like Sheila was. The Silver Orchestra did not want him to leave the city and reveal to the world what he had seen and done inside. Captivity was another price to pay for what he had perpetrated.

At the dawn of one of the rare sunny days in *Der Kristall Hochburg*, after saying his morning prayers, Keramat went from his house to the lab building. He met only a handful of the nightshift guards on the way. The fresh air of the morning made him think of starting a new project, something that could compensate for his last failure and clear his conscience. But the events of the day told him that he still had unfinished business.

Walking through the passage, he heard distressing moans from one of the rooms. It sounded like a man in a lot of pain. Keramat tried the door. It was open. Entering, he saw a man lying on a bed, begging for help and tossing as if in unbearable pain. Before he could ask the patient any questions, a guard entered in the room and closed the door behind him. Keramat waited to hear an alarm. But the guard locked the door and approached him.

'We need to talk, Doctor,' said the guard.

'I was just going to my lab,' said Keramat, trying to justify his presence in a room which he was not supposed to be in. 'I heard this man moaning and crying.'

'Dr. Keramat, you don't need to be scared. I'm not going to report this.'

'Then what were you going to talk to me about?'

'About this man. What do you think has happened to him?'

A note-pad was hanging on the wall beside the bed. At the top was written:

Subject No.11
Clinical reports
Day 2
Attending Doctor: Dr. Mao

Subject's complaints:
1. **Double vision**
2. **Muscle weakness**
3. **Drooping eyelids**
4. **Difficulty speaking**

Observations:
Minor Dyspnea

'What does Dyspnea mean, Doctor?' asked the guard.

'It means the movement of the muscles of the respiratory system has been reduced. He cannot breathe normally.'

'Is it dangerous?'

'It is. In severe cases it can lead to respiratory failure, due to the build-up of unexhaled carbon dioxide and its resulting depressant effect on the brain. This may lead to coma and eventually death if untreated.'

'Poor guy!'

'Do you know him?'

'He arrived three days ago. And since yesterday he has been on this bed,' said the guard. 'What do you think has caused his condition?'

'According to the symptoms on this chart, he could be affected by something really strong.'

'Like what?'

'I guess it's botulism. A milligram of it can kill a human being. He is lucky to be alive after two days,' Keramat said, 'but how do you think he has taken it here?'

'I need to tell you something,' the guard whispered, stepping closer to Keramat. 'The day he arrived they injected him with something and since then he has been like this.'

'Who ordered the injection?'

'Dr. Mao. He looks creepy. The guy really freaks me out.'

'What do you know about this man?' The man on the bed moaned even more loudly.

'I checked his records. He is a POW.'

'A prisoner of war?'

'Yes, sir. And I believe, based on your diagnosis, that he has been brought here as the subject of a medical experiment.'

'Oh, my god!' Keramat exclaimed.

'I'm sorry to tell you this. But as you probably realized, they are testing a dangerous bio-agent on him.'

'If they don't inject him with the anti-toxin, he will die. Even now it's too late.'

'The worst thing is, he is not the first and he will not be the last.'

'What am I hearing?' Keramat said. 'Tell me this is all a dream.'

'Unfortunately, it's not. Dr. Keramat, I have always known that you are different from these people. I need you to trust me now.'

'What are going to do?'

'I have already contacted WMST. And this morning I was called by one of their commanders. Colonel Beig.'

'What did he say?'

'He asked me to stay here and learn more about the sinister stuff The Silver Orchestra is doing in secret.'

'And you want me to the same thing?'

'No. I will help you leave *Der Kristall Hochburg*. They don't trust you any more and they are done with you. If you stay, you know the rest.'

'I will be expendable. Right?'

'I'm afraid so.'

'When are we leaving?'

'Very soon. I will contact the colonel and when the arrangements are made outside, take you to a safe location. I'll let you know the plan. Meanwhile, you need to be extra careful. Don't trust anyone except me. They are watching you closely.'

A week later, Keramat was transported out of the city, hiding in one of the trash cars. The driver pulled over on the road passing through the woods. Keramat stood alone at the spot where he was supposed to be picked up by a WMST agent. He stayed in the woods the whole night, but the agent did not show up. Something must be wrong. The next morning he walked along the road. It did not take long before he found an Audi beside the narrow road's shoulder. The driver's door was wide open and the front lights were still on. He checked the surroundings. Fear ran over his body when he found a man lying in a pool of blood behind the bushes. He took the photo of the agent he was supposed to meet from his pocket. It was him. They had got to his savior before he did.

He ran into the woods, staying away from the road. The Silver Orchestra was not a firm to make life sweet for future generations. They were murderers. They killed people for their own gain. But something was still missing. How could have they have found the agent and killed him in cold blood before finding Keramat? Was it his fate to walk helplessly in the woods and not be found by these savages?

Along the road Keramat found a small shop where he bought food and water. He had a long way to walk in the woods. A quick visit to the store to get the supplies he needed for the journey involved less risk than travelling on a public vehicle. He remembered the guard's words: they are watching you closely. Do not trust anyone.

A terrible new thought crossed his mind. They must have got to the poor guard. He could have been murdered by now.

Walking in the woods, to get as far as he could from *Der Kristall Hochburg*, Keramat was brought to a halt by the unlikely sound of a nightingale. The sound wasn't coming from the branches above his head. Its source was somewhere behind a wild raspberry bush. He looked around the area and finally found the bird. Its wing was damaged and it couldn't fly. Keramat somehow felt the communications of the little nightingale through its miserable song. The bird wanted help. How could he let this pretty creature die here alone or be hunted? He vowed henceforth to protect vulnerable creatures from the monsters who would do them harm.

Walking by day and sleeping under the trees at night, Keramat found himself on the slopes of a magnificent hill. He could see a river that was protected by tall trees. The purple, blue and green leaves of the trees in millions of different shades on the river banks looked like an extended colorful road to a larger source of natural beauty. He walked by that extraordinary wall of splendor and reached its source, a village. A pick-up, filled in the back with orange boxes, was leaving the village. The driver stopped his car when he reached Keramat.

'*Bonjiorno, signor!*' The driver removed his cowboy hat.

'*Bonjiorno*,' said Keramat. 'What is this place called?'

'Welcome to Oria,' said the man.

Keramat went to a small inn by the river. Days passed and he realized that he was getting low on his savings. He did not dare to withdraw money from his bank account because there was a strong chance that The Silver Orchestra could trace him, using the influence they had in government. If he wanted to stay in the village, he had to make money and for that he had to get a job. Observing the hard-working villagers spending days in the farms and orchards, he decided to return to his idyllic previous job, gardening. Keramat started to work in a citrus orchard. The owner was quickly charmed by his knowledge of farming alongside his imaginative ideas for running the marketing side of the business. In under six months the village council invited him to join them. And a year later, Keramat became the Mayor of Oria.

CHAPTER 30

The pilot on the Swiss Air flight, announced that they had three hours left before landing at Zurich Airport. Adam was watching the news on the screen before him. It was showing clips of a hospital, filled with infected people. The botulism agent had killed over six hundred; it was just the beginning of the tragedy as mentioned by Dr. Keramat, the second phase of the attacks. Thousands of farm and domestic animals had been killed, affected by the toxin. If the terror wasn't stopped, millions of innocent people would die.

'Why don't they besiege *Der Kristall Hochburg* to stop this madness?' asked Rose.

'Because they will find no proof linking The Silver Orchestra to these attacks,' said Keramat. 'The toxin was produced in their labs, but, according to Colonel Beig, they have transported it to unknown locations all over the Western Europe. Nobody knows how and where they are spreading the toxin.'

'Did they ever ask you to join them in this operation?' asked Adam.

'Long ago; but I ran away before they could make me,' Keramat said. 'The sad part is, it is almost impossible for governments to find a link between The Silver Orchestra and the present terrorist activities.'

'They are still presenting themselves as the saviors of future generations, guardians of science or the heroes of tomorrow's world,' said Rose.

'Grandpa, it's strange that you have been living quite near them for all these years and they couldn't reach you earlier,' Adam said.

'Judging by recent events and their activities within the last year, I guess they have always known where I was living. Maybe from the first day I moved into Oria.'

'So why didn't they harm you?'

'Because they realized I was no threat to them. They had even been watching you the whole time. That's how they learned you resembled the young Beethoven when you were fifteen.'

'And when it came to the right time, they abducted you and absorbed me.' Rose shifted in her seat.

'Exactly.'

'But now, you are both threats to them,' Rose said, frowning.

'That's why we should be extra careful in Zurich,' said Keramat. 'If they find us, God knows what will happen.'

WMST Headquarters

Colonel Ahmad Beig was sitting in his operations room, surrounded by monitors, computers and his technical unit staff. They had kept Adelheid's and Dr. Mao's activities under surveillance since they had been released from the custody of German Intelligence. Their phone calls were traced and recorded, their emails were read and even their moves on the ground were watched through military satellite feeds. But since the start of the release of the bio-agent in the water sources, none of the The Silver Orchestra's actions could be reliably connected to the unfolding tragedy. The colonel knew that Adelheid was still hoping to announce her firm's success in producing the clone of Ludwig Van Beethoven and developing it into a globally recognized musical genius.

'Dr. Keramat and his grandson are currently on a flight to Zurich,' said the colonel on the phone to his agent who was standing by at Zurich Airport. 'The Swiss police have declared full co-operation with us to protect them.'

'Yes, sir,' said the agent. 'We will escort Dr. Keramat and his companions to the university.'

'Report any suspicious activity to me,' the colonel ordered. To his team in the operations room he said, 'Look for anything unusual in the last six hours reported by airport securities in the Middle East and Europe.'

'Colonel,' said one of his staff, 'there is something you should see.'

'What is it?'

'2235. Isn't that the flight number of the plane in which Dr. Keramat is right now?'

'It is. What did you find sergeant?'

'I was checking the passenger manifest of the flight. There is something wrong about this airline security officer.'

'Tell me, for God's sake,'

'His name is Ali Samedani. According to the Iranian health organization database, he is in hospital in Tehran because of severe poisoning. And according to the flight manifest, he is on board.'

'It may be another person with the same name.'

'No, sir, I checked the social number for both of them. It is the same person. And also he has not been reported absent from work in the last ten days.'

'The airline doesn't know he is in hospital and someone, most probably disguised themselves to look like him, using his identity, is right now on the flight. So what do we extract from these two facts?'

'A terrorist attack, or perhaps a plot to capture Dr. Keramat, but the point is . . .'

'They are doing it midflight,' the colonel interrupted. 'Get the pilot on the line. We need to warn him.'

'Sir,' said another officer, 'European air traffic control just announced that they have lost contact with Flight 2235.'

'Is the plane on the radar?'

'Yes, sir, but the pilot is not responding. And they have changed the air corridor of the flight.'

'We have a hi-jacked plane.' Colonel Beig studied the satellite radar monitor closely.

The operations room did not rest for three hours, searching to track the plane above the green continent. The hijackers made no contact. Flight 2235 finally landed at Barcelona Airport. WMST forces and the Spanish police surrounded the plane, waiting for the passengers to leave the aircraft. As they appeared one after another on the steps, they were taken to a private lounge to be questioned. Snipers and officers waited for sight of the hijackers coming out of the plane. But nobody showed up, except the passengers and the crew. Special WMST agent Victor Ventura tried to spot Dr. Keramat and his companions among the terrified passengers, without success.

'Victor,' said the colonel on the intercom, 'do you have a visual on our friends?'

'No, sir,' said Victor. 'The plane is entirely evacuated. They were not among the passengers.'

'They were on that plane, Victor,' said the colonel. 'How can you possibly have missed them?'

'Sir, how many people are on the flight manifest?'

'Three hundred ten, including the crew and pilot.'

'We have three hundred five in the lounge, sir.'

Later, the Spanish counter-terrorist unit interviewed the passengers and figured out that Dr. Keramat, Adam, Rose, Ali Samedani and another airline security person were missing. Witnesses said that the two hijackers and their hostages walked to the back cabin and nobody saw them again. They said the attackers began the hijack by taking Keramat hostage and told all the security personnel to hand over their weapons and lie down on the floor. A thorough search of the plane led the police to a single explanation: they had jumped off the plane, midflight.

Keramat, Adam and Rose heard the locks on the harnesses outside the lavatory cabin being picked. Coming out of the cabin, they found a parachute linked to the cabin. Adam remembered watching the bungee jumpers flying down the deep hole in Spring Valley. He had never imagined that one day he would be thrown off a plane in a lavatory with his grandfather and his best friend. They had landed by a mountain, parachuting down thirty-thousand feet in the cabin.

Adam saw the hijacker taking a mask of Samedani off his face. The other one was examining Keramat's body to see if he had been injured during the rough landing.

They were on the green slopes of a mountainside. Disorientated by the events of the past hour, Adam spotted in the distance men on horses riding towards them. The closer the riders came, the more panic spread over Adam. He remembered Frodo Baggins being chased and stabbed by the black riders. The echo of the horses' hooves grew louder, until he found himself surrounded by the animals. The masked riders dismounted. The horses looked tired and thirsty. Meanwhile, the riders laughed, showing their satisfaction at having accomplished the operation to capture Adam Keramat.

'Who are you people?' asked Dr. Keramat.

'We are here to take you home, Doc,' said one of the riders, uncovering his face. He stroked his mare's muzzle to quieten her.

'Home?' said Adam. 'You could have killed us. You threw us off the plane!'

'The Silver Orchestra wants its old allies back in one piece, young man.'

'Allies?' said Keramat. 'I thought we were the betrayers.'

'Lady Adelheid always says that our objectives are so huge that we cannot afford to turn on each other.'

'So you know her well,' Adam said.

'Yes, and she has important business to finish with you, Mr. Adam Keramat.'

'She is gonna kill me? Is that what you mean by "important business"?'

'If she wanted you dead, you wouldn't be standing here right now after falling thirty-thousand feet.'

'What happened to the plane?' asked Rose. 'What about the other passengers?'

'They all landed safely in Barcelona,' said the rider. 'You see? It just cost Swiss Air an extra flight from Barcelona to Zurich. No life was endangered.'

Three of the riders made room for their horrified captives on their saddles, while the other three escorted them down the green mountainside and then through the forests. Adam knew where he was being taken. He had been there before. Once following a river on foot, and the other times by plane. There was no road ending at *Der Kristall Hochburg*. It was all surrounded by woods.

The ride below the branches of the trees and through the pastures took them four hours. They did not stop at all. Eventually, they came to the gate of the glass city and passed between the two seven meter female statues. The figures reminded Adam of the sense of community underneath the innovative glass skin. The riders saluted the city guards and handed over their three precious deliveries. The guards immediately drove the captives to the mansion, where Adelheid was waiting to meet them. Adam was led to a BMW, but his grandfather and Rose were manhandled into a SUV. He was not surprised when the two cars drove off in different directions.

Soon after arrival, Adam found himself at the dining-table with Adelheid. She looked calm and patient, as she had always looked.

'How was your flight, honey?' she asked, smiling.

Adam struggled to hide his fears, but he could not prevent his voice from trembling. 'Don't call me that!' he said.

'It's such a delight to sit here with you again,' Adelheid said, unmoved.

'Please don't do this,' said Adam, this time more loudly. 'Where did you take them?'

'They are safe and being treated as my very special guests. But it is up to you to determine what happens to them.'

'When you first asked me to work with you, there was no way I could have known about this grand deception.' Adam knew he was in trouble.

'I'm not deceitful.' Adelheid's patience and gentle voice were driving Adam crazy. 'I just couldn't reveal my plans at the beginning. I have to give people some time to understand them by themselves.'

'For god's sake!' said Adam, almost shouting. 'What do you want from me?'

'A concert.' She laid her hand on his. 'And then you will be free to go anywhere you wish. With your grandfather and the lovely Rose.'

'Is that all you want me to do?'

'Almost.'

'I can't believe you started those attacks.'

'Not yet, Adam. Not yet.' She spoke as if she was talking to herself rather than Adam. 'Indeed, I never meant to start any attack.'

'Hundreds of people have been killed.'

'It was just a preliminary. The problem is, things just got a little out of control.'

'A little? You know what this is called? 'Adam removed his hand from her clasp. 'Bio-terrorism.'

'Why do you believe that old man's nonsense?'

'Then you tell me, please. A biological attack on innocent civilians. A preliminary to what?'

'To show the world that we can do it anytime we wish.' Adelheid stood up.

'You can do what? Murder?'

'We have the power to create and we have the power to put an end to life.' Her voice had hardened.

'And being praised like God. Is that what you want?' Adam asked.

'The world doesn't need a god. She needs a wise leader.'

'An emperor?'

'We will have the time to discuss that later. Now I need you to come with me. We are going to see an amazing project together.'

In the car, Adelheid showed Adam a photograph. The discolored image had a corner missing and was scored by lines from having been folded. A man was standing in front of a massive old building with a gigantic dome.

'That is my grandfather,' said Adelheid. 'Franz Fester.'

'I know the place,' said Adam. 'That is the Pantheon in Rome.'

'He really liked this place,' she said, reminiscing. 'So did the Fuhrer.'

'What?'

'My grandfather was a Nazi officer. A commander close to Albert Speer, the Fuhrer's special architect.'

'He died in the war?'

'When Berlin was secured by the Russian Red Army and the Third Reich collapsed,' she said, talking again directly to Adam, 'the night that the Fuhrer and his wife, Eva, put bullets in their heads in the bunker below the Third Reich building, my grandfather took his wife and son out of the city.'

'Your father was in Berlin that night?'

'He was just a child. My grandfather was killed by the Russians on their way out of Germany but they let my father and grandmother go.'

'Where did they go?'

'Wien. My father grew up there and married my mother.'

'I don't understand. You own Sama record in the US, but you were raised in Vienna?'

'My father got really sick when I was seven. Mom took us to California. She believed I could have a future there.'

'What kind of sick?'

'He became schizophrenic. He dressed like Nazis, talked like them, draped SS flags all over the house. Above our porch he put a sign :*Ein* Volk, *ein Reich, ein Führer*

'One People, One Nation, One Leader,' Adam translated. 'That was Hitler's motto.'

'And years later, my father's,' said Adelheid. 'We took him to a mental hospital in LA. He stayed there for two years.'

'He was cured?'

'Committed suicide,' Adelheid said. 'He lived his life in a dream.'

'And you decided to make the dream come true.'

'In fact, I managed to do it.'

'When did the record company start, then?'

'Painting was my passion and later I switched to architecture. But I did not pursue either as a field of study.'

'What did you study?'

'UCLA admitted me for an MBA. And after graduation I started a small record company in LA. It did not take long before Sama Records swallowed the market.'

The car arrived at a hilly area covered by grass and surrounded by a high fence. Adelheid and Adam got out of the car. They were standing about ten meters away from the fence. Adelheid reached into her pocket and took out a remote control device.

'You are not gonna blow the place up, are you?' Adam said.

'You name it, dear Adam. You are about to witness a historical dream coming true.' And she pressed the button on the remote.

Adam could in no way anticipate what he was about to see. He heard heavy engines running below the ground. The pasture started to roll away at four sides of the hill. In a few moments there was no hill at all inside the fences. From below the artificial grass surface emerged a gigantic pantheon-shaped building, seemingly made of glass and aluminum. Each side of the construction's length was about half a kilometer. Above the entrance to the building was written: ONE LEADER, ONE WORLD.

'Welcome to Crystal Forum,' said Adelheid.

'Is this where I'm going to give this concert?' asked Adam once he had recovered from the shock.

'Before an audience of thirty thousand from all over the world,' Adelaide confirmed.

Above the dome of the forum, the crystal figure of an eagle holding the earth in its claws shone brilliantly in the sun.

WMST HEADQUARTERS

Colonel Beig was briefing the field agents and commandos of WMST on the raid operation. A huge screen showed a live satellite feed of *Der Kristall Hochburg*. The finest of WMST would be taking part in an operation to infiltrate the city and find proof of terrorist activities, at the same time rescuing Adam Keramat and his grandfather.

'Today, for the first time in thirty years,' said the colonel, 'we have succeeded in getting satellite images as a proof of the real nature of The Silver Orchestra's activities in *Der Kristall Hochburg.*'

'What we see in the field,' said an analyst standing by the screen, 'is a huge building they have been constructing inside an underground compound. We are not aware of its interior features. But we do know what it represents.'

'This is the beginning of Project Germania,' said the colonel. 'This forum was originally designed by Hitler himself. He wanted it to be an auditorium for his speeches as the earth's emperor, to address the world.'

The screen showed the small city of Germania.

'Germania, from The German Federal Archives
(Bundesarchiv)'

'Hitler and his special architect, Albert Speer, designed
Germania,' said the analyst, 'a city that would be built on the
ruins of Berlin. 'Germania was not a novel city in design.
It consisted of huge buildings, mostly inspired by those in
other nations, like The Pantheon in Rome or the *Arc de
Triomphe* in Paris.

'Hitler intended to bring them all into the reshaped
Berlin,' said the analyst, 'building a city made of stone, using
no modern construction material.'

'This was based on his Theory of Ruin Value,' said the colonel. 'He believed that when people are silent, the stones speak. That means when after thousands of years the city is destroyed, the remains of the great stone constructions will show the power which has once existed in the empire. Like those that remnants of the Roman Empire.

'What brings us here today is the threat that if we don't stop this project, it will start a round of terror, maybe much more horrifying than World War II.

'We believe that The Silver Orchestra is holding Adam Keramat and his grandfather,' said the colonel. 'They are planning to give a concert in the forum and introduce a new empire of Nazis to the world.'

'The new intel shows us that The Silver Orchestra is not a neo—Nazi group,' said the analyst. 'They *are* Nazis, revitalized and with greater power and knowledge.'

The screen showed an image of Adelheid. She was being followed by most of the intelligence agencies around the world. None had succeeded in finding proof of the allegations against her until the moment when she would reveal the Crystal Forum to all the military satellites. The moment that was intended to be the announcement of a mighty war.

'Her full name is Adelheid Fester,' said the colonel. 'She is the granddaughter of Franz Fester, one of the Nazi officers close to Hitler.'

'Fifty-seven years old,' said the analyst, 'she was born in Austria and moved to the USA as a child.'

'She has been leading The Silver Orchestra for thirty years,' the colonel said. 'She is highly intelligent and deceitful. She has a narcissistic personality and that is why she is unable to love.'

'A sociopath capable of ordering the killing of thousands of people, using biological warfare,' said the analyst, 'just to accomplish what once her grandfather couldn't.'

'Gentlemen,' said the colonel, 'we need to stop her before she starts the holocaust. Agent Ventura will give you the details of the raid operation.'

Der Kristall Hochburg

Adelheid and Adam walked towards the Crystal Forum. Throughout the long walk around the circular masterpiece, Adam noticed various types of glass work, both on the surface and within the structure. The huge dome was in some places covered by aluminum. Enjoying the magnificent exterior view of the forum, they reached the entrance porch of the building. At a considerable height above their heads was a gigantic crystal roof room, supported by fifteen transparent pillars and shining in the sun.

'Unlike the Fuhrer, I don't believe in stones,' Adelheid stated as they stood before the entrance to the greatest work of art Adam had ever seen.

They walked past the illuminated pillars and went through the enormous gate. The huge dome above them, with a diagonal of about four hundred meters, was decorated by mirrors. Glass statues stood all over the place, gazing mockingly at the astonished visitors. Adam looked beneath his feet; it felt as if he was walking on light. The floor was covered by a type of ceramic indistinguishable from glass.

Adelheid banged her heels on the floor.

'As reflective as mirror, as hard as steel,' she said. 'Even a nuclear bomb would not easily destroy this place.'

At the far end of the hall, technical staff where setting up the sound equipment and a couple of huge 3D screens. Workers were carrying chairs through another door that opened to a tunnel. Others were joining the huge sections of platform to form the stage.

'Soon your history-making concert in this place will be broadcast to the world.'

Adam could not help being impressed. But he said, 'Will you hurt my grandfather and Rose if I don't agree to the concert?'

'Let's not think about it like that,' said Adelheid. 'Look on the bright side, Adam. Don't you realize where your concert will be held?'

That night, Adam pictured every step of his strange journey from the village to the Crystal Forum. He had started the trip thinking only of saving the villagers from a year of famine. But now he was trapped in the middle of an enormous global conspiracy. He had never envisaged himself and his grandfather in positions such as they had been during these past months.

He hadn't found a chance to play his instrument for a long time. Taking the silver violin, he went to the balcony of his flat where it looked out over the picturesque gardens of *Der Kristall Hochburg*. He rested his chin on the instrument and started to move the bow on the strings. Having no particular note in mind, he began composing a new piece. He named it 'The Man on The Boat'. He imagined a young man sailing on a boat, alone in the middle of a lake. One side of the lake was surrounded by hills with a country road; on the other side the lights of an exotic city could be seen. The boat was circling around by itself, drifting on the lake without direction. The music evoked the ups and downs of the boy's journey from behind the hills to the middle of the lake at midnight. The same motif was repeated and repeated as he tried to choose which side of the lake to go to. The reflection of the city lights shimmered on the water and the Crystal Forum shone like a vast diamond in the middle of the city. Adam had a single thought in mind: playing on the stage of the Forum, the world admiring him. Finally, he set his feet in the direction of the city.

There were three days left to the grand concert. Guests were flying in from all over the world to be present at the event. Special arrangements had been laid on to transfer visitors from European airports to *Der Kristall Hochburg* by helicopters. Five thousand were already in the city, with fifteen thousand about to arrive. Each visitor would get to visit the modern houses, gardens and the controversial science labs. The replica of *Beethoven Haus* seemed to amaze everybody. They could stand in the place which had grown the second successful human clone into a great musician, just like his cell donor. They were also taken to the underground operating theatre in which Sheila had given birth to her baby. *Der Kristall Hochburg* was about to be revealed to the world as a city of advanced science; a city whose citizens were scientists and investors intent upon improving life for future generations.

Adam's car passed through the main gate of Adelheid's mansion *en route* for the Crystal Forum, where the final rehearsal for the concert was to take place. He could see people all over the streets, walking and enjoying the sights of the city. In three days, he thought, he would get his grandfather and Rose out of captivity.

On the way to the Forum, the driver reached into his pocket and took out a small envelope.

'This is for you, Mr. Keramat,' he said.

Opening the envelope, Adam unfolded the small piece of paper inside and read the message:

Tonight at 11. The chopper will extract you at Victory Arch.
Ahmad Beig

Adam had expected something like this.

'How about my grandfather and Rose?' he asked the driver.

'They will be free by then. You will meet them in the chopper.'

On stage, holding his violin, he could see the only audience present in the Forum: the glass statues, all together watching the artists. He played the pieces with the band for the last time before the concert. At the solo part, Adam played his new piece, 'Man in The Boat'. He played it over and over, each time making the band put more emotion into it.

'Mr. Keramat,' said the pianist, 'I think you are all set on 'Man in The Boat'. Can I ask you something?'

'Sure,' said Adam, already sensing the question.

'What makes you so nervous about this piece?'

'Sometimes the whole of life depends on one moment. The moment in which we choose where to direct the boat on the lake.'

That was the end of the questions, although nobody understood what he meant. None of the band's members knew about the real nature of The Silver Orchestra. As before, they had been invited from different countries to play with Adam. He was sure that even if they knew everything, they would not know whether to leave or stay.

It was almost eight in the evening when Adam was driven back to the mansion.

'We all set for tonight?' asked the driver.

'Just be sure that my grandfather and Dr. Illiano leave the city safely.'

'All arrangements are made, Mr. Keramat.'

'And give my regards to the colonel.'

'What do you mean, sir? You are not coming with us?"

'No,' said Adam. 'The journey I started is not over yet.'

'Sir, I think I need to contact Colonel Beig immediately.' The driver looked anxious.

'No, don't. Just leave without me,' Adam said.

'Sir, you will be in absolute danger here. Aren't you aware of that?'

'I am, but I think I'm the one to decide whether to stay or leave.'

Four hours later Adam was woken by Adelheid who came to his door. Adam had decided to drug himself to sleep while his grandfather and Rose were being rescued. He thought it would be easier if they did not say goodbye or have second thoughts. Opening the door, he faced Adelheid and a couple of guards.

'I made my choice,' he said. 'The concert will go well. I promise.'

Lyon, France—the G8 Summit

All routine flights to Saint-Exupery International Airport were canceled. The security level in and around the airport and all over the town was high. Every street was guarded by French police cars and a large number of the intelligence forces of all eight countries. Diplomatic planes landed one after another at the airport. People were gathered on the sidewalks, holding banners above their heads. The most conspicuous of them read: **NO MORE WAR, NO MORE FUHRER.**

The president of France was at the airport to greet his guests before the leaders of the eight countries were transported to the banks of the Saone River, where the first meeting of the G8 summit was about to be held.

The leaders were there to discuss the latest advances of the bio—terrorists which had cost the lives of hundreds of innocent civilians. Colonel Beig was reporting on the latest intelligence to the members of the most powerful countries in the world.

'We have long witnessed the activities of this mysterious but well—known company,' said the colonel, 'which we all know as The Silver Orchestra.'

'We know that they are giving a big concert in the city tomorrow,' said the French president.

'Yes, sir,' said the colonel. 'We managed to free two of their hostages, Dr. Keramat and Dr. Illiano. But unfortunately Adam Keramat had been compromised.'

'So a raid on *Der Kristall Hochburg* would risk his life,' said the American president.

'Also the lives of twenty thousand civilians who are currently there for the concert,' said the German chancellor.

'Adelheid Fester,' said the Russian president. 'With all due respect, she was brought to this dangerous point by the support of multinationals inside your countries. She should have been stopped long ago.'

'What proof do we have of her connection to the attacks?' asked the American president.

'The attack plot was hatched by her years ago,' said the colonel, 'but we could find no proof of her or any of her people operating it.'

The meeting went on for four hours and the final resolution to the crisis wrenched at the colonel's heart.

Poor Adam, he thought, why had this happened to a caring person like him?

They had decided to wait until the visitors left the city. And then the WMST military aircrafts would bombard the Crystal Forum and the Glass Victory Arch. Colonel Beig was appointed to command the covert raid that would put the life of every resident of *Der Kristall Hochburg* on the line.

CHAPTER 31

It was six in the evening of the momentous Thursday. There were just two hours left before the concert. Crowds of excited people were passing through the high, glass pillars to the gigantic entrance gate of the Crystal Forum. Everyone held a program with a list of the pieces. On its cover was depicted the Forum's shiny dome, held in the claws of an eagle, his extended wings spread wide. News reporters from many international channels were filming and interviewing the people queuing outside the building. Inside, it felt like being at the heart of a sparkling diamond. Everywhere glowed with the reflection of the lights. The light shone through the whole place even before the concert had started.

At last everyone was seated. Backstage, Adam heard his name being called by the presenter. He walked up the stairs and stood behind the transparent wall which made any object behind it appear on the other side in 3D. The audience started to applaud when they saw the huge three-dimensional figure of Adam on the magical screen. Adam waved at the crowd and the applause intensified. The magical glass screen started to move upward and Adam appeared on the stage holding his violin.

The interior lights of the Forum dimmed. Adam stood on a diamond-shaped spotlight, created by several light sources. Everyone was silent. He put the violin under his chin and started to move the bow slowly on the strings to play the first piece. It was called 'Spring Valley'. The melody evoked the feeling of sitting on the grassy slopes of a hill, with trees and grass and colorful flowers in the foreground. The melody was reminiscent of streams flowing down the hillside. When it was finished, everybody in the hall stood and applauded.

The second piece was called 'The Birds Are Coming'. All the violinists in the orchestra started with strikes of the bow on the strings. Like Vivaldi's 'Winter', the rhythm created images of snowflakes and drizzle in the mind at the beginning. Adam envisaged the flock of dark-feathered crows in the sky above the village, fleeing from the helicopter blades. Adam remembered how the dark, bird-filled sky had turned day into night.

The audience's warm applause made Adam play 'Fly To The Moon'. The piece started with a festive melody, bringing to mind birthday parties, engagement dances or the spirit of New Year. In the happiest part of the piece, Adam started to do a little dance on the stage as he held his violin, playing hard. It was then that he could see the smiles of happiness on every single person's face. He could feel the joy in their hearts; the joy that he had created.

The fourth piece was 'The Man in The Boat'. The music started with the recorded sound of ocean waves hitting rocks on the shore. The sound echoed all over the Forum, taking the listeners to seashore memories. This music was followed by a rhythm evoking the sensations of the man who was going to sea for the first time. Throughout the piece, the audience could hear waves hitting the boat and the calls of seabirds.

Adam sent everyone a poll question via Bluetooth. The audience could choose one famous piece among ten, and the one with the highest number of votes would be played. The winner was the magnificent music from the movie, *Schindler's List*. The piece reminded Adam how Schindler had dedicated his life to saving the lives of innocent Jews. He remembered the motto expressed in the movie: If you save one human, you have saved the world.' Adam could feel again his extraordinary emotions as he was leaving Oria in search of his grandfather. He remembered how he had abandoned all his dreams of saving the people of Oria. At that moment he felt a great distance between the Adam at the beginning of that journey and the Adam standing on the stage of the Forum made by Nazis, trying to become the emperor of the world's musicians. He tried to picture the faces of his grandfather and Rose when they realized were leaving without him. How did they really feel, hearing he had decided to stay?

In the later parts of the piece, he was so overwhelmed that he could not continue with the music and he had no choice but to stop playing. When that happened, the director of the show had the bullet-proof glass of the stage turned opaque and the orchestra vanished.

The next thing the audience saw on the stage was the presenter.

'Ladies and gentlemen,' he said, 'we are about to welcome someone on the stage, the person who has funded this magnificent forum. Please welcome Lady Adelheid Fester!'

Adelheid walked on to the stage. Remembering events at the end of the concert in *Beethoven Halle*, she lost no time in coming to the main point of her speech, Project Beethoven. A film was shown on a huge screen. It showed the old pictures from the secret lab in which the cloning had been performed. The news pictures of the announcement of the project after the clone's birth, press reports about it and short extracts of interviews with Keramat and Adelheid made everyone stare at the screen with wonder.

'I'm honored to announce,' said Adelheid as the film finished and the spotlight fell on her, 'that Adam Keramat, the musician who has captured the hearts of all of us with his extraordinary skill, is the clone of Ludwig Van Beethoven.'

The Forum was filled with an absolute silence. It was as if everyone was waiting for the moment when they would wake up from a dream. But it soon became obvious that it was no dream when Adelheid repeated the words.

'Yes, we grew the clone of the musical genius into a musician just like himself,' said Adelheid. 'We did it!'

And this time everyone stood and applauded. The clapping went on for several minutes.

Backstage, Adam could hear the cheers of audience from the auditorium. He knew that, they were not applauding him. Adelheid had finally introduced The Silver Orchestra's breakthrough. In less than twenty-four hours, everyone in the world would hear the news.

When the concert was over, a large number of the audience were waiting in the foyer to get Adam's autograph, the man who had just become the best-known musician in the world. But the star did not appear. Adam was sitting in the dressing-room, gazing at the window, not speaking.

'Sir,' said the guard, stepping into the room, 'lots of folks are expecting you out there.'

Adam did not reply. He just stared out through the window.

'Sir, are you all right?' Again he received no answer.

Adelheid entered the room, closing the door behind her. She asked the guard to leave and sat on the wooden bench beside Adam.

'Honey,' she said, 'you were extraordinary tonight!'

'The fame I won tonight has cost me my soul,' he said.

'Stop thinking like that.' Adelheid touched his shoulder. 'You know that is not true.'

'How is it not true?' Adam looked back from the window. 'I'm a Nazi now.'

'Adam, let me make something clear for you once and for all.' Adelheid took his hands, looking deep into his eyes. 'There is a huge difference between us and the Nazis back in the nineteen-thirties.'

'What's that? You live inside glass mansions and they lived by the dead stones?'

'No, of course not. The difference is, we are not criminals.'

'About seven hundred have been murdered. You don't call that a crime?'

'I told you before, we did not want that to happen. Things just got out of control. All we did was a biological test on a designated farm that we even quarantined.'

'Then who did kill those people?' Adam shouted.

'It wasn't us, Adam,' Adelheid shouted back. 'It wasn't us. And you are not a criminal. You are just in the right place at the right time.'

'The AAFH operation was designed by you years ago. I know everything about that.'

'But we are not operating it right now.'

'Then who is?'

CHAPTER 32

Paris

When his meeting in Lyon with the G8 leaders was over, Colonel Ahmad Beig decided to meet some people in his confidence in Paris before getting back to WMST headquarters. In a café by the river where the chairs all faced towards the city of Paris, Colonel Beig and three companions were sitting at a table, sipping at coffee cups. A public place in the hectic city seemed like the best place for a secret meeting.

'Gentlemen,' said Colonel Beig, 'as you are aware, the G8 leaders have ordered an air assault operation against *Der Kristall Hochburg.*'

'Finally the decision is made,' said one man. 'If only they had done it sooner!'

'I'm afraid that it is going to be a big mistake,' said the colonel. 'We have very new intel which says that some people in one of the G8 country's governments are behind the bio-attacks and The Silver Orchestra had no part in it.'

'What?'

'The source is pretty reliable.'

'Are the G8 leaders aware of this?'

'I don't think so,' said the colonel. 'I have just been informed myself.'

'Adelheid is showing off Germania, Hitler's dream city, to the world. Do we need stronger proof than this to attack the city?'

'There is a multinational corporation which has been supporting The Silver Orchestra all these years; one of their greatest founders. Now that Adelheid and *Der Kristall Hochburg* are going down, these people want to be off the hook.'

'So they want Adelheid, her people and the city destroyed before she goes on any trial?'

'Exactly.' The colonel wiped his mouth discreetly. 'They will not hesitate to kill the innocent people who are currently in the city.'

'Colonel, I understand your feelings. But don't you think this is the time to eliminate this group and all their terrible plans?"

'I would not hesitate to do so for all she has done. But I believe WMST had been manipulated to take action against The Silver Orchestra. There are those who want The Silver Orchestra to be taken out immediately.'

'Colonel, I will make the call and I will let you know in an hour.' The man and his companion shook hands with the colonel and left the café.

Walking through the Place Saint-Michel, Ahmad Beig stood at the bridge and felt the cold breeze rising off the Seine on his cheeks. A cruise boat was moving gently on the water, showing tourists the sights of Paris. The faces of the tourists, all gazing in awe at the Gothic construction behind Beig, made him turn back to look at the masterpiece. Meanwhile, the huge bell above the building started to toll. People from all around the world were walking towards the cathedral to become lost inside the holy edifice. Ahmad Beig was no exception. Before him stood the vivid statement of faith, Notre Dame. She was a jewel in the center of Paris with her two gigantic towers, the circular rose window between them and the ninety-three meter spire above her. The colonel was standing in front of the three portals of the cathedral, above which were three arches, supporting the gallery of kings. The door panels were crafted with iron work and above the middle one was sculpted the life of Holy Mary. Her youth, her marriage to Joseph, the day she gave birth to Jesus, her entry into glory and her crowning in the heaven were displayed above the great doors. Above them was a circular window, the Rose window, which carried a message of incarnation and the image of a circular earthly world.

Ahmad Beig passed through the portals and entered the building. He walked down the aisle that was lined with massive stone pillars on both sides. He found himself standing before the statue of the Virgin Mary, holding her dead son in her lap, and behind her the golden cross of glory. The holy music had enchanted him and it was at the foot of the statue of Mary that he felt his heart touched. He realized that God existed everywhere at every time to anyone who wanted to feel his glory and kindness. Notre Dame de Paris, Our Lady of Paris, was the place where Ahmad Beig felt God's closeness again after a long time. The last time had been when he had risked his life to save his soldiers who were trapped by Iraqi troops. When he had secured his camp, he had felt God standing right next to him.

The colonel left the cathedral, the polyphonic organ music still in his head. There was one thought in his mind, and that was to free Adam and save the people from the terror that was about to hit their towns. Just as he thought about this, his phone started to ring.

'Colonel,' said the man he had met in the café 'wheel up in sixty minutes. The operation is on for tomorrow morning. They were not convinced. I'm deeply sorry!'

'Can't we postpone the attack just one more day?' Beig asked. 'Just give me one day and I'll give you the names of those who were behind the attacks.'

'I'm sorry, Colonel,' said the man, 'the decision is made. *Der Kristall Hochburg* must be destroyed tomorrow morning.'

'At least let me get Adam and the rest of the civilians out of the city,' the Colonel said.

'I wish I could comply with your request. Sorry, that will be all for now, Colonel.'

Thinking hard, Colonel Beig resumed walking along the rue Saint-Michel. He was ready to leave for the airport where the WMST jet was awaiting him. As he walked, he dialed a number on his satellite phone.

'Let the bird sing by the organ before the house is on fire,' he said, and disconnected.

A black car pulled over just beside him and a couple of bulky men, their faces concealed by dark masks, got out.

'Colonel Ahmad Beig,' said one. 'You must come with us.'

Beig got into the car. He knew that the truth behind the bio-attacks could be revealed to him within the next few minutes, but he was not sure he would leave the car alive. If he did not make it to his office in WMST headquarters, the UN Security Council would have no choice but to appoint a new commander for the treaty.

The G8 are not aware of the civilians in *Kristall Hochburg*, the colonel thought. The firm wants the city destroyed the first thing in the morning, regardless of the innocent people there.

The next morning, Adam Keramat was preparing to leave the mansion to go to the glass Arch of Victory. Under the Arch the orchestra was about to shoot a music video as a promotion for Adam's new album. Adelheid was headed there also, to supervise the final shooting of the video which would introduce *Der Kristall Hochburg* to the world, following the successful concert.

'Sir,' the driver said to Adam. 'I have news for you from Colonel Beig.'

'Go on!' said Adam. 'Another pick-up point?'

'Actually, yes,' said the driver. 'In less than an hour the city will be attacked by WMST fighters and choppers.'

'What?' This would be disaster.

'The colonel asked me to tell you that the only safe place will be by the organ.'

'The organ?'

'Is there a church here? That's where an organ would be found.'

'You mean you don't know where the organ is?"

'No, sir. I will be lifted out before the assault starts. But Colonel Beig sounded pretty sure that you would know the location.'

'The organ.' Adam thought hard. 'Of course! I know where it is. There's only one organ here. It's in the *Beethoven Haus*.'

'Then be sure to be there before the attack begins,' the driver said.

'How come he is attacking the city without letting innocent people leave first?'

'As I understand it, there have been some problems in the G8 and the colonel is not completely in charge of the operation.'

'You mean, sending me this message is all he could do to warn me?'

'Unfortunately, yes.'

At the Arch of Victory, Adam could not see Adelheid among the crowds. He waited anxiously for a dozen minutes, but she did not show up. The bitch must know about the attack, he thought. He grabbed the video director's loudspeaker and climbed on the car's hood.

'Everybody, attention please,' said Adam. Within a few seconds the hum of voices had quietened, everyone listening to him. 'In a few minutes the city will be bombed. Everyone who stays out will burn to death.'

The people had not so far taken his words seriously. It sounded too farfetched. They probably thought that he wanted to promote the band in an outrageous way. But when he asked the crowd to follow his car, one by one they started to believe him and an atmosphere of alarm ran through the crowd. Adam and his driver made for the replica of *Beethoven Haus*, while the film crew and the band members followed in vans. Adam knew that many, like himself, were picturing fighter aircraft in the sky above the city, shooting their rockets towards them, tearing their bodies into unrecognizable parts. Some were silent, imagining their flesh burning, with nobody to help or even hear them.

The cars reached the walls of the secret garden. A van driver asked his passengers to leave the vehicle and stand aside from the building. Then he drove the van at speed into the gate, hitting it hard and smashing it to pieces. He did this over and over, making the awful noise of metal on metal. Finally, the van shattered one of the gates, throwing fragments inside the garden. Everybody swarmed in. At the entrance to the main building, Adam remembered that there was no need to smash the windows. He stood before the camera and, as soon as his face was recognized, the glass door opened. He walked in and the frightened film crew followed him inside. Breathing fast, he walked quickly to the organ.

'As long as we stay in this room together, we will be safe,' he said when he was sure everyone was in the building.

The sound of fighter jets tore through the sky over the city. Nobody spoke. Inside the room there was just silence and fear. The noise increased, until the roar of the engines shattered the air above the secret garden. Everyone was expecting a missile, cutting the roof of the building open and killing everybody within. But then the planes flew past the garden and headed toward the center of the city, and the sense of fear receded.

'This is Falcon One,' said the pilot on the radio. 'I have the visual on the Arch.'

'Falcon One, do you have the target in missile range?' said his commander.

'Affirmative.'

'Take the arch out,' said the commander. 'I repeat, take the arch out.'

The first missile was fired and then the second, third and fourth. All four missiles hit the glass arch and in less than three seconds the whole construction turned into a mountain of glass fragments, flying through the air. The second fighter dropped a bomb at the site of the arch and, after a huge explosion, all the fragments started to burn and melt into ash. The attackers knew that nothing at all should remain.

The people in the organ room started to shout immediately they heard the explosion. The noise of the fighter's engines could still be heard, not too far off.

Adam went towards the organ and sat behind it. He started to play one of the polyphonic pieces he had composed in a mosque in Kerman, listening to the rhythm of Azan being played on the mosque's loudspeaker. As he became lost in the music, everyone in the room dropped on to their knees, praying for safety. Adam had just come to the middle of the piece when the second explosion shook the *Beethoven Haus*. The blast sounded bigger this time, and nearer. The Crystal Forum, Adam thought. They had hit it. For a few seconds he stopped playing, remembering his magnificent concert in the building. But it did not take long before he was lost in the organ music again.

The explosions went on for about half-an-hour. The fighters struck at all the buildings in the city, demolishing it completely. Inside the rose-adorned city walls, the only thing that could be seen was ashes. Everything had been destroyed, except the secret garden and the building inside it. Once the sound of the planes' engines could no longer be heard in the sky, people started cautiously to leave the building. Before them they found a scene from a nightmare. The entire city had turned into rubble. The scent of fields and flowers had given way to that of gunpowder and flames.

Adam was the last to leave the building. He was afraid of facing the sight of that inimitable beauty destroyed. But eventually he joined the crowds and watched the city burning. The sound of a chopper's blades approaching them brought renewed panic. The chopper appeared from out of the black smoke in the sky. It came towards them in a zigzag flight, as if the pilot was not skilful enough to control it. After several tries, it landed by the crowd. The clatter of the rotors drowned out every other sound, but Adam could see the Humvees getting close to them. His driver rushed towards him and seized his hand.

'We should leave, Mr. Keramat,' he said. 'The cars are after you. Get in the chopper now.'

Adam did not hesitate and climbed aboard the chopper; the driver and a girl he thought was probably an undercover agent with WMST followed him. The pilot, dressed in military uniform, and a soldier helped them in and immediately slid the door closed. The chopper looked old and overused, not like one of WMST's state-of-the-art ones. The pilot grabbed the control handle and moved it back to take the helicopter off the ground. Shaking severely, it rose in the air, but seemed not to be able fly to a high altitude. Meanwhile, the Hummers were closing on the troubled flying bird. Adam heard gun shots again. The firing came from the Hummers, pursuing them on the ground. A bullet hit the helicopter and it lurched badly. Through the window,

Adam could see the burning city turning around them. The chopper descended lower and lower until it hit a tree. The driver opened the door and pushed Adam and the girl out, then jumped out himself.

'Run! Run!' he shouted.

The three of them ran and hid behind a bombed-out building as the man in the Hummer fired a rocket at the chopper, blowing it up with the pilot and the soldier inside. Hummers halted by the blasted building and about a dozen men in black suits got out of them. They started to search the place, tracking Adam and his two companions. The driver began to run on tiptoe by the wall, Adam and the girl following him. They ran towards a farming area, covered by burning trees. Trying to hide amongst these was futile. They ran as fast as they could, the men chasing them, shooting at them from time to time. Adam sensed that the driver was no longer with him but he had no time to look back and search for him.

'He is shot!' cried the girl. 'Run! Run!'

These were her last words. She dropped, bleeding profusely. Adam heard another shot and felt a fierce pain in his leg. He came to an abrupt halt and fell to the ground. His pants were wet with blood and he could not feel his left leg. A man appeared from behind a tree, holding a machine gun. He walked towards the girl and Adam as they crawled away in a last desperate effort to escape. He aimed his gun at the girl's chest and fired. Then he walked over to Adam, held his gun pointing at the sky and fired. Two other men appeared.

'Arthur!' one of them called. 'Are we done here?'

'Keramat is dead,' said Arthur. 'So are his driver and the girl.'

The men walked towards the girl, who lay with her chest opened by the bullets. Then one of them stepped close to Adam. He pointed his gun at his head. Adam had closed his eyes, trying to hold his breath so that they would believe him to be dead. But the man was determined to finish the young musician off. He put his finger on the trigger and aimed at Adam's head. There was nothing Adam could do. Any movement would push him closer to death.

'Drop it, man!' said Arthur.

'Don't be crazy,' said the man.

Arthur did not let him finish his sentence and fired the machine gun at his chest. The other man tried to fire at Arthur, but Arthur was quicker and he fell to the ground, dead.

Adam started to breathe normally and moved his head to see the face of his rescuer.

'Sorry about your leg,' said Arthur. 'I had no choice.'

Adam's vision had begun to blur cold and in a moment everything went dark and a cold feeling spread over his body.

CHAPTER 33

Adam opened his eyes briefly. He realized that he was lying on a stretcher, inside the cabin of a helicopter. His leg was bandaged and he could see a blood bag hung above his head, its tube fixed into a vein in his hand. He found it difficult to focus. Thick leather ear protectors had been placed over his ears, so that he would not be disturbed by the noise of the rotors. Arthur was sitting opposite to him and gave him a smile. But soon Adam had to close his eyes again.

It was midnight. He was lying on the marble floor of his temple. The river's melody was the only sound he could hear. Everywhere was pitch dark and the tree branches were dancing in the wind. Among the shadows of night, something in the distance drew his attention and he rubbed his eyes to see it more plainly. It was the hazy image of a shining spot in the depths of the darkness. Sleep deserted him. He stood up and walked quickly towards the shining spot.

As he made his way down to the river through the darkness, the shining white spot grew bigger and bigger. The blur of the light source dissolved gently and the midnight mystery was revealed. It was another temple, made from white marble and covered by white curtains. The slight wind was making the curtains move slowly and a light flickered behind them. His heartbeat slowed when he heard the soft voice of a woman singing inside the temple. He stepped closer and stretched his hand to the curtain, which slid aside gently. He had no fear of being seen by those inside the temple, for he felt safe with them. He pushed the curtain aside to look more deeply into the temple.

A mother and her baby were sitting on a chair made of a precious stone. The mother was sitting with her back to Adam, stroking her baby to sleep. Three angels, all dressed in white and with long brown hair, were standing around them. One was playing a violin, another a flute, and the third was singing in a very soft voice. Adam, the master of all sounds and voices, was in no doubt that the voice and song he had chanced to hear were from the skies. The woman turned her back calmly with no fear of his presence, as if she had been aware of his eyes on her the entire time.

And the gift reached to its perfect state of divinity when she turned around. The angels stopped their song. The woman was his mother.

'Play your violin for me, darling!' she said. 'Play it, my son!'

When Adam opened his eyes, he was lying on his bed in his grandfather's house. Through the window he could see the beautiful orchards of Oria. He could hear the laughter of the village children, playing on the field in front of Keramat's house. Now he was able to sit up in the bed for a while. The door opened and his grandfather entered.

'Adam,' said Keramat, 'you're awake, my dear boy!' He rushed to Adam and hugged him.

'Grandpa!' said Adam, tears rolling down his cheeks. 'I'm so sorry! I'm so sorry!'

'Rose!' shouted Keramat. 'Get in here! Adam is awake.'

Rose ran upstairs, stumbling on the stairs twice, but she did not care and rushed in to Adam's room. She joined the embrace of grandfather and grandson, squeezing them in her arms.

As they drew apart, Adam took Rose's hand and his grandfather's and said, 'I'm truly sorry to have left you like that.'

'I understand, said Keramat. 'You just happened not to be yourself.'

Adam managed to get out of bed that day, trying to walk after several days under sedation. He met Oria's people, coming to visit him with flowers and congratulating him on his concerts. He spent the day walking by the river with Rose, chatting to the villagers and meeting the school children's band. He could not be further from all those adventures and conspiracies which had started with a world tour. Oria and its enchanting countryside took Adam and Rose back to the days of their childhood. They planned to visit Spring Valley, but the pain in Adam's leg did not let them walk that far.

These days of respite did not take long. The peace of village life with his loved ones was broken one morning when there was a knock on the village chief's door. Looking through the window, Keramat could see dozens of reporters gathering outside. Press vans were parked by the river with satellite dishes above them, while cameramen were trying to get the best shot of the mayor's house before he appeared.

Opening the door, Karim Keramat found the cameras zooming in on his face and reporters shoving each other aside in their urgency to be the first to ask a question. But of course he was not the only one they were looking for and they had driven all the way to meet. That was Adam Keramat, the world-famous musician and survivor of the airstrike on *Der Kristall Hochburg*. In less than an hour, a press conference was to be held in front of Keramat's house and Adam would reveal all he knew to the world.

Adam was in his room dressing when the phone rang.

Mr. Keramat,' said the caller, 'you were so lucky that Arthur was compromised.'

Adam had heard the voice before. He could remember every word he had said at their last encounter. It was the guy in the dark suit, the one who had chased him after the chopper had exploded. It was the same man who had shouted, 'Shoot him on sight! Keramat must not leave here alive!' The same man who had been appointed to kill him after the airstrike. Adam shivered. He could not speak to ask the man what he wanted.

'Dear Adam,' said the man. 'Here is a thought: the reporters are gonna ask you what happed that day in *Der Kristall Hochburg*. You are going to tell them that The Silver Orchestra was bombarded by WMST fighters and then you were rescued and transported to Oria by them.'

'Why did you want me dead?' Adam asked finally, trying to hide his fear.

'That doesn't matter now,' said the man. 'You tell them something other than what I said, you know what happens next.' He disconnected the phone.

Keramat, who had come into the room, was looking at Adam curiously, waiting for an explanation.

'Grandpa,' said Adam, 'they are after us! I'm so scared.'

'Come here.' Keramat hugged Adam. 'Who are they?'

'I just know that they are not WMST or The Silver Orchestra. They tried to kill me in *Der Kristall Hochburg*. And they have been behind the bio-attacks.'

'That's what I thought,' said Keramat. 'Colonel Beig would not have started the attack before getting the civilians out of the city.'

The press conference started with half-an-hour's delay. Adam was bombarded, this time by questions, about how it felt to be the clone of Beethoven.

'I respect The Silver Orchestra's project of cloning Beethoven which was performed twenty-nine years ago,' Adam said, 'but I'm sorry to announce that I'm in possession of very strong evidence proving that the project failed and I am not the clone.'

'Mr. Keramat,' asked a reporter, 'in your most recent concert in The Crystal Forum, Lady Adelheid Fester introduced you as the clone of Ludwig Beethoven and you did not reject her statement.'

'Unfortunately, this has been a matter of conflict between The Silver Orchestra and me for a while,' said Adam after a pause, 'but what I claim can easily be confirmed.'

'You mean by a DNA test?'

'Yes,' Adam said. 'Dr. Keramat, my grandfather, has invited a medical team over to do the test. A representative from the Beethoven Study Center of San Jose University will be here, too, with a strand of Beethoven's hair.'

'Mr. Keramat, two days after your concert, nobody was allowed to get near *Der Kristall Hochburg* for a twenty kilometer radius around the city, including journalists. What can you say about that?'

And that was the moment that Adam remembered the whole terrible events of the airstrike. He remembered the faces of his driver and that of the girl agent, covered with blood. He remembered hearing the voice of the man who had been ordered to kill him. He remembered word for word what the man had told him on the phone.

'Mr. Keramat?' the reporter prompted him.

'I'm afraid that,' Adam paused again, 'on the day that you mentioned, there was a military operation against The Silver Orchestra in the city by WMST.'

'And that's where you got your leg injured?' asked someone else.

'Yes.'

'Sir . . .'

Adam did not let the reporter ask his question. 'The medical team will be here tomorrow,' he said, 'and I want all of you here when the result of the DNA test is ready. That will be all for now.'

Lying on his bed, Adam had an opportunity to look at the sky and the stars. He bore in mind that sometimes we see in the sky the shapes that we really long to see, deep within our soul. And at that moment he made up his own constellation: one that looked like his temple of music. He thought about the day his grandfather finished building the temple, the day on which Adam had gained a special spot to sit in and been drawn into the fabulous world of creating melodies. The temple was located beside the river on a curve so that the flow of water passed around three sides of it; just like a private peninsula.

Adam had put some big stones in the river by the temple so that he could hear the melody of the water flow clear and loud. It was the loudest sound he could hear there. The tree which stood opposite his temple on the other side of the small river had purple leaves and the one beside it violet and the next one greenish and dark brown foliage, the full range of the color spectrum. In the valley it was only him and his beloved instrument and hours of envisaging different aspects of his small and beautiful world and composing and playing music based on them. As well as the summer that he spent in the village, he would visit the valley at other times of the year. The compositions he created throughout the year differed from each other, reflecting the diverse weather conditions of the village and his different moods. One piece he named 'The Blue Storm.' It had been composed when he found that some of his college mates had acted to conceal news of the students' music festival from him, for they all envied his outstanding musical talent and they did not want to see him playing on the stage at the festival.

A couple of days after Adam found out about the conspiracy, he went to the village. The first thing he did after meeting his grandfather was to go to the temple and compose the piece. It was almost spring, so he found the light breeze on his cheeks soothing. He put the bow on the strings and moved it. He was so overwhelmed by the emotions he had experienced through his so-called friends' conspiracy that he wanted to express his anger in the form of a calm melody. In the event, he expressed both rage and calm in the piece, which was why he named it 'The Blue Storm'. He could never explain where he had got the idea of expressing anger in the form of a relaxing creation; he could not do so even to himself. However, later, he discovered that artistic creation works as a remedy to anger and fear. Hence, he was happy that his creation was not a savage one. The piece did not represent anger, though it had been inspired by it. 'The Blue Storm' was a conversation between madness and a pure source of calm. There were some parts in it that evoked the feeling of chaos in the listener's mind, but soon these were followed by a tranquilizing reply from the music.

'The Blue Storm'! That is what he needed to play right now. He took out the silver violin and started to play the piece. He had not played it for a very long time, maybe seven years. However, he remembered all the notes exactly as he had written them in the first place. He played the piece over and over. He listened to the conversation that led into serenity, a calm after a devastating hurricane, without letting it unsettle him. He needed that in the present situation. The storm was over and another was about to begin. What he needed most was to be prepared and sensible.

He drew back the curtain and looked at the sky. He started to play the silver violin again. In the sky, he saw a silver line which connected five shining stars. His grandfather had shown him that constellation before and told him that it called Cassiopeia. The five stars were the right shoulder, heart, waist, knee and ankle of a queen called Lady Cassiopeia. She was a mythical queen, notoriously vain, who sat on a throne fussing with her hair. Adam could see her clearly in the sky. She was sitting on her throne, proud and dignified. She had all the glory and mystery he had found in Adelheid. His grandfather had shown him the sky queen over many nights, telling him the myth about her, describing how she lay on the throne to observe the whole world and how the inhabitants of the earth were drawn to her splendor. All men on earth were attracted to the sky queen, but they could never reach her and that was why they were looking for a woman like her on their own planet. That was the real power of a myth heard in childhood; it would be embedded in a person's mind, always with him, like his own shadow.

At that moment, Adam realized why he had given in so easily to Adelheid and her desires. Until Adelheid had turned out to be something totally different from the sky queen he had desired for such a long time. Maybe he had sensed this about her and that was why he had lost his feelings for her, or maybe he had never had that feeling in the first place and it was all his subconscious desire, shaped by the myth, that attracted him to the queen of The Silver Orchestra.

CHAPTER 34

The twelfth floor of the hotel had the most perfect view of the Liberty Island and the magnificent Statue of Liberty. Adelheid was switching TV channels to find the one with live coverage of the investigation into the news about Project Beethoven. Finally, she found the right channel. The broadcaster was standing on the field before Keramat's house in Oria. He was outlining the press conference that was about to be held there. Adelheid, waiting for the event, knew that all she had built in the past thirty years was gone. But there was still one thing she cared about: Adam's image in the world. The young musician undoubtedly owed a great part of his fame to her.

Adelheid kept watching the picture of the field, which was used for all public gatherings. Then the medical team appeared on the stage. Adam and Keramat followed. The doctor, ready to speak into the microphone, was holding an envelope in his hands. Adelheid knew what the envelope contained. The result of the DNA test could destroy the fantasy that she had been living with for so many years.

'Ladies and gentlemen,' said the doctor, 'here I pronounce the result of the DNA matching test we performed on

Mr. Adam Keramat's DNA and the DNA of Ludwig Van Beethoven, obtained from his hair strands, which were brought to our mobile lab here in Oria from San Jose State University.'

Adelheid felt sick with apprehension. The terrible moment of facing the fact that Project Beethoven had failed was almost upon her. Without *Der Kristall Hochburg* and with the news she was about to receive, she would be completely ruined.

The doctor opened the envelope and took out a small yellow paper.

'The result of the test is positive,' he said.

'What?' Keramat gasped. 'That's impossible.'

Adelheid sat rigid in her chair. She couldn't believe it either.

'Dr. Keramat,' said the doctor, 'there is no question of the accuracy of the test we performed. Mr. Adam Keramat is definitely the clone of Ludwig Van Beethoven.'

'I was there when the clone died.' Keramat could not hide his anger. 'Adam is my grandson.'

'I was there, too,' whispered Adelheid in her lonely hotel room. 'What the hell is going on?'

Adelheid knew that the TV coverage would be cut any minute and it happened sooner than she had expected. She could make no phone calls as herself, for she was believed to be dead. But the more time passed, the more she wanted to find out what was going on in Oria.

She went to the mirror and checked her appearance once again. With the mask Dr. Mao had made for her in the bio-lab, she looked twenty years younger. She picked up the phone.

'This is Veronica Christi,' she said to the receptionist. 'I'm checking out.'

Adam's DNA test and the storm of controversy around it had put Oria into the headlines. Reporters were all over the village, making documentaries, interviewing people about Adam's life and his grandfather's. The proof had been presented to them and they had no doubt that the young world-famous musician who had grown up in the village was Beethoven's clone. They could get anyone to go on camera, to show their excitement about the news except Adam and his grandfather. Both strongly denied the result of the test and kept telling the reporters, 'The clone died years ago.'

Day by day, Adam's leg was getting better. And finally one morning he decided to walk to Spring Valley; the very first place in which he fell in love and where he had realized his gift for creating music. Dr. Keramat went with him. They spent the day in the valley and it was on the way back to the village that Keramat asked Adam to sit by the river.

They gazed at the river's flow. Adam knew that, unlike himself, his grandfather was not a man who took breaks in the middle of something.

'Adam,' said Keramat, looking at Adam with pain in his eyes. 'I need to tell you something before we get to the village. I was trying to do it during the day, but I couldn't.'

Please don't tell me that I'm the clone and you knew it the whole time, Adam prayed silently.

'What is it, Grandpa?' he asked.

'If I did not reveal this before, it was for your own safety. And also hers.'

'Hers?' Adam said, surprised. 'Who are you talking about?'

'Your mother.'

'My mother?'

'Adam, your mother is alive.'

By now Adam was almost used to receiving the most unexpected information about himself. But this sounded quite different. For a moment, he questioned whether he was awake or not.

'Angela is alive and she been asking about you during all these years,' said Keramat, clearly relieving himself of the great secret.

'I'm so confused,' said Adam. 'Why should her existence have been a secret? And what about the DNA test?'

'The test result has baffled me, too. Something is certainly missing here,' his grandfather said. 'We cannot, even with your mother's presence or that tape of Adelheid's, gainsay evidence such as a DNA test. But . . .'

'But what?'

'This is between us,' said Keramat, his face relaxed now that the pain had gone. 'With the threat gone, I can let you and your mother meet.'

Adam sat watching the river as it flowed past them.

'Grandpa.' He broke the silence. 'I will need to have some time. I've been living my whole life with a mental image of my mother. I can't just meet her all of a sudden.'

'You are right to ask for all the time in the world, my boy,' said Kermat, smiling. 'I told you as soon as I could, knowing that it won't endanger your life any more.'

They walked the rest of the way to Oria in silence. But inside their heads, Adam asked thousands of questions and Keramat answered them all.

It was three days later that Adam knocked on the door of his grandfather's library.

'Grandpa,' Adam said, 'I'm ready to go. Let's meet her.'

Keramat smiled at him. Without a word, he went to his computer and sent Angela the email that she had been awaiting for twenty-nine years.

> Dear Angela,
>
> I guess the circumstances are now right for you and Adam to meet.
>
> Please let me know if you can come to Oria next Sunday. I'm sure you have been following the news of the recent DNA test.
>
> Adam and I hope to see you soon.
>
> Best wishes,
> Karim Keramat

Just an hour later, Angela replied, expressing her excitement at the prospect of meeting her son after all those years of living apart from him.

CHAPTER 35

Two hours after Angela's plane had landed in Rome, Adam and Keramat were waiting at the narrow road through the woods that ended at Oria, to welcome her to the family which had for many years thought her dead. Adam did not know how he should act at the sight of his mother. The night before he had cried himself to sleep, trying to find a way to welcome her, but without success. Standing by the road, he was still searching his mind. The mother whom he had never met could seem like a total stranger. He was so confused after the DNA test that found everything and everyone hard to believe. Not even his grandfather could help him.

Adam spotted the white vehicle in the distance, coming towards them. Watching the taxi becoming bigger and bigger, he hoped for one of those moments that comes out of nowhere and brings all the solutions along with itself.

The cab pulled over by the road. The back door opened and a woman got out. She stood by the roadside staring at Adam, who was silent and motionless on the opposite side.

Adam stared back, still without speaking.

And then the other back door opened and another woman stepped out of the car.

'Oh, my god!' Keramat exclaimed. 'What the hell is happening?'

'What's wrong, Grandpa?' asked Adam.

'Do you recognize both of these women?'

'That's Angela, but much older than her photos,' said Adam. 'Actually, the second one looks really familiar.'

'You have seen her in the photographs. Beside me and Adelheid.' Keramat's voice sounded muffled. 'But what is she doing here?'

Photographs? All at once, Adam recalled the face. He had forgotten about finding a way to treat his mother. Instead, he was trying to figure out what had brought the two women together, standing on the other side of the road, gazing at him and wiping the tears off their faces, as a mother would. She was standing by Grandpa in the photo, holding me. Adelheid was there, too. They were in the lab. Oh, my god! The woman is Sheila!

Holding his breath, Adam walked with his grandfather towards the women. Nobody spoke. Adam sensed that his grandfather was as confused as he was. And it seemed to him that his mother and Sheila were struggling to find a way to start the explanation they owed him.

During the walk to Keramat's house, Angela talked mostly about Adam's concerts and how proud she had been of him as she followed the news of his achievements in the media. But when they got to the house, Keramat asked the question that was on everybody's mind.

'Angela,' said Keramat, 'it's not so surprising that you and Sheila know one another or that you could have met over these years. But how come you are together now?'

'I will never forget those days of solitude in that underground clinic, Dr. Keramat,' said Sheila. 'You were the only friend and support I had. You were like a father to me.'

'Thank you, Sheila,' said Keramat. 'So were you like a family to me. They were my days of loneliness, too.'

'It all happened in that hospital in Rome,' said Angela. 'It was a terrible night.'

'What night, Angela?' Keramat asked.

'It was three weeks after Adam's birthday,' she said. 'He was burning with fever, so we took him to the same hospital he was born in.'

'Three weeks?' said Keramat. 'Sheila was there at that time; so were the press.'

'They ran tests on the baby. The doctors told us that our son wouldn't live beyond a year.' Angela's voice started to tremble.

'What?' Keramat said, shocked.

'That was the night I met Angela for the first time,' said Sheila. 'She was sitting alone in the hospital's cafeteria, holding her head in her hands and crying.'

'Sheila came to me,' said Angela, 'and I told her everything.'

'And then we made the deal,' Sheila said.

'What deal?' Adam was trying to get his head round this.

'When I agreed to be the surrogate mother for Project Beethoven, I was so excited,' said Sheila, 'but when I gave birth to the child, I had one single feeling, day and night. I wanted to protect my child from any danger.'

'She offered and I accepted.' Angela smiled.

'I knew that my child would be an object of scientific study for his whole life, like a lab rat,' Sheila said. 'I wanted him to live a normal life, in a family.'

'Oh, my god!' said Keramat. 'Don't tell me that . . .'

'Yes,' said Sheila. 'That night we swapped the babies.'

'I wanted to raise my child and she wanted to protect hers,' said Angela. 'That was the deal that only two desperate mothers could make.'

'So the test,' said Adam, hardly able to finish the question, 'the test result was correct?'

'Yes, my dear.' Angela's eyes filled with tears. 'Your real mother is Sheila.'

'And he is the clone,' Keramat said.

'But I don't understand,' complained Adam. 'If you wanted to raise a child that badly, why did you leave me?'

'Only to protect you, Adam,' Angela told him.

'Protect me from who?' said Adam. 'There was no threat in Oria!'

'From Adelheid.' Angela paused briefly. 'Dr. Keramat, there is something else I should tell you.'

'Not another deal that you two made?'

'No, this one doesn't concern Sheila,' said Angela. 'Actually, it's about Adelheid.'

'What about her?'

'I was working with The Silver Orchestra, years before you met me.'

'You were working for Adelheid?' Adam felt himself choking with rage.

'Dr. Keramat, I met your son for the first time by the order of Adelheid,' said Angela. 'I was on a mission to infiltrate your family and observe you and your whereabouts. But I really fell in love with him. My marriage to him was because of love. My child was the result of love and my maternal feelings towards the child were real.'

'I'm not moved, Mother,' Adam muttered.

'Three years after Adam's birth, when you were Oria's mayor, I told Adelheid that I wanted to stop working with her. I pushed her hard on it. But she would not agree. And . . .' Angela whispered the words, 'they had your son murdered in a faked accident.'

'Murdered?' asked Keramat, agitated. 'And you kept this from me the whole time?'

'They threatened that they would kill me and Adam, too.' She started to cry. 'I just wanted Adam's safety. I had to stay away from Adam to protect him.'

'You mean the whole time I was hiding in Oria, Adelheid knew where I lived?' Adam couldn't believe it.

'That's how she knew that Adam looked like Beethoven as a child,' said Sheila.

'And she tried to make me a musician,' Adam said.

CHAPTER 36

The next morning Adam was woken up just after dawn by a knock on the door. He rushed downstairs and pulled the wooden door open. Before him stood one of the children from the school orchestra.

'Sorry to disturb you at this ungodly hour, Mr. Keramat,' said the boy, who was holding a box. 'I have a delivery for you. He said it will rot if I don't bring it to you right away.'

'What is inside?' asked Adam, rubbing his eyes to wake himself up. 'Who gave this to you?'

'One of those men we see these days around the village, in a black car,' said the boy. 'He didn't say anything else.'

'Ok, thank you.' Adam took the box and went back inside the house.

The box was wrapped up in paper. Once he had removed this, Adam took a knife to cut the box open. Inside was something wrapped in a towel. He undid the towel. Seeing what it contained, he jumped back in horror, letting out such a cry of terror that it woke the two women, his grandfather and Rose. They all hurried to the living-room.

Adam couldn't bring himself to hold the thing in his hands. The eyes were wide open, staring. The forehead was covered with blood and the disfigured mouth was unable to say a word. Blood was still dripping from the veins of the neck. The head belonged to the last man Adam had met in *Der Kristall Hochburg*.

Dear god! It was Arthur.

The women clung on to one another, screaming.

'Who is this, Adam?' Rose managed, her hand over her mouth.

'The man who saved my life.' It was too horrific to take in.

Keramat reached into the box and took out a piece of paper. Unfolding the sticky note, he read the message.

Dear Adam,

This is what happened to your savior.

Open your mouth, and you will wish for your death.

'Oh god!' said Keramat. 'What do you know, Adam?'

'It's about the attack on the city.' He began to tremble.

'What about it?' Rose asked.

'The last time I talked to Adelheid, she mentioned that The Silver Orchestra had never started the bio-attack.'

'How is that even possible?' asked Keramat. 'Who did then?'

'The same people who tried to kill me there, on the day of the air strike. She said they were government.'

'What government?'

'I don't know that, Grandpa! I really don't.'

Keramat sat down on the sofa, deep in thought.

'The fact is,' said Angela, 'The Silver Orchestra and their dirty plots are gone for ever.'

'Their destruction cost the lives of hundreds of innocent people who died during the bio-attack and those who burned alive in the Crystal Forum on the day of the air strike.'

'Lives that The Silver Orchestra never intended to take,' Adam said.

'The price that innocents paid for a dictator who never became one,' Rose added.

'She should have been stopped long ago, before any of these things happened,' said Keramat sadly.

Adam's cell phone alerted him to a new SMS.

Another threat?

He opened the message. It was from his bank.

15,000,000 EURS has been transferred to your account by Veronica Christi.

Adam, unable to make sense of this, gave the phone to his grandfather.

'Are they bribing and threatening me at the same time?' he asked.

'It doesn't make sense,' said Keramat. 'Do you know this Veronica Christi?'

'Never heard the name.' Adam frowned. 'How can I find out who she is?'

'Why don't you call the bank?' his grandfather suggested.

Adam placed a call to his bank, asking about the identity of the woman who had made him a multi-millionaire but they would not disclose any information other than what Adam already knew. Information like that was confidential and couldn't be given over the phone, he was told.

'You need to come here in person, with a court order, to learn the whereabouts of this individual,' the bank representative said.

'If the money has come from the same people who sent you the head,' said Rose, 'they will contact you soon.'

Rose's voice reminded Adam of the days they had spent together in Spring Valley. And once again he wished that he had no global fame or multimillion-euro wealth, and that in return he could spend one more day in Spring Valley, free from worries. A day on which he would think about nothing, except Rose, and receive nothing but her kindness.

Dr. Keramat remembered that once he had been led to escape from The Silver Orchestra's custody and the guard who worked undercover for Colonel Beig had given him a phone number. It was a secret line, belonging to the colonel himself. Keramat searched in his address book and pressed out the number.

'You have reached the GBS Bank of Cyprus,' said an automated voice. 'Please dial the extension number you require. To leave a message, please dial ten.'

Keramat followed the instruction, setting the phone on loudspeaker.

'My silver account has just expired,' he said. 'I need to talk to someone about it.'

On the phone's LCD screen, Adam could see the call being diverted immediately after his grandfather left the voice message.

Someone picked up the phone. His deep voice was so familiar to Adam, especially when he said, 'My dear Keramat, please tell me that Adam is ok and safe by your side.'

Colonel Ahmad Beig!

'Adam is safe and well, Colonel,' said Keramat. 'Thanks to you.'

'I'm glad to hear that,' said the colonel. 'What can I do for you, my friend?'

'We need to find out who transferred money to Adam's account.'

'I have some connections,' the colonel said. 'Just give me the name and the account number. I guess it's connected to Adam's involvement in The Silver Orchestra. I will let you know ASAP. Take care of the young man.'

An hour later the phone rang.

'The account belongs to Veronica Christi, as you know,' said Colonel Beig. 'The address registered to her is in Rome. I had a colleague go there. But the house has been sold.'

'Rome?' Keramat was surprised. 'She is this close to us?'

'Indeed. And there is something else,' said the colonel. 'I cross—checked her name with the border agency's list of arrivals to the country. She flew into Italy just yesterday.'

'Thank you, Colonel,' said Keramat. 'Is there anyway we can meet this generous lady?'

'I should tell you that you need to be extra cautious about her,' said Beig. 'She used a fake passport to open the account and she left the USA with the same passport.'

'Oh, god!' This information unnerved Keramat. 'She is like a ghost around us. We meet her only when she says so?'

'Exactly! I will be in Oria with you very soon.'

'Thank you again, Colonel. Have a safe trip.'

'The only woman I know capable of doing something like this is Adelheid,' said Adam, having listened to the whole conversation, 'but we don't know whether she is dead or alive. Plus her empire is finished and she can't have that kind of money.'

'I have no idea, Adam,' said Keramat. 'Whoever she is, she wants you to have the money. And she won't ask for a refund.'

'But she will ask for a favor,' said Rose.

'Exactly,' said Keramat.

'All Adelheid has ever asked of me was giving concerts. What can she possibly want from me now?'

It had been weeks since the gusts of autumn wind had started to blow in Spring Valley and make its way through the orchards of the village. But the wind in Oria was much different from the year before; it felt warmer and gentler, as it had always been before the cold spell. Especially for the woman who got off the bus at the entrance to the village and was making her way to the guest center. She intended to stay there for the night and attend the mid-autumn celebration the next day. She had left New York wearing a long raincoat and a woolen scarf around her neck. As she walked, limping slightly, she felt warm inside the coat but preferred to have it on. She was still even wearing a scarf. She did not feel safe taking the coat off and carrying it. The coat was her security. She did not look up to see the others making their way to the center, not daring to risk them looking at her face.

Night had fallen and the celebration field was filled with people working hard to prepare the ground for the next day's event. For the first time in Oria, on the very day of the mid-autumn celebration, a concert was being given. This year, apart from the villagers, guests were invited to the village. The concert would bring a profit to the village, money which Oria desperately needed after a year's loss of income for the farmers and farm owners. Adam had promised to give a concert for three straight nights and donate all the proceeds to the village. The donation wouldn't save the farms, but it would be a sympathetic gesture to the villagers. They needed a lot more to be able to keep their farms and afford the necessary expenditure for the coming year.

The new arrival had checked into her room at the center and was sitting quietly on her bed, gazing at the darkness of the night through the window. She was thought to be dead by all those who had heard her world-famous name. She was living with a face that was not hers and spoke with a voice made by a small machine, in her larynx. She looked like a stranger to people who had once known her very well.

On the morning of the celebration, she went to the field. She was not the only despairing soul in the crowd. Almost all the villagers looked miserable, owing to the terrible economic crash which they had experienced. She was not sure that Adam's concert and the magic he did with the violin could make those glum-faced folks happy. They needed something more than the momentary pleasure of a concert; something more solid that could save their livelihoods.

She spotted Adam standing by the colonel, talking to him by the first row of seats on the field. She still believed that if one person could act like a hero and bring back the joy to the villagers' lives, it was Adam.

If only he knew what he can do for them, she thought.

She walked towards him, determined to convince him.

'Mr. Keramat,' she said. 'I'm a huge fan of yours.'

'Thank you, madam,' said Adam, not realizing who was talking to him behind that artificial face and voice. 'Welcome to our celebration!'

'Can I have a word with you alone?' she asked.

They walked away from the crowd, leaving Dr. Keramat and the colonel busy welcoming their guests.

'I have a message for you from a friend,' she said.

'Oh, no!' Adam was fed up with the secret messages and threats. 'You are not here for the concert?'

'I am,' she said. 'Do not feel alarmed, Adam. My name is Veronica Christi.'

'What?' Adam cried, searching among the crowd to find his grandfather.

'I'm a friend of Adelheid's, dear!'

'Is she alive?' he asked.

'Yes, she is alive,' she said, wincing as if in pain.

'What does she want from me?'

'She just wants you to have the money that belongs to you after those concerts. That's all yours, Adam.'

Photographers appeared from out of nowhere and surrounded Adam. He forced a smile for them. His face was going on to the cover of countless magazines, introducing him as the world-famous musician who was about to help run a small village.

When the flashes had ceased, Adam looked among all the faces around him, but he could not see the woman any more. He walked over to the crowds. She was not there either. Veronica was gone, just like a shadow.

Having played a couple of his pieces to begin the celebration, Adam gave the stage to the master of ceremonies.

And he invited Dr. Keramat to the stage for his annual speech.

'When I walked into this magnificent place twenty-seven years ago,' said Keramat, 'I was separated from my family, friends, job and all I once had. But you people became my everything and I have been honored to serve you as mayor for all these years.'

Warm applause broke out from the crowd.

'Now it is time for me to step down from this duty and leave the responsibility to someone younger, filled with a fresh enthusiasm to provide you lovely people with the best that you deserve.' Tears glimmered in his eyes.

'As some of you know, my grandson has announced his candidature to become Oria's mayor. He has my blood in his veins and the heart to love and serve you people and do whatever is in his power to make you happy.'

As Keramat left the stage, the crowd were on their feet, applauding him enthusiastically, their eyes moist.

Adam returned to the stage and stood behind the microphone.

'Actually I am more saddened than you are by the news of my grandfather's resignation,' he said to the now silent audience. 'Because he is not just stepping down from this the duty, he is leaving Oria, too. And I cannot make him change his mind about going back to his home town in Iran and teaching in the university again as an honored professor.

'I do not intend to talk about the mayoral election now. I will instead dedicate today's concert to my grandfather and all he has done for me and all of us throughout all these years.'

His speech was greeted by clapping from the villagers, who were all crying with him at the same time.

'I grew up in this village and I composed my best songs here in the beauty of its nature,' said Adam. 'I have enjoyed your company and living among you, and I believe I owe a lot to you.'

Adelheid was standing behind the back row of the chairs, weeping quietly as she listened to Adam's speech.

'Recently I have received the sum of fifteen million euros as payment for my world tours,' said Adam, suddenly spotting Veronica in the crowd, her gaze fixed on him. 'I would like to donate this money to Oria's council so that we can keep the farms and save the village from total bankruptcy.'

'Here's to Adam Keramat!' said the master of ceremonies. 'The man who will make flowers flourish in Oria again.'

The first one who walked to Adam to show him gratitude for his new decision was Rose. During the celebration speeches, deep within her heart she felt the pleasant bounding with the village, its people and most of all with Adam. Thinking about staying in Oria with Adam, smile did not vanish from her face for a single moment. Walking on the pastures of the Spring Valley hand in hand with Adam and a peaceful life in the picturesque village, intrigued Rose so much that she was ready to let Adam hold her hands and never let go.

'Adam,' she said 'I'm really glad you made this decision. Only a great human being can dedicate his life to his people this way.'

'Thank you Rose,' Adam was desperate to express how willing he was to have Rose by his side in Oria 'will you do something?'

'Do what honey?' she tried hard to avoid tears rolling down her cheeks.

'Stay in Oria with me.'

'Adam,' she had to say the words that she did not really wanted to say 'I have a job at the university.'

'Don't say that you are leaving too!'

'I need to finish a project, but I hope we will find each other again one day.'

A week after the celebration, when all the guests had returned to their homes, Adam was sitting on his stone chair under the dome of his music temple. His grandfather had left early in the morning for Rome and in less then half a day he would be in Kerman to raise flowers in the gardens of the desert city. Colonel Ahmad Beig had left for his headquarters with the intention of handing in his resignation and spending his days in retirement. And Rose had bade farewell to Adam to return to her university job.

Adam was playing his violin for the last time as the violinst of Oria. The next day he would be officially inaugurated as the new mayor of the village. He did not know whether he would get a chance to play in the peace of his temple any more or not. The wind was making the trees move with the movements of the bow on the strings of his violin. He was lost in the music and the beauty of the countryside around him.

But the peace did not last long. He could hear chopper blades coming close to his temple. He stopped playing when the black helicopter hovered above his temple. The door of the machine slid open and a bag was thrown out. When the black bird left, Adam reached for the bag, undid the zip and took out the envelope inside. Cutting it open, he recoiled in horror. The severed finger of a middle—aged man adorned with a ring holding a big turquoise stone fell on to the stone floor of the temple. The only person Adam knew who wore such a ring was Colonel Ahmad Beig.

On the highest level of the highest tower of the world, Adelheid, under the face and name of Verocina Chritsi was sitting at a table with a bunch of shareholders of the multinational companies. They had the view of Persian Gulf on one side, and the LCD on which the project was being presented on the other. The men present in the meeting did not know that the lady, they were having a secret debate with, was Adelheid Fester, herself.

'Ms.Christi,' said the man 'we managed to let Adelheid and her Germania vanish forever. Adelheid will not be walking on this earth anymore.'

'You all did a great job,' said Adelheid 'convincing the G8 to order the air strike, was not an easy task'

'We need to thank you for your perfect plot and your support in the last three months to destroy The Silver Orcehstra.'

'Adelheid and her crystal city had to be eliminated,' said Adelheid 'Now we need to move on from all these and focous on the project.'

'What did you name the project Ms.Christi?' asked a man

'Project 123,' said Adelheid as she looked the green waves of the gulf hiting against the shore.

The End

AFTERWORDS AND ACKNOWLEDGMENTS

A dolf Hitler began building his dream city, Germania, on the ruins of Berlin, a city that would become the capital of the Nazis' global empire.

The secret city of *Kristall Hochburg* and The Silver Orchestra organization are completely fictional and such a society does not exist.

The first successful human cloning project was performed in Clonaid organization. Eve, the first successful human clone was born in an undisclosed location in 2003.

This book is a work of fiction. Any resemblance of the characters and organizations in this book to actual ones is purely coincidental.

The Beethoven's Skull Fragments journey is real and the fragments exist at the time of publishing this book. The names of the fragments owner and his ancestor are changed to fictitious names due to his request.

My grateful acknowledgements are made to:

Dr. William Meredith, the director of the Beethoven Study Center of San Jose State University

Beethoven Haus, Bonn

Beethoven Halle, Bonn

My editor and advisor, Dr. Hilary Johnson
The Kermanology Center, Kerman
The London School of Journalism
The German Federal Archives